SYLVIA WAS A
PRETTY LITTLE THING . . .

And Longarm was powerfully attracted. But there were suddenly little fireflies swimming before his eyes and he didn't think it was the right time for romancin'. More to get rid of her than anything else, he reached out and caressed her.

She stiffened. "Am I to take that as a compliment or a challenge, Mr. Long?"

He didn't answer. He couldn't answer. The room was spinning. He was going to be sick . . .

And then he was in this funny big room with red velvet drapes and a mess of undraped women were coming at him from all directions. They had painted faces and high-heeled shoes and they were grinning fit to bust. But they were grinning evil and they had guns in their hands . . .

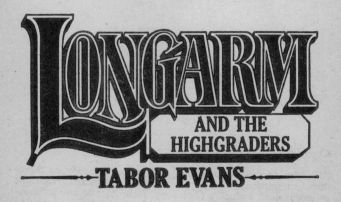

LONGARM
AND THE HIGHGRADERS

TABOR EVANS

A JOVE BOOK

Printed in the United States of America

Library of Congress Catalog Card Number: 78-70788

First Jove edition published April 1979

10 9 8 7 6 5

Jove books are published by Jove Publications, Inc., 200 Madison Avenue, New York, NY 10016

Chapter 1

Longarm entered the Manzanita Saloon to the lilting strains of "Garryowen," being played very fast on what sounded like tin pans. Had he come through the front entrance, he'd have been able to see who or what was making all that racket an hour before noon. But when a shifty-eyed stranger tells a lawman that someone is waiting for him in a saloon, then darts away before he can be questioned further, common sense dictates a prudent avenue of approach. So Longarm came in the back door.

There was a pantry to his right. The kitchen to his left was deserted. Longarm nodded. Drawing the .44-caliber Colt Model T he carried for just such mysteries as this, he eased toward the barroom on the balls of his feet. He moved quietly for a man of his size, but the music out front was so loud that he probably could have ridden a horse along the corridor without being noticed. It was a noisy place, considering that it seemed to be empty.

That was something to ponder. August was hotter than the hinges of hell in the Sierra foothills, and the dusty streets of Manzanita were devoid of life as the siesta hour approached. He'd only been in town about a half hour, and hadn't climbed up on a soapbox to announce his arrival. Yet the rat-faced little cowhand had been waiting in the empty street as Longarm had come out of the livery after leaving his army issue gelding in a cool stall. The hand had just said something about Longarm's being wanted over at the saloon, and then had slithered away like a sidewinder seeking shade under a flat rock.

Who in thunder could know he was in Manzanita? They were expecting him up at the mine, and he'd intended to pay a courtesy call on the local law before beginning his investigation, but he'd deliberately arrived two days early. It was surprising what a lawman could stumble over that way. Yet he'd been spotted the moment he had ridden in. Someone probably had a reason for watching the trail from Angel's Camp.

There was a bead curtain across the doorway into the barroom. The tall deputy stood in the shadows behind it as he studied the barnlike space on the other side of the beads. There was no bartender behind the long oak bar to his right. The rinkytink music was coming from a coin-operated harmonium against the wall to his left. In the middle of the room, seated at a table with his back to Longarm, was a dark figure in a brocaded charro outfit. A black sombrero hung on his back between his shoulders. The exposed hair was dishwater-blonde. Some Anglo had apparently taken to the Old California style, which made no never-mind to Longarm, but he did think the double-barreled shotgun the stranger held trained on the swinging doors to the sunlit street was a proper thing for any lawman to take an interest in.

Training his .44 on the man at the table, Longarm said, "You just freeze in place and listen, friend. I've got the drop on you. A sudden sneeze could get you killed. You got that much of my message, old son?"

Without moving a muscle, the man in the charro costume asked, "Is that you, Longarm?"

"Deputy U.S. Marshal Custis Long, at your service. In a minute, we'll palaver about who *you* might be, and why you have a scatter gun trained on the doorway you invited me through. Right now I want you to slide your chair back away from that gun on the table. Then I reckon you'd best put both hands on top of your golden locks and stand up slow and easy. I'll tell you when I want you to turn around."

The man at the table didn't do as he was told. He crabbed sideways off his chair, shotgun and all, and pivoted on one knee to fire.

He didn't make it. The twin barrels were three-quarters of the way around when the Colt kicked in Longarm's palm and the lawman's first slug slammed into the man's chest. The shotgun went off, blowing a hole in the baseboard of a corner as Longarm fired again. Between the recoil of the twelve-gauge and the .44 slug that caught him just under one eye, the would-be ambusher was thrown flat on his back to the sawdust-covered planks. A booted heel drummed mindlessly a few times, as if dancing to the music box, and then the corpse lay very still, staring up into the drifting blue gunsmoke with a bemused smile.

Longarm parted the beads and strode over to stare down at the man he'd just shot. He was a total stranger. Longarm reached into the side pocket of his Prince Albert coat for two fresh rounds as he studied the odd situation. The harmonium tinkled merrily on as he thumbed the spent brass from his cooling weapon, wondering how to go about shutting the infernal contraption off. He muttered to the dead stranger, "You likely thought you were as smart as an old he-coon in a hen-house when you put a penny in and cranked her up, huh? What was I supposed to think it was, a piano being played in a crowded saloon?"

Holding the Colt in his right hand, Longarm dropped to one knee, being careful not to get the spreading blood on his tobacco-brown tweed as he went through the dead man's pockets with his free hand. The man he'd shot was about thirty, with one of those uninteresting faces you see every day. He'd backed his shotgun with a brace of Smith & Wesson .45s in a silver-mounted gunbelt. Longarm noticed that one of the ivory grips had been notched four times. He sighed and muttered, "Jesus, you've been reading Buntline for sure. No calluses worth mention on your gun hand, so despite the vaquero outfit, you ain't a dally roper. You're tanned enough to have been out in the sun a few years, so you ain't some loco Easterner playing big bad cowboy, either. But those notches don't make you look like anyone with a lick of sense. Who were you trying to scare?"

At that moment a shadow appeared in the front doorway and a voice called out, "What's going on in here? You are talking to the law!"

Longarm looked up at the worried-looking newcomer in the doorway and replied, "I'm law, too. Just shot it out with this cuss for some fool reason. I'm still trying to find out why." He reached into his inside coat pocket. Producing his wallet, he flipped it open. His badge glittered dully in the dim light filtering in from the street. "Custis Long," he said. "Deputy U.S. marshal out of Denver. Now who the hell are you?"

The Manzanita lawman came in to join him, introducing himself as one Constable Lovejoy. As he got his first good look at the body, he said, "Oh, Jesus H. Christ! You've shot the Calico Kid!"

"Is that who he was? The name doesn't mean much to me, Constable. I pride myself on a tolerable memory, but if any wanted fliers on a so-called Calico Kid have ever come my way, I disremember seeing them."

Lovejoy said, "God, this is awful! We have a nice, quiet little town here, and I don't have deputy-one who'd go up against the Calico Kid and all."

Longarm got to his feet, dusting off his trousers and holstering his sixgun as he studied the concerned-looking smaller man. Lovejoy was gray around the edges and had a slight pot. He had the kind of politician's face that seemed to be made for smiling a lot. But right now he looked as if he were getting ready to burst out crying. Longarm said, "He did seem to think he was one mean fellow, but I doubt that he'll give anyone any more trouble. You reckon he really shot four men like he bragged?"

"Hell, it's more like a dozen. I'm going to have to do something about this mess, Longarm."

Longarm managed not to raise an eyebrow. He had no memory of having told the constable his nickname. Counting the dead man at his feet, that made at least three people in Manzanita who had been expecting him to ride in early.

Playing dumb, the tall deputy said, "Well, it was open-and-shut self-defense, even if I wasn't packing a federal badge. I'll make a statement for the county before I mosey on."

Lovejoy said flatly, "Longarm, you ain't going nowhere in *this* county! You just shot the Calico Kid!"

Longarm pushed his Stetson back from his forehead. "You keep saying that like it's important. Who was he, the bully of the town?"

"Damn it, he was a killer. Meanest son of a bitch we've had in these parts since Joaquin Murietta rode through in '53!"

"Well, don't get your balls in an uproar. His killing days are over."

"Hell, I'm talking about his friends, Longarm!"

Longarm looked down at the glassy-eyed corpse and shrugged as he mused, "He had friends? Well, anything's possible, I reckon. The way it seems to read right now is that he recognized me as I rode in and decided to build his rep some more with an easy murder. If his plan had worked, you'd likely be telling him right now what a serious thing he'd just done. I've got friends, too. They call themselves the U.S. Justice Department."

The constable was sweating profusely now. "Yeah, but *your* friends ain't likely to ride in shooting in the next hour or so. The Calico Kid's friends *are!* You take my meaning?"

"I'm not sure. Since I don't have the calling for raising folks from the dead, what is it you've got in mind?"

"I want you to *git,* damn it! If you've a lick of sense, you'll fork that pony you have over at the livery and ride out sudden and far!"

Longarm shook his head and said, "Can't. My outfit sent me here to do a job and I don't aim to ride anywhere till it's done. I'll help you put what happened here on paper, then I've got to head up to the Lost Chinaman diggings. I was aiming to poke around here in town for a spell before I rode up for a look-see at the mine itself. But since everyone seems to know Uncle Sam has a man in the field already, I don't reckon it's worth my time to jaw with the local barber and such."

Lovejoy hesitated. Then he nodded and said, "I figured you were on that case. We'd best go over to my office. If you won't leave peaceable, we may as well take down your statement and at least get you out on the trail. Calico rode with a mean bunch and at least one of them knows you just killed him."

Longarm thought, *Strike two!* but didn't say anything aloud as he followed the constable out the door.

Other men were standing in the street now, and Lovejoy called to one of them, "Hawkins, go fetch Doc Forbes and tell him we got a fellow who needs planting. Me and this deputy U.S. marshal will be at the jailhouse if you need us."

The little crowd parted as they crossed the street to the shady overhang of the opposing frame buildings. Longarm was now aware that the local law knew how he'd been set up. Yet he didn't remember having told Lovejoy about the rat-faced hand by the livery. That could be taken several ways. Lovejoy might have heard it from the stablehands. It seemed a bit soon to conclude that he was in cahoots with the gang against a fellow lawman.

The Manzanita jail was a thick-walled adobe structure with a redwood-shingled roof. Lovejoy ushered him in and Longarm saw that it was a one-room building partitioned by iron bars. A morose-looking Indian sat crosslegged on the floor of the lockup. He didn't look at them as they entered.

The office was furnished with a rolltop desk and some bentwood chairs. There was a typewriter on the green blotter of the desk. Beside it stood a funny-looking contraption of a kind that Longarm had never seen before. He asked, "Is that one of Professor Bell's newfangled talking telegraphs?"

"It sure is," Lovejoy said proudly. "We're up to date in California. Got us a line running all the way to Sacramento, now."

Longarm was impressed. "You must have some budget. My boss, Marshal Vail, has been trying to get him one of those back in Denver. Washington keeps telling him it's a passing fad."

Lovejoy put a sheet of paper in the typewriter and began to hunt and peck, standing. Longarm snorted and said, "Hell, let me type it up for you. I ain't got all day."

"You know how to play a typewriter?" Lovejoy said incredulously.

"Some. I've been fooling with the one in the office in Denver."

He sat down at the desk and began to hunt and peck a bit faster than the constable had, but not much. For the life of him, he couldn't see why everyone was in such an all-fired hurry to change things. He'd been writing his reports in longhand for six or eight years and nobody had ever said they couldn't read his Palmer penmanship.

He had typed out, *REPORT BY CUSTIS LONG, DEPUTY U.S. MARSHAL, DISTRICT COURT OF DENVER,* before Constable Lovejoy got up the nerve to place the muzzle of his revolver against the nape of Longarm's neck.

Longarm stopped typing. He asked, "Do you have a reason for whatever you're trying to pull, Lovejoy?"

The constable licked his lips and said, "You just keep them hands up there. I don't want no trouble, Longarm."

Longarm said, "Hell, old son, you've already *got* trouble." But he did as he was told. As Lovejoy held the muzzle of the revolver against the base of Longarm's skull with one hand, he frisked and disarmed him with the other. As Lovejoy took the derringer from Longarm's right-hand vest pocket, the lawman nodded and sighed, "Yeah, they gave you a pretty good rundown on me, didn't they? Not many folks know about the derringer on my watch chain. Who are you working for, those jaspers who've been stealing high-grade from the Lost Chinaman?"

"State of California," Lovejoy said, adding, "You could have rode out like I asked, but they said in Sacramento that you was a stubborn cuss. You get up, now, and move slow for the lockup. I don't want to shoot you, but . . ."

Longarm rose slowly to his feet, the gun pressing against his back, but he protested, "Lovejoy, you are starting to piss me off a mite. You can't lock me up."

Lovejoy cut him off. "You ain't the law in California. You're out of your jurisdiction, and Justice Field, down in Sacramento, says you have no call to mess in local matters."

As the constable opened the jail door and shoved him inside, Longarm snorted, "Hell, if you mean Justice Stephen Field, *he's* in trouble too! I wasn't ordered out here by the Denver office. I'm on a special assignment from Washington! It seems they've been wondering why the federal marshals out here can't seem to get a handle on those missing gold shipments." As the door slammed shut, he added, "We're talking about gold being sent to the U.S. Mint in San Francisco, Lovejoy. We're talking about Uncle Sam's money. Savvy?"

"Look, I just do my job as best I know how. Sacramento says your badge don't mean shit on this side of the Sierras and, damn it, it was your own idea to go and shoot the Calico Kid!"

"Come on, the silly son of a bitch was trying to murder me!"

"Maybe. We'll see about it at your trial."

"My *what?* What the hell charges are you holding me on, God damn it?"

The constable holstered his sixgun. "Don't know. Maybe murder. Maybe manslaughter. That'll be up to the district attorney, won't it?"

Longarm laughed, still more puzzled than alarmed, and said, "Lovejoy, this ain't going to work. I know you old boys up here in the Mother Lode play rough, but we're not talking about jumping some greenhorn's claim

13

or robbing a Mexican. We're talking about over a dozen gold shipments sidetracked between here and the mint. You don't seem to grasp that it's federal gold we're talking about!"

Lovejoy shrugged and turned away. One of the townies came to the door and yelled in something about the undertaker. Lovejoy said, "I'll talk to him. Keep an eye on the jail, will you?"

As Lovejoy left, Longarm called out, "They'll send someone else, you damned fool! Even if you kill me, you're going to be combing U.S. deputies out of your hair until Justice finds out where all that ore's been shipped!"

And then the constable was gone. The man he'd deputized to take his place went over to the desk and sat down with his back to the lockup. He put his feet up on the desk and lit a smoke. Longarm asked, "You mind telling me something, friend?"

The man didn't answer. Longarm swore softly and turned away from the bars. The Indian on the floor said, "I am not a bad person. Don't hurt me."

Longarm went over to the fold-down bunk and sat down, saying, "I'm not a bad person, either. What are you in for?"

"My name is Bitter Water. I am a Miwok. What you Saltu call a Digger Indian."

Longarm had recently come to know and respect these groups of foraging Indians contemptuously called Diggers. They were peaceable, graceful, and intelligent peoples who were often ruthlessly exterminated or driven from their lands by avaricious whites. He had recently had occasion to help a group of Paiutes in eastern Nevada whose stores of their staple food— pinyon nuts—were being destroyed by uncontrolled, illegal logging. Longarm extended a large, callused hand toward Bitter Water, and the small Indian shook it firmly. "Well, I'm Custis Long," he said, "and I'll call you a Miwok. You didn't say why they arrested you."

"Yes I did. I told you I was an Indian."

"Is that against the law?"

"In this county? Yes. Some Saltu came to the valley where my people have always gathered acorns. They said it was *their* valley now. They said they had a paper from Wa Sentan telling them they could keep cows there. When I asked to see the paper, they hit me. So I ran away."

"I'm sorry, Bitter Water. I hope you don't think all of my people are like that. But how'd you wind up in this jail if you got away?"

"You have a good heart, but you do not listen. I said I ran away. I did not say I *got* away. While I was running from the men with cows, I crossed some other Saltus' mining claim. They caught me with a rope and brought me here. They say I have been stealing gold. Someone has been stealing gold around here, and, as I said, I am an Indian." Bitter Water shrugged as he added, "I think they will hang both of us as soon as it gets dark."

Longarm shot a glance out front. Lovejoy had taken his watch along with his badge, gun, and last three smokes, but he could see it was still early afternoon. Turning back to the Indian, he said, "Lovejoy said something about a trial. How often does the circuit judge come over from the county seat?"

"I don't know. It does not matter. They will not hear of us over in San Andreas. The men in Manzanita who hang people call themselves vigilantes. It is said nobody knows who they are, but I think this is a lie."

Longarm frowned thoughtfully. Then he got up and went over to the bars again, calling out, "Hey, this fellow says you have a vigilance committee in this town. I thought that sort of thing went out with the forty-niners."

The deputy, if that was what he was, didn't answer. Longarm insisted, "Look, I don't know if Lovejoy told you boys the facts of life, but I am a federal officer. You just try lynching a federal man and you won't have to worry about the Justice Department. You'll have the U.S. army up here asking all sorts of questions."

Again, there was no reply. Apparently the man at the desk knew how hard it is not to give anything away, once you start talking. The people behind this had their henchmen well-trained.

All right, he decided, *let's take as gloomy a look at this mess as possible and see where that leaves everyone.* His investigation had been nipped in the bud, either by some very clever plotting indeed or just a bit of quick thinking on the part of a skunk wearing a badge. It didn't matter whether the late Calico Kid had been in on it or not. By shooting the inept gunman, he'd delivered himself into their hands. The Indian's idea made sense, too, damn it. Longarm knew there was no way they'd ever hang a murder charge on him in open court. On the other hand, if he and Bitter Water were killed, by vigilantes, friends of the Calico Kid, or simply "trying to escape" . . .

"It still won't work," he called out, adding, "My office knows I'm here in Calaveras County. The Lost Chinaman is fixing to ship another carload of high-grade ore down to the stamping mills, and if I don't ride in with the gold, they'll send in another team."

No answer.

Longarm insisted, "Sure, you and your pals might steal at least one more shipment, but then what? You're spreading yourselves a mite thin already, you know. I figure even if we're talking about the highest grade of ore, it still can't run more than a few thousand dollars

16

a trainload, before it's refined. I can see you've bought your own law all the way down to the state capital, but, like I said, there's only so much gold and there are a lot of palms to grease."

Hoping the silent man was at least listening, he insisted, "Look, you can bribe almost anyone to look the other way about a trainload of ore. But the rates go up as soon as you start killing folks, and a deputy U.S. marshal comes high as hell. I know you won't answer, but I want you to study on my words. Up to now, I don't have a thing on anyone. But once the government starts getting serious about you boys, it's all over. You have too many people in on it. One of you, only one, just has to get worried about his own hide, or maybe pissed off because he thinks he should have had a bigger share and——"

The man at the desk swung his boots to the floor and turned around to snap, "You just *hush*, mister! You don't know what you're talking about!"

Longarm was a bit relieved to see that the man wasn't deaf. "The hell I don't. I'm talking about a U.S. deputy being hindered, or worse. You're not going to like it in Leavenworth, boy."

"God damn it, you got no call to say I'm a thief. I've never stole a penny in my born days. Me and every other honest man in the county is as riled as you are about them jaspers robbing the ore trains, and I'll not be tarred with the same brush as them!"

Longarm saw that the man was young and rather simple-looking. He smiled and asked, "Why are you holding me, then? Can't you see you're helping the highgraders, even if you're not in on it?"

The guard shook his head and said, "Don't fun with me, mister. You know you shot the Calico Kid."

"Then you must be one of *his* friends, right?" Longarm prodded him.

"Hell, I just said I was an honest man. I got no truck with them wild gunslicks Calico used to ride with."

Longarm shook his head wearily and marveled, "Loco. The whole bunch has busted out to nibble locoweed, unless I missed a turn a ways back. If you and Lovejoy ain't with the highgraders, and you ain't with the Calico Kid's bunch, what in thunder am I doing behind these bars?"

"You're in jail 'cause it's where you belong, damn it. You had no call to come here and stir up trouble."

"I'd say the trouble sort of came my way. I was only trying to do my job."

"No, you wasn't. You don't belong in these parts, mister. We got a town constable and a county sheriff. We got our own federal marshals down to Sacramento. You're just a durned old carpetbagger! Nobody around here ever asked you to stick your nose into our business, did they?"

"I hate to call such an honest man a liar, but you are purely full of shit. I *was* asked to investigate those gold robberies. Uncle Sam asked me, real polite. Are you saying Calaveras County's not part of these United States?"

The youth hesitated. Then he said, "You're trying to mix me up," and turned away again. This time he meant it. Longarm tried reason. He tried argument. He tried saying mean things about the man's mother. Nothing worked. After a while he got tired of talking to the back of an obviously thick skull and went back to the bunk. As he sat down again, the Indian muttered, "We have nothing to worry about as long as they are guarding us."

Longarm started to ask what Bitter Water meant. Then he nodded in sick understanding. He'd investigated enough lynchings to know the form.

If that was indeed the plan, Constable Lovejoy would

go through the motions for the rest of the day. A rural community like Manzanita went to bed early. Or at least, the honest elements did. Later, in the dark of the moon, Lovejoy would probably be called away from the jail on some obscure mission. That was when the night riders would arrive.

Later, some luckier lawman might put it all together and they'd know at last whether the late Custis Long had been lynched by men in the pay of the gold thieves, by pals of the Calico Kid, or by someone he hadn't figured out yet. Yeah, they'd get to the bottom of it, in time. You don't steal federal gold and murder federal marshals and hope to get away with it forever. But he didn't have forever. He had maybe eight or ten hours if he intended to crack the case himself. It wasn't a bit comforting to think some other lawmen might track down the answers, after he was dead.

The Indian's voice was soft as he asked, "Would you get mad at me if I made a suggestion?"

Longarm smiled and said, "No. I think it's a good idea."

Bitter Water looked puzzled as he asked, "Do you read my words before they are spoken?"

"Hell, if you're thinking about anything *but* busting out of here you must be loco, too. What's your plan?"

Bitter Water suddenly looked even more dejected. "I was hoping *you* had one. All I know is that we can't stay here overnight. Right after dark would be the best time, don't you think?"

Longarm shook his head and said, "That's when they'll be expecting us to try and bust out. One of the oldest tricks around is to leave a prisoner unguarded and sort of let him think he's escaping."

Morosely, Bitter Water studied the floor between his knees for a time before he sighed, "Heya! Waiting outside with rifles. Forgive me for being stupid. I have spent little time in Saltu jails. When do *you* think we should get away?"

"Right about now would suit me just fine. It's mid-afternoon and hot as hell out there. Half the town'll be taking a siesta, and the restless souls are likely holding a funeral for the cuss I just shot."

"I agree. But I don't see how we can get out of this place. If I had a knife I could dig through the adobe wall, but—"

"It'd take too long," Longarm interrupted. "I think we'd better try an old trick and hope that jasper out front is as dumb as he looks. The old prison fight would never work on anyone who's worked as a guard for six weeks, but he might not have heard of it."

"He does look stupid," Bitter Water agreed. "But what is this trick you speak of?"

"Oh, you're going to start beating me up. I don't think he'd care if *I* started slapping *you* around, but—"

The suggestion caused a flicker of enthusiasm to brighten the Indian's features. "Yes. No Saltu is going to stand by and allow a brother to be bested by a dirty Indian. But what are we supposed to be fighting about?"

"Hmmm, we'll have to make it look a mite serious, won't we? Let's see now. What's a good old boy likely to have strong feelings about? I'll tell you what, Bitter Water. Take off your pants."

The Indian looked thunderstruck and muttered, "You are making a joke. What do you take me for?"

"That ain't important. It's what we want *him* to take you for. I want you to act like a wild, crazy Indian with a hard-on. Come on, old son, I know you ain't a jail-wolf."

Bitter Water shrugged and stood up, turning out to be taller than the lawman had expected. The Indian dropped his ragged britches and stepped out of them, naked from the waist down. Longarm shouted, "You ain't gonna do no such thing, you crazy red bastard!" and then he grabbed the startled Indian by the shirt and pulled him against his own frame, crying out, "Help! This crazy Digger's after my white ass!"

The guard swung around to stare openmouthed as the two men rolled over and over on the floor. Then he sprang to his feet and shouted, "Hey, what the hell kind of jail do you think we're running here? We don't allow that sort of thing in Manzanita, boys!"

Longarm whimpered, "Get him off me, then! He's as strong as a goddamned elephant and I reckon he'd fuck one, given the chance!"

The guard fished a key from his ring and fumbled with the lock, saying, "Hit back, damn it! You're a white man!"

"He's killing me! He must have been chewing that crazy Indian medicine they use to get riled up!"

The door was open and the guard stepped in, muttering, "Oh, for God's sake," as he drew his gun. Longarm saw what was coming and tried to shove Bitter Water out of the way, but the gun barrel slammed down against the side of the Miwok's head and Longarm felt him go limp. He rolled the Indian off, hooked a toe behind the guard's ankle, and kicked him hard in the kneecap with the other booted heel.

The guard went down, gasping in pain, but still holding on to the gun as Longarm rolled to his hands and knees and dove headfirst over his victim's thrashing legs. He landed with all his considerable weight on the man's chest and grabbed for the wrist of his gun hand as he kneed the guard viciously. The man gasped in pain. Longarm grabbed his hair and pounded his head on the floor until he lay limp and silent. Then Longarm hit him once for luck and got up with the other man's gun in his own hand.

He stood for a moment, listening. The sounds of the struggle didn't seem to be drawing any attention from the blazing furnace of the town outside. Both Bitter Water and the guard were breathing, but were obviously out of it for some time to come.

The Indian looked sort of silly lying there with no pants on, but his appearance was the least of Longarm's worries. He stuck the gun in his waistband and picked up the Indian's discarded pants. As he knelt to fumble them on over Bitter Water's big feet, the Indian opened his eyes and asked, "What are you doing?"

"Trying to get you dressed and out of here."

Bitter Water sat up and said, "I can do that. Why didn't you run away as soon as you had the chance? Didn't you think he knocked me out?"

"You mean he didn't?" Longarm asked, astonished.

"No. I was only dazed. It came to me as I lay there that I would be wise to let you run away and then leave myself. You are a good person, but you are Saltu."

"You mean you figured you could lose yourself in the timber easier without a white man tagging along?"

"Of course," Bitter Water replied with assurance. "No white man can track me in my native hills. But you did not run away. You stayed to help me. This is a new thing I must consider."

Longarm shrugged and said, "You light out on your own if you've a mind to. I've got to see if I can find my gun and badge."

But as he went out front to rummage through the constable's desk, the Indian, now dressed, took his arm and said, "Come, Saltu brother. The siesta will be ending and we must have at least an hour's start on them through the trees."

Longarm looked at Bitter Water with some surprise. "I thought you aimed to make it on your own, Bitter Water. Just let me find my stuff, and—"

"You are a good person, but a fool. You *had* your badge and they arrested you! When they find their friend unconscious, the whole town will be after us!"

"*Us?* All for one and one for all?"

The Miwok nodded. "You have me in your debt. Come with me and no Saltu will ever cut your trail."

"Well, maybe if I can get a few miles off and study my next move a spell . . . " Longarm speculated.

"Come. I will show you things no Saltu knows about these hills. Later, you can go back to Wa Sentan. Agreed?"

Longarm nodded, but then he said, "Not hardly. This case is just getting interesting."

"You mean to come back to this place? Without your badge? Without your gun? Without a friend in the county?"

"Hell, old son, I've got a gun. The other odds just promise to make the game a mite more interesting."

In a white man's town, wearing a white man's cast-off rags, Bitter Water had seemed a rather shabby specimen. But crouched on a granite outcropping beside the lawman, the Miwok was a wild creature in its own element. The Mother Lode country lay in the oak-covered foothills of the Sierras, rather than in the ever-green slopes he'd half expected, so they were no higher than the Colorado prairie he was used to, yet Longarm was out of breath. His Indian companion had set a killing pace since they'd skulked out of Manzanita. Bitter Water had led them downslope for a time, which made sense, since anyone trying to cut their trail would figure they'd made a beeline for the high country. But then he'd led them in a series of hairpin turns through canyons thick with undergrowth and over hogback ridges too steep for a billy goat to consider, and, except for knowing that they were somewhere to the south of, and slightly higher than Manzanita, Longarm was completely lost.

He could only hope that anyone following them was as bushed and mixed-up as he was. As he rested his cramped calves by sprawling on the granite on one elbow, Longarm began to recover his bearings as well as his breath. The lookout Bitter Water had selected was a cunning choice. Longarm knew most men moved to the highest ground they could find when they wanted to see out across the world. The Miwok had led them to one of many boulders running in a horizontal band two-thirds of the way up this particular ridge. Anyone sweeping the high country with field glasses from the valley below would have no particular reason to study the rocks they were on, and their outlines were well below the skyline.

At the same time, they had a spectacular view to the west, north, and south. The sun was low and blazing red as it headed for China. The tawny, rolling foothills lay below them like some huge, wrinkled carpet, stitched together by the Great Spirit from odds and ends of animal skins—mostly cougar. The ridges ran north and south, under a cover of cheat grass and wild mustard, in rounded muscular curves that reminded one of the feminine strength of a great cat. It was easy to see, from up here, why California was earthquake country. The lower slopes of the Sierra looked as if they were about to spring at the North Pole. The folds between the smooth rolls of the slopes were dark with canyon oak and manzanita. To his left and right, the land grew rougher as the slopes became steeper, with a darker pelt of ponderosa pines and other evergreens disputing the claim of the lowland vegetation. He couldn't see the snow-covered crests of the High Sierra behind them, for the range climbed to the timberline in graduated waves, steeper toward the east and gentler toward the sunset. The western slope of the Sierra would hardly have been noticeable, in fact, had not time and the patient running waters of a million brooks carved the main slopes into thousands of smaller ridges and canyons.

Bitter Water was watching one of the brush-choked canyons. They had come through it on the way here, and he was worried about his attempts to hide their sign. He'd called the place Spider Valley. Longarm remembered it as a winding stretch of dusty hell where he'd crawled on his hands and knees under waist-high twisted branches that smelled like medicine. He didn't remember seeing any spiders in Spider Valley, but the place had been crawling with sassy little lizards who stuck their tongues out before they darted away along the branches.

He couldn't locate it now. Spider Valley could have been any of those wrinkles down there, sinking into twilight well ahead of the still brightly illuminated ridges. He squinted his eyes against the red sun and managed to make out the distant flatness of the Great Valley between where they stood and the lower coastal ranges. The lowlands shimmered under a flat haze of dull orange and woodsmoke gray as the late afternoon breeze moved in from the invisible Pacific, beyond the horizon. He knew Sacramento was down there, some-where. That son-of-a-bitch federal judge who'd disputed his jurisdiction was probably watching a nice sunset and planning a night on the town. In a state notorious for political corruption, Justice Stephen Field had gained a reputation for innovative crookedness.

The trouble with federal judges, Longarm mused, was that they were appointed for life and were often given the job as a reward for getting out the vote in-stead of for juridical literacy. Justice Field was one of those oldtimers who'd come West to do good, and he had done a lot of it—for himself. They said he'd killed a few men in his day, and he was widely known for his draconian views on the rights of Greasers, Chinks, Niggers, or Injuns, as he called them. He was reputed to be thick with the railroad barons and bankers. He'd elevated the art of land-grabbing and claim-jumping to a fine science. This very year, at a place called Mussel Slough, U.S. marshals from the judge's district had done battle with a group of small ranchers and farmers who had failed to see the justice in their homesteads being seized by Justice Field for his richer cronies. Longarm was glad he hadn't been assigned to that case. The Battle of Mussel Slough had been a bloodbath California was going to remember. Five settlers had been gunned down by federal deputies, but they had taken two members of the attacking forces with them before losing their lands. It was easy to see why someone in Washington had asked for a deputy from another district. The California marshals had said they had no idea who had been stealing that gold bound for the San Francisco Mint. Longarm wondered if they were all in on it, or if he only had a few key men in high places to worry about. He felt a certain sense of loyalty to his fellow deputies, but in truth, he knew his own good reputation was mostly the result of his having a certain amount of common sense in an outfit tending to hire cheap help. He knew a lot of federal deputies who didn't have sense enough to pour piss out of their boots. They'd go where they were told and see what they were told to see. The cover-up that Washington suspected was pretty obvious. Yet, wasn't it a mite *too* obvious?

Longarm chewed thoughtfully on the edge of his full, dark brown mustache. Aloud, he muttered, "I don't understand it. We just ain't talking about all that much money!"

Beside him, Bitter Water asked, "What money are you talking about?"

Longarm said, "I've been thinking about those gold shipments. A federal judge is expensive and I've been adding it up. Those highgraders haven't been running off with gold bullion; they've been stealing whole train-loads of ore. You know what ore is, don't you?" Bitter Water looked at Longarm a bit reproachfully.

"Of course. My people roamed the Mother Lode before the Saltu found out there was gold in that band of yellow-brown quartz that runs north and south through these hills." He chuckled softly and added, "We used to make arrowheads out of it. If the Saltu were less unfriendly, we could show them places where the flecks of gold in the rock are visible to the naked eye. We never had any use for it. Gold is softer than lead; it makes very poor tools. In the old days our children used to find the beads of gold washed out of the rocks by running water and, being children, they'd bring them to their mothers. Once, when I was a boy, I found a nugget as big as my thumb. My mother said not to be foolish. It was the time of the year to be gathering acorns."

Longarm nodded and said, "I sometimes wonder myself why so many men have gone crazy over the stuff. Though I don't hold with eating acorns. Pinyon nuts ain't bad, but acorns are bitter as hell."

The Miwok laughed and pointed a finger at Longarm. "You are a Saltu. You don't know how to wash the bitterness from our food. Your people have no patience; you only eat what's easy. Over to our west, there is a valley where a whole party of your people starved to death many years ago. They were very crazy. They starved surrounded by food, had they but seen fit to gather it. Yet they cried like women and started to eat one another. My people have often joked about those crazy Saltu."

Longarm frowned and asked, "Are you talking about the Donner party, back in the gold rush?"

"I think that was what they were called. They got lost in the High Sierra and were snowed in for the winter. There were roots and nuts all around them, but they ate each other. The ways of your people are very strange."

Longarm had had this same conversation with other Indians, so he didn't want to get into it. Unlike some whites he knew, Longarm liked most Indians. But he didn't buy the "noble savage" myth. As a man who'd lived with, slept with, and fought with Indians, he knew them better than either the bigots who hated them or the poetic writers who, never having swapped shots with Apache, tended to picture them as misunderstood supermen. The tragedy of the American Indian was simply that, save for a few tribes he could think of, they saw the world they shared with the white man as something *different*—something no white man could fully understand. Bitter Water seemed neighborly enough, and they were in this mess together. But Longarm knew that, no matter how it all turned out, they'd never really understand each other, so he didn't waste time trying.

He said, "The sun's going down. You aim to spend the night up here on this rock like some big-assed bird?"

The Miwok shrugged and said, "One part of this country is as good as any other. I don't see dust against the sunset. If they are trailing us, they are on foot."

Longarm stood up, shook the kinks out of his leg muscles, and stretched in the red glow of the setting sun.

"I could have told you that. We went through places

no pony could have gone. Come to think of it, I wouldn't have laid odds on a mountain goat."

"If I had run off alone," Bitter Water continued, "I would not think anyone was taking the trouble to search for me. They consider us pests rather than game worthy of a great hunt. But you seemed important to them. From what you have told me this day, important people want you out of the way. There may be a reward offered for your capture. Saltu will do anything for money."

The tall deputy nodded grimly. "That's for damned sure. But you purely puzzle me, Bitter Water. You *know* what money is."

"Of course. Did you think I was a stupid person? You know I speak your tongue. 'Fuck' and 'money' are the first words anyone learns around you people."

Longarm chuckled. "Well, maybe 'son of a bitch' comes almost as early. Where'd you pick up English, at some mission school?"

"No, my band avoided the padres when Mexico owned California. They were nearly as cruel as your people. When I was young, I was captured by some gold miners. They made me work for them one summer. Your tongue is less complicated than my own. You Saltu speak a sort of baby-talk with very few words. It was easy to learn your speech, although your ways will always be a mystery to me."

"White folks keep surprising me a mite, too," Longarm admitted. "But what do you mean about us talking like babies? I know your old ones like to make long speeches. Most Indians I've met could talk the horns off a billy goat. But where'd you get such a big vocabulary with no books or telegraph lines?"

The Miwok shrugged and said, "We talk about things your people do not seem to find important. When Saltu speak, they only skim the surface. For instance, you only have one word for a horse."

"Wait a minute. We have lots of words for the critters. We call them horses, ponies, studs, mares, pintos, roans, all sorts of things."

Bitter Water waved this away with an imperious gesture. "Bah. Those words only deal with the surface. You say the same word for the poor animal no matter what it's *doing!*"

The lawman looked puzzled. "I don't follow you."

"Of course you don't. Suppose I said I saw a horse. What would this mean to you?"

Longarm stared down into the low country and asked, "*Do* you see a horse down there?"

"No. I am hoping that when it gets dark, anyone following us may build a fire and give his position away. To a Miwok, the word 'horse' would have little meaning. He would want to know how old the horse was and which way it was going. He would want to know if the horse had a rider. He would want to know if it was running, walking, or standing still. He would have no word that simply meant 'horse.'"

"You mean in your lingo you use a different *word* for a horse running and a horse standing?"

Bitter Water nodded. "Also for every other thing a horse can do. We have no word that means 'woman.' To a Miwok, it is important whether a woman is young or old, ugly or pretty, awake or asleep, and so forth. No Miwok would ever ever say he had a woman. He would say he had a pretty woman who'd had children and made good acorn mush, or—"

Comprehension flickered in Longarm's blue-gray eyes. "I'm getting your drift. That's why when I ask what you folks call a man, I get all sorts of answers, right? I mean, as far as I can grasp your lingo, a 'ho,' a 'wa,' a 'pai,' or a 'ute' are the same critter!"

"They are all men, doing different things," Bitter Water concurred. "Your wise men are very funny.

They keep writing down names of things they call tribes. They don't understand that when they asked the so-called Paiute, Ute, Hopi, and so forth what they were, they were given the same answer. We all call ourselves 'people.' What the wise men wrote down was simply what the people they met were doing, or felt like, that day."

"Well, I thank you for the language lesson, but I never came out here to study Indians. I'm looking for some jaspers given to stealing federal gold. For some reason, you have as much trouble grasping the idea of money as I do understanding Miwok."

"I understand money. I just see no use for it," the Indian said.

"That's what I mean. Hell, can't you see that a couple of dollars would buy you a decent set of jeans instead of those rags you're wearing?"

Bitter Water shrugged and said, "I wear cotton this time of the year because it is cool on the skin in the heat. Later, when it's cold, I will wear skins. In the green of spring I will go naked. It seems very sensible to me."

"Sure," Longarm persisted, "but if you had money you could buy all sorts of outfits and have them ready as the seasons changed."

"You speak foolishly. Why should any man carry everything he might need for all the months he can't possibly need them?"

Longarm started to argue. Then he reconsidered and nodded. Since the Diggers wandered constantly, following the game and harvests of wild vegetables, it *did* make sense to travel light. But he saw a hole in that argument and, even though he knew better, he asked, "Haven't you folks ever considered sort of staying put? I mean, you ain't dumb and you must see the advantages of a permanent home, with maybe a garden and some livestock. Farm folks don't have to wander all over creation just to rustle up a meal."

The Miwok grimaced and asked, "Would you have us live like some sort of Mexicans? Even if we were content to spend all our days looking at the same hills and trees, drinking water that always tasted the same, smelling flowers that always smelled the same, eating food that always tasted the same, would we be left to enjoy our new bland lives?"

"Well, the Indian agency would protect you, on a proper reservation."

Anger darkened the Indian's features. "As a caged bear is protected by its keepers? No, thank you. There were villages of my people in the Great Valley when the gold seekers came. They had learned farming from the Mexicans. They ate well, as you say. Then a general called Fremont came over the Sierra to fight the Mexicans. The Mexicans had guns and knew how to fight back. So your Fremont had his war with the mission Indians. He killed many. Today their farms are owned by Saltu. They boast that they won their homesteads from wild Indians."

Longarm said, "You win. It's nigh dark enough for anyone on our trail to be thinking of setting up camp for the night. You think we can find your village in the dark?"

"My people have no villages. They wander. They sleep wherever they are when it's time to sleep."

"Then how do you expect to find your band?" Longarm asked.

Bitter Water shrugged and said, "We shall meet when we meet. There are only so many valleys where a person can find food. At this time of the year my people will be gathering manzanita. I know where it grows thickly. If I don't find them in the manzanita groves, they will be harvesting acorns soon."

Longarm started to say he'd tasted one of the little crabapple things off a manzanita bush once, and never intended to try again. Instead, he pointed with his chin and said, "Smoke. Over there to our right, behind that saddleback ridge." The distant plume of smoke was tinted violet by the setting sun.

"I see it. It is a Saltu fire. You people put too much wood on when you make camp. It is very foolish. A Miwok builds a small fire and sits over it, keeping warm. Saltu build big fires and have to sit back, roasting their fronts and freezing their backs. From the smoke, I would say there are a lot of men in the party. The fools are mounted. We have nothing to worry about."

Longarm was getting tired of being treated like a greenhorn, so he tried to figure some things out for himself. He wasn't a bad woodsman, if he said so himself, but he'd have missed the part about horses, had not the Miwok made him study on it for a spell.

He said, "You're right. They must be mounted. I can see how the land rolls gentle on the other side of that saddleback. They've been following the natural lay of the land, hoping to cut our trail as they rode. If they don't give up come morning, they'll likely ride up that draw to the north. I'd say they're about four miles away right now, as the crow flies. But they're riding ponies instead of crows, so the grain of these hills will carry them directly away from this rock."

Bitter Water said, "I know. Why did you think I led you this way?"

Longarm laughed and said, "I thought you were aiming to kill me. I can see now how you folks can stay so wild right on the edges of settled country. It's a good thing for our side that you old boys are less warlike than Apache. I'd hate to try and lead an army patrol after you poor primitive bastards."

Bitter Water smiled grimly and said, "The idea has

been discussed around our campfires. We are not a warlike people, but many of your people are evil. Just a few years ago some men of our kind, led by a breed called Captain Jack, tried fighting you, to the north of here."

"I heard about the Modoc War. Your Captain Jack and his braves made the army look sort of silly."

Bitter Water shrugged and sighed. "It didn't matter. In the end, they were all killed. It is better just to avoid your kind."

Longarm suddenly understood something he'd started to wonder about. He had a gun, though, so it was as good a time as any to have it out. He said, "You have no intention of leading me any closer to your own kith and kin, right?"

Bitter Water kept his face blank as he answered, "I am in your debt. My people are not. You are a good person, I think, but they would want to kill you if we met them far from any settlement."

"I've heard that white men have a habit of sort of vanishing in the high country from time to time. But what are we supposed to do, walk hand in hand through these bushes forever?"

"When I am sure we have lost those who wish you dead, I will take you to a place called Murphy. There you can steal a horse and be on your way. Will you be going back to Wa Sentan?"

"Not hardly. Nobody seems to savvy that I came out here to do a job."

"You keep saying that. If you go back to Manzanita, they will kill you and all of my efforts will have been wasted."

Longarm shook his head and explained, "I ain't as dumb as I look. I've been studying on my next best move. Can you put me on a trail that leads to San Francisco?"

"Of course. You can go down to Sacramento, then catch a steamboat to the big bay."

"No. I don't think they like me in the capital. I've got to get to Frisco without anyone in Sacramento knowing about it. Can you do it?"

The Miwok thought for a moment before he nodded and said, "Yes. We will move along the ridges until we are well south of Sacramento. Then I will lead you to a Mexican village in the valley. They are good people and may give you a horse. From there you simply ride due west toward Mount Diablo, on the coast. San Francisco is on the other side. Are you going there to get help?"

Longarm shook his head and said, "Not exactly. I'm going over Judge Field's head. You see, he's only the *second* biggest crook in California. If I can make a deal with the *biggest* crook, I might uphold some law around here yet!"

Chapter 2

They called him "The Blind Boss," but this appellation was only partly accurate. Christopher Buckley was getting on in years and had cataracts, but he could see well enough with his ghastly gray eyes, and didn't miss one hell of a lot. Boss Buckley was the undisputed owner, lock, stock, and barrel, of the California Democrat Party, and who was in the White House made no difference to him and his henchmen, a band of boisterous bullies known as Buckley's Lambs. Finding out where Boss Buckley was, the night Longarm arrived in San Francisco, was no problem. Getting to see him was a bit more difficult.

Longarm caught up with Buckley at a whorehouse near the waterfront. It was late evening. The cobbled streets at the foot of Telegraph Hill were dark, and a peasoup fog was rolling in through the Golden Gate. Longarm was on foot and tired of chasing false leads by the time he got to the frame house and knocked, as instructed, on an alley entrance. The door opened a slit and a wary-looking Chinese asked who'd sent him.

Longarm said, "Marty, the bellhop at the Palace Hotel. I have to talk to Boss Buckley."

The doorkeeper said, "No savvy," and tried to close the door. Longarm stiff-armed it open, Chinese and all, and stepped inside, saying, "Sure you do. Where is he, upstairs or in the parlor?"

The Chinese yelled something in his own language and a trio of his countrymen boiled out of the woodwork, yelling.

Longarm sighed, punched the doorkeeper flat, and waded into the others, swinging. Since nobody seemed to be waving a gun at anyone, he decided to settle for a friendly fight.

The confrontation was short, savage, and noisy. Longarm emerged with a split lip, leaving four Orientals stretched out on the red carpet in various states of disrepair. As he sucked a knuckle and got his breath back, a tall, statuesque blonde wearing little more than red garters and a wisp of black lace appeared in the nearest doorway to observe, "Hell, honey, if you want to get laid that badly, you should have made an appointment."

Longarm smiled at the tall whore and said, "I didn't come for that, this time. I have to see Boss Buckley."

"Oh, now I see why Wang attacked you. You'd better get lost, handsome. We only do business in this place. We don't introduce customers to one another."

"Where is he? It'd save time and furniture if folks would be more neighborly hereabouts."

The whore insisted, "Honey, if I were you, I'd fold my tent and steal silently away. Since I don't want you to beat me up, I'll tell you all you really need to know. The boss is holding a meeting in a side room, and he has a couple of his lambs with him. So what are you waiting for? *Run,* you damned fool!"

Longarm started toward her. She noted the look in his eyes and got out of the way, but yelled out, "Hey, Curly! There's trouble headed your way, and he's a *big* son of a bitch!"

Longarm found himself in a high-ceilinged stairwell,

appointed richly with brocaded wallpaper and, for some reason, a suit of armor. A door across the way opened, and a man only slightly smaller than a steam locomotive appeared. He had curly red hair, so Longarm didn't wait to be introduced. He swung as hard as he could and connected firmly with the bodyguard's lantern jaw.

Nothing happened.

Curly not only looked like a locomotive; he seemed to be made of the same materials. He shook his head as if dimly aware of the blow and then, as the deputy hit him again, he simply reached out and hugged Longarm like a big bear, crooning, "Now, Jasus, me bucko, is it trouble you've come for? Faith, and it's trouble you've found, for it's in the bay I'll be after putting you, dead or alive."

Longarm tried to knee the monstrous redhead as he felt the breath being squeezed out of his creaking ribs. But Curly had his knees together against such a move and sighed, "Now, is that a dacent way for a wee thing like you t'act?"

Longarm butted his forehead into Curly's mouth, as hard as he could. Curly roared like an annoyed grizzly and warned, "You're beginning to *annoy* me, bucko! You jist come quiet, and I may be after depositin' you in the water alive. Another trick like that and it's a dead man you'll be!"

Longarm felt his feet leave the carpet as the giant started waltzing him toward the front door. He reached down with the only hand he could move, got a firm grip on Curly's family jewels, and started to twist them off.

The bigger man howled and literally threw Longarm across the hall into the suit of armor, shouting, "Jasus! Now I really am starting to dislike you!" as the lawman sprawled in a welter of disjointed steel plates. He crabbed sideways, clattering and scattering bits of armor as Curly charged. The big man crashed into the wall as Longarm got to his feet, holding the battle mace he'd found on the carpet amid the debris. As Curly moved in on him, growling low in his throat, Longarm could only hope the studded steel club might stop him.

He never found out. A new voice whipcracked, "What in hell is going on out here?" and Longarm recognized the white-eyed older man standing in the doorway. He said, "Buckley, I'm a deputy U.S. marshal. If you don't call that gorilla off, I'm going to have to pull a gun on him!"

Boss Buckley said, "Back off, Curly." But Curly said, "He went after me privates. I'm going to tear off his arms and legs. I'm going to twist off his head. And then . . . I'm going to kill him!"

Buckley laughed and said, "Later. After I hear what he has on his mind. What's this all about, Deputy?"

"I've come to ask a favor," Longarm gasped as he tried to regain his breath.

"You and everyone else. Let's go inside and sit down. Would you mind telling me how you found me here?"

"Like to. Can't. The man who told me where to find you made me promise not to tell on him. I can see why."

Buckley led the way to another room. It was expensively furnished and smelled musty. Buckley had a cigar in one hand, but there was no smell of tobacco smoke in the small room, so Longarm knew he'd been taken to one the boss hadn't been in that evening. The political meeting he'd been holding in some other part of the house must have been private indeed. But it was none of his business, so he didn't comment.

The boss waved Longarm to a chair and took a seat across from him, near a marble fireplace that smelled of damp ashes. He leaned back and fixed the lawman with a shrewd look from his oyster-colored, half-blind eyes, saying, "All right, this had better be good."

Longarm told his story, beginning with his assignment to the case and ending with a brief sketch of his escape. When he'd finished, the boss said, "I think you're barking up the wrong tree if you think Steve Field is in on it, son. I happen to know he's about to be made a justice of the Supreme Court."

Longarm exhaled heavily and shook his head. "God help the country!"

"Now cool down, son," the old boss admonished him. "I know old Steve. He's twice as tough and almost as mean as they say he is, but he wouldn't take a bribe from penny-ante thieves."

"What about *big* thieves, Mr. Buckley? Are you saying Field hasn't his price?"

Boss Buckley chuckled and said, "Of course he has his price. As does everyone, which makes my career so interesting. But a man slated for the Supreme Court's bench has expensive tastes—too expensive for what you have in mind. I know the Mother Lode like the back of my hand. The Bonanza reefs are played out. In fact, the Lost Chinaman bottomed out a good ten years or more ago. There can't be enough gold in that whole mountain to buy Steve Field—or even me."

Longarm chuckled and said, "I wouldn't know what your price is, sir, but you're dead wrong about the mine being played out. I read the reports from the assay office. It's true the original owners hit bottom back in the fifties. At least, they thought they'd hit bottom, but we live in changing times. The oldtimers just skimmed the cream when they found the Mother Lode. They took the stuff you can wash out with running water. The new owners up there use chemicals the forty-niners never heard of and they found the veins weren't all that pinched out after all."

Buckley nodded. "I know about the cyanide process. I've shoveled, hydraulicked, and cradled gold in my time. These newfangled methods explain why they've been shipping the ore down the mountain instead of stamping it out on the site, eh?"

"Yes sir. The old-fashioned stamping mills up in the gold fields can't extract enough gold from the country rock to make it a paying deal. So the Lost Chinaman's been sending it by narrow-gauge down to Sacramento where it's supposed to be leached out, melted down to bullion, and transferred here to the mint. But like I said, it ain't been getting here."

"So I heard," the boss said. "Where are the trains being held up?"

Longarm wondered if he dared ask the man for a smoke, but decided against it, and said, "That's the spooky part they sent me to find out about, Mr. Buckley. You see, the trains ain't being held up. They leave Manzanita with a shipment, chug down through the hills right peaceably, then turn up in Sacramento with worthless rock. Our government assay boys say the highgraders are substituting the same salmon-colored quartz the gold is found inside, only it's worthless. It looks like gold ore, but it ain't."

Boss Buckley puffed his cigar thoughtfully and said, "I give up. How the hell do you suppose they manage such a slick trick?"

"I don't know. You're right about its being slick. If the jaspers just stopped the train and rode off with the stuff, we'd have some notion where to cut their trail. But by switching worthless rock for gold-bearing ore somewhere along the way, they leave us with some sixty-odd miles of trackside to study." He paused for a moment before adding, "If I could get some cooperation around here for a few days, I might be able to answer better."

Buckley ignored the hint. "Do you suppose they have a railroad siding up there somewhere? You can't unload and then reload an ore car while it's moving. The only way I can see it is that they have a set of duplicate cars, loaded with dross rock and waiting along the right-of-way. Somehow, they must be uncoupling the ore cars, switching them for the others, and— Yeah, you'd only need to start with one string of empties. Each time you switched cars you'd wind up with more empty ones for the next time. You'd best start looking for a siding near a tunnel or switchback. Maybe someplace where they stop the train to jerk boiler water."

Longarm took the bull by the horns and said, "I'd like to. But I need your help, Mr. Buckley."

The older man snorted. "*My* help? Before we go a step deeper, I'd like you to tell me why. You're working for those shit-for-brains Republicans the voters were dumb enough to put in, last election. I wouldn't want this to get around, but I run the Democrats in this state!"

"I know. That's why I came to you. Most of the folks up near the diggings are Republicans. If any government people are mixed up in this highgrading, I should think you'd want me to expose them before it's time to vote again."

Boss Buckley chuckled and said, "I admire your gall. You must have been told by now that I'm supposed to be a scoundrel and a thief."

"Yes sir, and if this was my assignment, and if I could prove half of what I've heard, I'd arrest you. But I catch my crooks one at a time, and right now I'm after those highgraders. If you could get the county government up there off my back, I'd likely get them, too."

"How do you know I'm not one of them?" Buckley asked pointedly.

Longarm shrugged. "Don't seem likely. The sheriff up there is a Republican. Another Republican named Lovejoy robbed me of my guns, my badge, my watch, a horse and saddle, and too much else to mention. He's welcome to all but my guns, watch, and badge, as long as he promises not to arrest me any more."

Buckley smoked a while, immersed in thought, and Longarm knew he'd aroused the older man's chess-playing instincts. Finally the boss asked, "What could I do if I was willing to? I run San Francisco, not Calaveras County, or even Sacramento."

"They'd listen to you, though. Every nail and barrel of flour they need up there in the Mother Lode comes through your port. I doubt whether a handful of deputies up near the mines would want to tangle with your lambs, either. I know I wouldn't!"

Buckley laughed expansively, and said, "Hell, old Curly is one of my *gentle* lambs. But I'm not about to loan you a posse of waterfront Irishmen."

Longarm leaned forward and asked intently, "What *are* you going to do, Mr. Buckley?"

The boss studied his cigar ash and replied, "I'm not sure. With Steve Field on his way to the Supreme Court, and a mention in your case report saying I've been helpful to the U.S. government, I might feel more comfortable about those Eastern senators who keep questioning the way we do things out here on the coast. You did say something about mentioning me in your report, didn't you?"

"I sure did, Mr. Buckley." Longarm smiled. "Now that you mention it, I don't see how I could have solved this case without your help. I disremember just what you did for me, though."

"You let me worry about the wheels of government,"

44

Buckley said. "Take your time getting back to the gold fields while I pass the word to a few people."

"Like Justice Field and the marshal in Sacramento?" Longarm prompted.

"I told you Steve Field's not a thief. I doubt if he knows you're alive."

"Somebody in his office does," the deputy pointed out. "They came down hard on a jurisdictional dispute and signaled the county to get rid of me."

"All right," Buckley relented, "let's say there's a crook or two in the marshal's office. Let's say that once the marshal's personal attention is drawn to the matter, a smart crook would crawfish off, grinning as innocent as a shit-eating dog. You give me a day or two and I'll be surprised as hell if anyone wearing a badge tries to give you a hard time."

"I'll be in your debt if you can, sir. That still leaves me with the highgraders, whoever they may be, and they say the late Calico Kid had lots of friends in the county."

The older man growled, "Don't press me, son. Despite what they say about me, I don't have much truck with outlaws and roughnecks I don't have on my payroll. I'll tell the sheriff's department up there that it might not be advisable to gun you down like a dog. You'll be on your own as far as anyone else up there is concerned!"

The Sacramento boat left San Francisco after dark to arrive upstream at the capital in the morning. It was comfortable, but a slow way to travel, even that far west.

On the other hand, he'd promised Boss Buckley that he'd take his time getting back to Manzanita, so what the hell.

He'd wired Denver for expense money and bought

himself some fresh duds before engaging a stateroom on the paddlewheel steamer. As the night boat puffed its way through the San Pablo narrows and headed for the tule marshes of the big inland delta, Longarm took a seat near a window in the dining salon and gave his order to an immaculate colored waiter who acted as important as Queen Victoria's head butler.

He was waiting for his steak and potatoes when a female voice at his side asked, "Forgive me, sir. Is anyone sitting at this table?"

Longarm smiled up at the expensive-looking brunette who'd spoken, and replied, "I'm sitting at it. You're welcome to that other chair across the table."

The girl smiled back at him and sat down, explaining, "A woman traveling alone has to be careful. The purser tells me you're a U.S. marshal."

"Only a deputy," he corrected her. "My handle is Custis Long."

"I'm Sylvia Baxter. Of the Boston Baxters, that is."

Longarm studied her, wondering what a Boston Baxter was. She had a veil over her eyes, hanging from a perky little blue velvet hat, but he could see she was pretty, in a snooty sort of way. The hat had been chosen to match her wide-set eyes. A hat like that cost money, no matter what color it was. He said, "I was in Boston, once. Had to transport a prisoner back from there. I didn't get to see much of it, but the harbor was right pretty."

"I'm afraid we lived on the Back Bay. You do know what the Back Bay is, don't you?"

Longarm found her approach a trifle offensive, so he nodded and said, "I can read, too. If we ever get served, you might be surprised to learn that I don't eat with my fingers." He saw the uncertain look in her eyes and added, "Might use my bowie knife if the steak is tough, but I promise I won't shoot the waiter."

She smiled uncertainly, and said, "Dear me, we are getting off to a bad start, aren't we?"

Longarm was beginning to enjoy needling her. "Don't know. Where are we supposed to be headed?" he asked with a blank expression.

She replied huffily, "I simply introduced myself in what I felt was a proper manner, sir."

"Maybe. Folks out our way don't fret much about which side of the tracks a person comes from. I'll say right out I was born and brought up on a hard-scrabble West Virginia farm, and I'll take on any man who says that makes me less than he is."

The woman blinked, apparently taken aback by the marshal's directness. "My word! I certainly never intended to start a fight with you! Are you always so sensitive about your background?"

Longarm's mouth smiled, but his eyes remained expressionless. "Honey, I never had any background. We were too poor. As to what coming from Back Bay Boston makes you, all I really want to know is whether you aim to pay for your own dinner or whether you're expecting me to."

Sylvia Baxter flushed under her veil and snapped, "That's a churlish thing to say! Of course I had every intention of buying my own meal!"

He looked elaborately relieved and said, "In that case, let's just eat and say no more about it."

He saw the snooty waiter passing, apparently with no intention of taking her order, so he snapped his fingers.

The waiter didn't look their way, but the girl said, "Please, it's not polite to snap one's fingers at the help."

Longarm shrugged, drew his revolver, and aimed it at the ceiling. The girl gasped, "Oh, my God!" in a loud voice, and that did the trick. The waiter swung his head to see what was wrong and, noting the gun in

Longarm's hand, hurried over with a nervous smile, saying, "May I be of service, sir?"

He'd obviously been working here long enough to understand the frontier breed better than he'd been letting on. Longarm put the gun away, saying, "This lady wants to eat. So do I. Where in thunder is the steak I ordered?"

"It's coming right up, sir. Would madame care to order, now?"

Sylvia looked undecided and stammered, "Dear me, I haven't read the menu."

Longarm said, "Give her steak and potatoes, and tell them we ain't got all night."

As the waiter scurried away to do as he was told, the girl asked Longarm, "How did you know I wanted steak and potatoes, sir?"

"Everybody wants steak and potatoes. I read the menu. By the time you found anything worth ordering, we'd have likely starved to death."

The girl picked up the menu firmly and began to read it, trying to ignore Longarm. He tried in turn not to drum his fingers on the table. He was wondering what was wrong with him tonight. He was usually a friendly enough sort, and the girl was pretty, but he felt edgy, impatient, and out of sorts. Was he coming down with some ague? He didn't feel sick, just sort of raw-nerved about something. But what could it be? It wasn't the snooty little Boston gal. Any other time he'd simply have laughed her uppity notions off. They said ponies and other critters got like this when an earthquake was fixing to happen. Could he be sensing some disaster he couldn't see or smell?

The waiter returned with their orders, a nervous smile, and a bottle. He said; "We'd like you to accept a complimentary bottle of our California wine, Marshal. May I draw the cork for you?"

Longarm nodded and said, "Sure, you can draw it *and* quarter it." Then he shook his head to clear it, wondering, *What in thunder is wrong with you, old son? You're acting like a schoolboy sniggering at a dirty joke!*

He knew he wasn't given to rawhiding colored folks or playing big bad westerner to schoolmarmish little snoots. But he was fighting a terrific urge to draw the gun again and shoot up the overhead coal-oil lamps. The infernal lamps were too bright. They hurt his eyes. It seemed pretty silly when he thought about it. A high-plains rider who'd squinted against a searing sun for many a summer shouldn't be blinded by a little coal-oil flame in a smoke-glass globe.

The waiter poured a small amount of red wine into a long-stemmed glass and handed it to Longarm. The deputy remembered the form and took a sip before nodding. The nod was a lie, for the wine, if that was what it was, tasted like red ink mixed with vinegar. The waiter filled both their glasses, put the bottle on the table between them, and left with a relieved expression.

Sylvia Baxter tasted her wine and said, "My, it is good, isn't it? I mean, it would hardly pass for Bordeaux '53, but it has an amusing bouquet."

Longarm stared at the bottle as if it had played a dirty trick on him. The fancy label said it had been made in Riverside by some colony, but it didn't say what river the colony was beside. He remembered his manners and waited for her to start eating. But she kept dawdling with the godawful wine until he muttered, "Let's dig in," and started cutting his steak. She probably had him figured for a savage anyway and, what the hell, he'd never see her again. He intended to catch the stage in Sacramento in the morning, and take his own sweet time getting back to Manzanita. He only hoped Boss Buckley's word would arrive there ahead of him. If the word didn't help, he'd cross that bridge when it shot at him.

The steak tasted as though it had been fried in iodine, and he was about to say so when the girl smiled and said, "My, this *is* good, isn't it? I've been making do with shipboard fare since leaving Boston. Fresh meat is such a relief to my poor, tortured taste buds."

He didn't want to call the lady a liar, so he said, "Oh, you came around the Horn?"

She shook her head and explained, "No, I took the Vanderbilt line to Nicaragua, crossed to the Pacific by the Commodore's road, and arrived yesterday on the Matson clipper."

"You didn't get to see much of Frisco, then?"

"Forgive me for correcting you, but they tell me it's simply not called Frisco by gentlefolk."

He said, "Yeah," and took another bite. It was no use. The food was as bad as the wine and he was feeling . . . seasick?

That was impossible. They were steaming through a big flat swamp he could see outside in the moonlight. The night was dead calm and the water all around was as flat as a millpond. He could feel the vibration of the big stern-mounted paddle and hear the hiss of the engine if he listened carefully, but they were moving as smoothly as silk up the winding, shallow Sacramento.

The girl was saying, "I am in a hurry to reach Manzanita, but I did a bit of sightseeing in San Francisco. I rode all the way to the top of Nob Hill on one of those new cable cars. I must say they're up-to-date out here. I'm afraid I expected California to be much more primitive."

"Some of it still is. You say you're headed for Manzanita, up in Calaveras County?"

"Yes. That's the place Mark Twain wrote about in that amusing piece about the jumping frogs, wasn't it?"

"Yep. I read it, too. The last time I was up there, though, they weren't betting on frogs worth mention. Uh, do you have kin or something up in Calaveras County?"

"I'm joining my brother," she told him. "He's a mining engineer interested in some properties near Manzanita."

"Oh? Did he come out ahead of you, then?"

She looked down, avoiding his eyes as she murmured, "I hadn't planned to come at all. But Ralph is the only family I have now. You see, our parents are gone and . . . well, if you must know, I just divorced a man I never should have married. Ralph told me he was no good, but would I listen?"

Longarm nodded, understanding her snooty act better now. Divorces were legal enough, but still shocked a lot of people, despite the changes that had rocked the world since Victoria had been in the catbird seat of proper society. Sylvia Baxter was acting as if her armpits smelled of violets because she'd probably had a few snide remarks spit at her. To comfort her, he said, "I'd say divorcing a skunk is more civilized than shooting him or putting flypaper in his coffee."

She looked startled and said, "Flypaper? In coffee?"

"Coffee, tea, or whatever. That sticky stuff on flypaper is a mix of honey and arsenic. You'd be surprised how many mean husbands have died young since flypaper was invented."

She laughed, for once not stiffly, and said, "I should have met you sooner. The papers I paid for cost much more than those I could have bought in any general store."

He laughed with her and said, "We live and learn. Maybe next time."

She said, "I'm not sure there'll be a next time. I've had all of marriage I care for, thank you very much."

"Don't thank me; I wasn't proposing. You'll be taking the Wells Fargo stage up to the Mother Lode, won't you?"

"I don't think so. My brother wrote that there's a narrow-gauge railway winding up from Valley Springs. I think I have to transfer from the main line at a place called Lodi, and—"

"It's the long way around, but likely more comfortable than the stage," he cut in. He was disappointed in one way, but relieved in another. Ordinarily he had an eye out for a well-turned ankle, but there was something about this woman that made him as broody as an old hen on a cold glass egg. Besides, he hadn't come all the way out here to spark divorcees. He'd been on the case nearly a week and, up to now, hadn't even managed to get within hailing distance of the goddamned mine he'd been sent to investigate.

He took another sip of wine, gagged, and suddenly knew he was going to throw up!

Without a word, he got up from the table, moved off at a trot, and just made it out to the promenade deck in time. He leaned out over the rail and gave everything he'd eaten in the past couple of years to the croaking frogs protesting in the tule reeds they were passing through.

He heaved at least five times before a couple of dry retches told him he'd hit bottom. A male voice to his left said, "If you taste hair, swallow fast, or you'll be throwing up your asshole!"

Longarm turned to the amused deckhand and asked mildly, "Can you swim, sailor?"

"Don't take it personal, cowboy. I've been seasick myself. Though, come to think of it, it was out at sea. Ain't the waves in this delta a caution?"

Longarm wiped his sweating brow with the back of

his hand and said, "I ain't seasick. I suspicion I've been poisoned. You have a sawbones on this tub?"

The deckhand shook his head and said, "Not in the crew. If you're really sick, I can ask the purser if there's a doctor on board."

Longarm shook his head and said, "I'll just go to my stateroom and flatten out. If I ain't dead by the time we make Sacramento, I likely threw up whatever it was."

He brushed past the amused deckhand and staggered to his stateroom, where he stripped without lighting the lamp, tore open the bottom bunk, and flopped face down on it, feeling as though he'd been run over by a Conestoga wagon. He ached all over, and though the California nights were cooler than he'd expected, he was sweating like a pig shoveling coal.

How in thunder had they done it? He hadn't had a thing to eat or drink at the whorehouse. The Boston gal hadn't been wearing any rings big enough to play a Borgia trick on him. It hardly seemed likely that the steamboat company had poisoned him. Could it have been those oysters he'd eaten for breakfast at the hotel?

He started feeling a little better. He'd most likely thrown up whatever it was, and it was time to reconsider living long enough to collect his pension.

Longarm got up, lurched over to the gunbelt he'd hung on a rusty nail, and drew the Colt he'd bought in San Francisco to replace the one the Manzanita constable had stolen from him. He hadn't had time to shorten the barrel or file off the front sight, but he thought he could manage a fast enough draw from under his pillow. The door to the deck outside was a flimsy-looking thing with jalousie slats for ventilation, but anyone busting through it would have to make some noise. Gun in hand, he walked naked to the door to slide the bolt in place.

The door opened before he could reach it.

Longarm whipped the muzzle of the gun up, trained it on the slim figure outlined in the moonlight, and snapped, "Freeze, you son of a bitch!"

Then he saw that it was Sylvia Baxter. She looked startled, which sort of made sense, even if nothing else did. Suddenly aware of his nakedness, he placed his free hand in front of his crotch and asked, "Don't folks knock in Boston, sis?"

"I did knock! What on earth is *wrong* with you, sir?"

"I've been shot at, thrown in jail, beat up, and poisoned. Now let's hear what's wrong with you. Are you in the habit of leaping at a person wearing nothing but his birthday suit?"

"Would you please stop pointing that gun at me? I only came to your cabin because you played a dirty trick on me back there in the dining salon. I had to pay for both of our dinners!"

He lowered the Colt, still covering his privates as he stepped back and said, "Come on in. My pants are hanging over there. You'll have to fish out my wallet and help yourself, because I've only got two hands."

She laughed nervously and said, "I know, but it's a little late now." Then she added, "Don't worry about it. I studied medicine for two years before they forced me out of it. I've seen naked men before."

He backed to the bunk and sat down, pulling the edge of the blanket over his thighs as she turned her back on him to go through his pockets. He was grateful that it was almost dark in the room, for he knew he must be beet-red. He said, "It's too bad you didn't graduate. I could use a doctor right now—even a female one."

She turned around and handed him his wallet, saying, "You owe me seventy-five cents plus the extra dime I tipped the waiter. I might have known you'd be like all the other men. Damn it, I would have been a *good* doctor! You men just don't seem to understand that a woman has a brain, too."

He put the gun under the pillow and took out a bill, saying, "I'll give you a whole dollar and we'll call it square. As to your brain, I ain't actually seen it, so I can't say whether you've got one or not."

She snatched the bill from him angrily and stuffed it into her purse as she sniffed, "I don't understand why a grown man should be afraid of a woman doctor. There are a lot of quacks and butchers who are men— name one who is a woman."

"Don't reckon I can," he concurred, not a little nonplussed by her belligerence. "Now look here," he continued. "First of all, I said I'd be right glad to see *any* doctor just about now—"

"Even a female one," she interrupted him acidly.

"Even a Paiute medicine man," he continued. "I'm purely sorry about the eighty-five cents, but I was a mite confused and in just a smidgin of a hurry. You wouldn't have cared for it much if I'd stayed."

To his surprise and further confusion, she sat down on the foot of the bed and said, "You know damned well it isn't the eighty-five cents; it's your whole attitude."

This conversation was starting to make his head spin even more. He said, "Up to a minute ago, I didn't have any attitude worth mention, but I'll admit I'm getting one pretty fast. Just to set the record straight, as a U.S. deputy sworn to uphold the Constitution, I can tell you I'd arrest anyone trying to deprive any citizen—yourself included—of his constitutional rights."

"There, you see?" she exploded. " '*His* constitutional rights'—it's even in the language."

"Afraid I can't take responsibility for that," he said. "I only talk it—I didn't make it up."

"What about the right to vote?" she pressed on, leaning closer to him and jabbing a finger into the thatch of hair on his solid chest.

Longarm was beginning to wonder seriously what her game was, and he decided to feed her some more rope. "I'll allow that most *men* don't have the sense to pour piss out of their boots—excuse me, ma'am—much less vote. I doubt that women would do much worse, and maybe someday, when the country simmers down and gets less hectic around the polls—"

He noticed that her face was growing flushed and little beads of perspiration had appeared on her upper lip as she asked, "Does the Constitution say only you men have the right to sow wild oats? There's a parlor house in every town across the country, and you know very well that no man sniggering with the others at the pool hall would ever admit that he was a virgin."

"Would you admit it?" he asked pointedly.

There was an unmistakable sparkle in her eyes as she replied, "It's hardly a problem. I told you I've been married."

"And since I don't visit parlor houses," he said, "I guess that more or less cancels out the entire issue."

Longarm felt now as if he were floating in the air a little distance above the bed. He knew he needed to lie down, with her or without her. As usual, his amorous parts were behaving as though they had a life of their own, and he could feel himself swelling beneath the blanket across his lap. Longarm decided, with fireflies glittering before his eyes, that it was time to call her play. He placed a hand on her knee. She glanced down at his hand without moving away, then shifted her gaze to the prominent bulge at his crotch. Her eyes rose to meet his, and she asked, "Am I to take that as a challenge or a compliment, Mr. Long?"

He didn't answer. He couldn't answer. Suddenly the room was spinning around and he felt as if he were about to puke all over them both. So he decided to lie down and die instead.

He was in this funny big room with red velvet drapes. A bunch of naked women were coming at him from all directions. They had painted faces and high-heeled shoes and they were all grinning from ear to ear. But their grins were evil and they had guns in their hands.

He reached for his own gun, but he wasn't wearing his cross-draw rig. He wasn't wearing anything at all. He was naked and had a monstrous erection, and the painted women were laughing at it. A big blonde with a mouthful of gold teeth and a Mexican gunbelt riding low on her naked hips grabbed at him as if she intended to milk him like a cow. He stepped back and discovered that another naked woman had knelt behind him on her hands and knees. He fell backward to the thick red carpet and the big blonde jumped over the girl who'd tripped him, placed her French heels to either side of his chest, and squatted. Her aim was perfect and he felt his shaft going deeply into her as she shouted, "Powder River and let 'er buck!!"

It felt too good to be real. He decided he was having a wet dream. He wondered if he'd get to come this time, before he awoke all the way. The trouble with wet dreams was that he always seemed to wake up just as they were getting interesting. He started pumping back, but he couldn't quite make it and he knew he'd open his eyes in the little furnished room by Cherry Creek and discover that he had to take a leak. It was purely frustrating to wake up with a hard-on and nobody there to share it with.

He opened his eyes. For a long moment he wondered where he was. Then he remembered that he was on a steamboat. The stateroom lamp was lit. Sylvia Baxter was beside him, sitting up in bed and doing something funny to his eyelids. She was stark naked. Built better than he'd expected, too. Those starched lace dickies that women wore down the front of their dresses sort of flattened things out. Her pink nipples were turned up like her nose.

He said, "What happened? The last time we met, you had all your duds on. Then I must have passed out. I had the damnedest dream."

"It was a dream for *me,* too!" she said. "I didn't know you were unconscious until a moment ago."

"You mean we—?"

She smiled languidly. "Yes, darling, and I must say, you're better by reflex action than my silly husband ever was wide awake. I think you've got a concussion. Has anyone hit you on the head recently?"

He grinned wanly, and said, "Now that you mention it, doc, I did have a tussle with a big Irish wharf rat last night. He hit me with the wall of a whorehouse."

She nodded and said, "That explains a lot. I didn't think you could be as crazy as you've been acting. Have you had sudden mood changes? Any nausea?"

"I threw up a while back. What do you reckon I should take for this concussion, doc?"

"There's nothing you can take. What you really need is a few nights of bed rest. If I'd known you were ill, I'd have . . . well, what's done is done."

He grinned and said, "The hell you say! If I really did what I dreamed I did, I've got some catching up to do in the real world."

As he put an arm around her, Sylvia drew back and insisted, "Not in your condition. Maybe later."

He said, "My condition right now is hard as a poker and, what the hell, it ain't like we're strangers!"

She was still insisting that he was too weak as he rolled her to the mattress and started to mount her.

Then, as he got his hips between her smooth ivory thighs, she went limp and breathed, "Do be careful, dear heart. I don't know what I'd do if you killed yourself with this foolishness!"

He got a hand between them and guided his shaft into her moist warmth, saying, "Yeah, it'd be a tough thrill to follow, wouldn't it? A gal who'd once come with a dead man in her would never be able to top it for an interesting experience!"

As he slid all the way into her, she gasped in mingled pleasure and annoyance. "I think I liked you better unconscious! Must you be so vulgar about it?"

He laughed and started moving. "Hell, lady, if you didn't want it he-man style, you never should have started it."

"I didn't start it. Oh, stop talking like a fool and *do* it!"

The fireflies were back again and the room was spinning like a merry-go-round, but he knew he wasn't going to black out. He gritted his teeth and muttered to himself, *Listen, God. I'm likely to take it personal if you don't let me do it right this time*.

This time, God listened.

Sylvia couldn't ride to Manzanita in the stage with him because her brother was meeting her at trackside in the mountains. So they kissed goodbye as the boat docked in Sacramento the next morning, and Longarm promised to look her up when he arrived in Manzanita.

He went to the Wells Fargo office and bought a ride to Manzanita. The agent told him he had a couple of hours to kill before the stage hauled out for the High Sierra. He had most of the background material he needed, but Marshal Vail and the treasury boys might have missed a thing or two, so he moseyed over to the land office to refresh his memory.

Longarm introduced himself to an elderly clerk as a deputy U.S. marshal, without mentioning what district court he worked for. The clerk was a friendly sort who didn't even ask to see his badge, which was just as well, since some son of a bitch had it up in the hills somewhere.

As he started pawing through the files, the clerk said, "I can tell you just about anything you'll find in there, Deputy. I came out here in '49."

"I'm interested in the Lost Chinaman claim, up in Calaveras County."

"Hell, son, I was washing color in the headwaters of the Stanislaus when Mark Twain wrote that fool story about the frog."

"You ever meet the frog?"

"Nope, but I met Mark Twain and Bret Harte when they was just starting to tell all them lies about us. You see, the gold rush started down here in the low country, when they found color washed down off the Sierra in the creek beds."

"I know about the gold rush, old son," Longarm told the man.

"No, you don't," the old clerk contradicted him. "Not if you been reading Harte and Twain. Like I said, we started washing color in the low country. By the fifties, we'd followed the gold up the streams and found the Mother Lode—a big, wide belt of gold quartz running a couple hundred miles up there. The color we'd found in the creeks was just what had washed out of the real lode. It was the hard-rock miners who had the capital to move mountains to get at the good stuff."

"How many mines are still in Bonanza up in Calaveras County, pop?" Longarm asked.

"Bonanza? Not a one. Most of the veins petered out some time ago. A man named Hearst has a working claim in Calaveras, a mine called Sheep Ranch. But he's hauling low-grade out these days. Hearst is a big boo who got in on the big Virginia City strike, on the other side of the Sierra. He's got the capital to crush his own ore. Angel Camp's about dead. Murphy has a low-grade mine nobody's interested in these days. They had a copper strike up there a while back, but it never amounted to much. Copper's too cheap to haul over all them ridges and they just couldn't compete with Arizona Territory."

"So let's talk about the Lost Chinaman. I understand the owner is a man named MacLeod?"

"That's right. Nice young jasper, for an Easterner. Him and his pretty little wife bought the mine for next to nothing. It seemed to bottom out a good six or eight years back, but MacLeod's some sort of geologist and he hit a vein the others overlooked. They say he's been shipping tolerable ore."

"He may be shipping it," the deputy agreed. "It's not getting anywhere, though. You got a railroad map of the county?"

The clerk nodded and slid open a wide, flat drawer, saying, "I know what you have in mind. Other marshals have been studying the same crazy situation. You won't find the siding everyone's looking for. Half of the old narrow-gauge tracks up there have been pulled up for scrap."

Longarm spread the map on a nearby table and ran his finger along a red line between Manzanita and the Big Valley. He mused aloud, "If there's unused track laying around up there to be claimed by any junkman, it wouldn't be impossible for somebody to build his own siding in some wooded stretch of canyon."

The clerk shook his head. "The other lawmen have been all up and down the line. Besides, the train crews say they've never stopped or been stopped between the mine tipple and the mills down here."

"What about this other fellow, Hearst?"

"George Hearst? He lives in Frisco. Ain't heard about him missing any gold. Like I said, they crush their own ore up at Sheep Ranch and ship it almost pure. They send it down in freight wagons, under guard. The way I hear tell, nobody wants to tangle with old Hearst. He's in politics in the city and thick with the Big Five. This young MacLeod likely don't have as many friends who'd back his play against high-graders."

Longarm smiled thinly. "He has the U.S. government in his corner. He contracted with the treasury to deliver his gold to the mint. Where does this Hearst jasper send his gold?"

The clerk shrugged. "Same place, of course. Nobody else buys gold in quantity on this coast." He saw Longarm's puzzled frown and asked, "Did I say something important, Deputy?"

"Maybe. These robberies have added up to a mess of gold, no matter what the quality of the stolen ore might have been. But you're right. You can't sell a real pile of gold to anyone but Uncle Sam—not without attracting a lot of attention."

"Mexico?" the clerk suggested.

The marshal tugged at a corner of his mustache. "Doubt it. For sure, they couldn't haul it that far as ore. They have to have a refinery we don't know about. If MacLeod's extracting with the cyanide process, it can't be just some backwoods stamping mill, either. You say the Hearst mine has its own mill?"

The old man shook his head. "Wrong tree, Deputy. The mill in Sheep Ranch is just a simple crusher that runs the slurry over mercury beds. They boil the mercury out of the results and wind up with rich dust. If the Lost Chinaman's ore needs cyanide to leach it from the rock, the Hearst mill couldn't extract it worth mention."

"How about those other ghost towns up there, like Angel's Camp?"

"They ain't quite dead, for one thing, so you'd have witnesses. There ain't no cyanide mills, either, so you'd get no gold."

"Try it this way. What if MacLeod's wrong? The ore might be rich enough to run through an old-fashioned mill and settle for half, letting whatever gold the cyanide might get out stay where it is?"

The man scratched his wispy-haired pate vigorously. "Well, highgraders is called highgraders 'cause they skim the cream. You could get some gold out of nigh *any* rock with a pan and running water. They're going to a lot of effort if that's their play, though. MacLeod's ore is marginal. Wouldn't be worth digging if they hadn't come up with new methods in the past few years. Hell, if *I* was up there highgrading, I'd rob George Hearst's mine. It's a third richer in color."

Longarm thanked the clerk and left. He went next to the offices of the *Sacramento Bee,* where he found another friendly cuss who was more than willing to jaw about the newspaper's back files.

He knew he was wasting time asking about the highgrading. If the case could have been solved by reading old reports on paper, the treasury never would have come bleating to Justice for a helping hand.

He asked about the Calico Kid and was told, "He got the name and the rep down near Los Angeles. Mining camp called Calico. Nobody knows who he was or where he came from before he started shooting folks as a hobby."

Longarm pursed his lips and said, "Hung out in mining country, did he? Now that's right interesting.

You got anything in the morgue about him robbing gold shipments?"

The reporter shook his head and said, "Nope. The way they tell it, he was just a wild saddle tramp. Rode with some other young owlhoots of the same stripe. They've shot up a few towns for the hell of it, and been run out of twice as many. But the kid never had any robbery pinned on him."

"What *did* he do for a living, then? Folks can't just ride around like something in a Ned Buntline novel with no visible means of support. Bullets cost a nickel apiece and drinks are three cents a shot!"

The reporter shrugged and said, "He probably let folks grubstake him some. Lots of people sort of like to stay on friendly terms with a mean-eyed jasper with a rep."

The deputy pondered this for a moment, then said, "I don't see him as a man who begged for handouts. If he didn't work, he must have been stealing for a living."

"Could be," the newspaperman agreed. "If he ever robbed anyone, they never saw fit to press charges, which isn't hard to understand. They say he had about five sidekicks riding with him, all of them just as mean as he was."

Longarm saw that he wasn't getting anywhere, and left. He found a café and had some chili and a beer. They both stayed down, so he figured he was getting over the set-to with Curly.

By the time he got to the Wells Fargo office again, the stage was loading up for its run up the slope. The jehu holding the reins was a fierce-looking old man of about seventy. The shotgun rider at his side was a consumptive-looking hunchback with a bullet hole in the brim of his dusty Stetson. Longarm saw that two passengers were already aboard, so he climbed in.

His fellow passengers were a tall man wearing a

business suit and a blonde mustache, seated across from a girl of about twenty-five. She wore black Spanish lace and her face was a dusky shade of rose. If she wasn't at least half Indian, he'd never met one. Her dark eyes smoldered angrily in a way that led Longarm to believe that anger was a natural condition with her, so he just smiled and sat beside her, introducing himself to the man in the opposite seat.

The man held out a hand and said, "I'm glad to know you, Deputy. I'm Kevin MacLeod."

Longarm blinked and asked, "The same Kevin Mac-Leod who owns the Lost Chinaman? I was beginning to think I'd never find you. This must be your pretty little wife I've heard so much about, right?"

The girl gasped in dismay and MacLeod said, "Not hardly. Allow me to present Señorita Felicidad Vallejo. One of the Vallejos of Old California."

The girl looked away, trying to ignore them both. MacLeod shrugged and said, "She doesn't like gringos very much."

Longarm refused to be snubbed, and he said, "It's an honor, ma'am. I read about your kinsman, General Vallejo. He sort of chased our army through a few canyons before they called the war off, didn't he?"

She didn't answer. So he shrugged and turned back to MacLeod as the jehu atop the stage cracked his whip and shouted, "*Move,* you oat-wastin' sons of bitches!"

The stage lurched into motion and took off in a cloud of dust, swaying on the rawhide thoroughbraces as if it were a small craft plunging through choppy water. MacLeod grinned and said, "It gets worse when we reach the high country. I think old Logan, up there, has been trying to die young. You can see he never made it, but it's not for lack of trying."

Longarm turned toward Señorita Vallejo, touched the brim of his Stetson, and asked, "Mind if I smoke, ma'am?" She kept her face averted, gazing out the window, and made no answer. The deputy shrugged and, taking her silence for consent, produced a cheroot from an inside coat pocket and planted it between his front teeth. He turned back to MacLeod and said, "Let's talk about rocks. Just how many shipments have we lost track of, so far?"

MacLeod's smile faded as he said, "Thirteen. I don't know what I'm going to do if you can't find out who's been doing it, Deputy. We've been digging damned decent stuff out of that mountain, but my men have to be paid and my wife and I are down to bread and beans. If they keep robbing us, we're just going to have to cash in our chips. Our original grubstake's about used up."

Longarm struck a match on the coach's window frame, and touched the flame to his cigar. "Haven't you made *any* money on the mine?"

"Not a red cent! I figure, allowing for a rough assay, we've shipped at least a quarter of a million in extractable ore since we reopened the mine. Not a speck of it's ever reached the mint."

Longarm blew out a large cloud of smoke that dissipated rapidly in the breeze from the window. He was tired of going over the same ground, so he didn't ask about the shipments. Instead he asked, "Do you know a mining engineer named Baxter?"

"Ralph Baxter? Sure. He's staying at the hotel in Manzanita. As a matter of fact, he's made me an offer for the Lost Chinaman."

The deputy's eyebrows rose slightly. "You don't say. Now that's sort of interesting."

"Not really," MacLeod said. "I have no intention of selling—not if I can help it. Baxter is fronting for an Eastern syndicate, and frankly he's been talking penny-ante. He knows what we have up there. I took him through the mine myself. You know what he offered us? A measly million dollars!"

Longarm whistled and asked, "You call that measly? For a man living on bread and beans, you think big, MacLeod!"

"Hell, I'd *be* big if they'd let me! The vein I opened promises to assay out a hundred times that amount. That reef of quartz shows no sign of having a bottom to it. Given the time and a little more backing, I can dig for gold all the way to China!"

"Maybe, but in the meantime we have to see about getting it to the mint. Have any others made you an offer for your mine? I've got reasons for asking."

MacLeod nodded and said, "I follow your drift. Ralph Baxter might be a crook, but I sort of doubt it. I checked out the people he works for. I'm not supposed to know who they are, but a man who's knocked around the mining business knows who to compare notes with. Baxter's outfit is made up of Boston bankers with solid reputations. I'd say his offer was legitimate, but it's way the hell too low to consider."

"How about the Hearst interests, over in Sheep Ranch? Do they seem interested?"

"They sent a man over to congratulate us when we hit pay dirt. He didn't make an offer. I showed him through the mine. He said the rock formation we're into isn't the same one Hearst is working. He said that was all he was really interested in. You see, some folks think the gold quartz runs all the way under the Sierra, clean over to the diggings in Nevada. But we agreed we'll have to dig some even to get near one another underground. Sheep Ranch is a good ten miles from Manzanita and the Lost Chinaman."

"Maybe. I'll ride over there and have a talk with them, though. From everything I've heard about

George Hearst, your mine's just the sort of thing he's been buying up on both sides of the range. Didn't it strike you as odd that they weren't interested in buying you out?"

MacLeod frowned and said, "Not at the time. Now that you mention it, though, Hearst has the capital and muscle to make the Lost Chinaman a paying proposition. You see, you usually lose money on opening a mine and organizing things. A lot of small operators go broke holding rich enough claims. It takes money to make money, once you're into hard-rock deep mining. But they have money, and they know we've opened a new vein. Do you think—?"

Longarm held up a cautioning hand. "Let's leave off thinking till we know some more. You eat the apple a bite at a time, in my business. I'd best start with the suspects closer to home."

They rode on in comparative silence for a time. The stage was jarring hell out of them all as it started hitting rougher road. The Mexican girl was pouting fit to bust, and Longarm was heartily sick of running over the details of the mysterious highgraders. It seemed that no matter who he met up with, they all had the same impossible tale to tell. He knew they'd all missed something. Something simple. Nobody could simply lift a running freight car filled with gold ore off the tracks in broad daylight without the train crew noticing it. Someone had missed something—something important. He'd just have to bull on through till he spotted something in the pattern that nobody had seen up until now.

They were a couple of hours out of Sacramento and had just topped a rise when Longarm felt the stage slow down and heard the jehu cry out, "Son of a bitch!"

His oath was followed by the crack of a rifle shot

and the sound of something or someone thudding to the dust outside. Then the stage was moving faster and a bullet slammed into the doorjamb near Longarm's head!

MacLeod gasped, "Road agents?" as he drew his own Smith & Wesson. Longarm didn't answer. He was leaning out the door he'd opened, gun in hand and looking back.

There were four of them, riding hard after the runaway stage and shooting from the saddle. Longarm spotted the body of the jehu on the trail as one of the road agents jumped his pony over it and kept coming. Longarm took aim and fired. He missed with his first shot. His second slug hit the pony he'd been aiming for and spilled the outlaw ass-over-teakettle into the dust.

He fired again, dropping another mount with its cursing rider, and then the survivors were reining in. One of them was shaking his fist.

Longarm climbed out on the side of the careening coach and looked up at the boot. There was nobody sitting up there, with or without the reins. He swore and climbed all the way to the top, holstering his gun as he crawled to the vacant seat. The shotgun rider was down in the boot, alive but bleeding like a stuck pig. Longarm saw that he'd managed to hang onto the traces, albeit with no control over the frightened mules. He said, "Good man!" and pried the blood-slicked reins from the shotgun's hand.

The hunchback made a gargling sound and tried to say something. Longarm said, "Just hold on, old son. You ain't hit bad. I'll have a looksee as soon as I get these infernal mules under control!"

He lied, of course. The poor bastard was done for, but he didn't think it would cheer the shotgun to hear it from him right now.

Longarm hauled back hard and kicked the brake rod, locking the wheels. The team dragged the coach a few yards, then came to a nervous, dancing stop. Longarm reached down with his free hand and groped for the shotgun wedged between the bulkhead and the dying guard. Then he looked quickly around in a full circle. They were alone on a stretch of rolling mustard meadow. Kevin MacLeod, gun in hand, stuck his head out and called up, "You seem to have driven them off, Deputy. What happened to the crew?"

Longarm said, "Both hit. The jehu didn't stop when they threw down on him. He was a good old man. Can you handle a scattergun?"

"Of course. Toss her down."

"Nope. You come up here and watch my ass while I turn the team around."

The mine owner joined him, gasping at the sight of the dying hunchback down in the boot. Longarm handed him the shotgun and said, "They may have given up. They may be back. They'll hit us from the rear if they hit us at all."

As Longarm hauled on the reins, MacLeod asked, "Where are we going, back to Sacramento?"

"Nope. Back to pick up the old man. Wouldn't be neighborly to leave him for the buzzards. There might be some sign to read back there, too."

MacLeod braced his heels on the boot above the moaning hunchback, and said, "I'm sure he's dead. I saw him hit the ground. But you're right. We can't just leave him."

Longarm swung the team back the way they'd just come and clucked them into motion, holding a tight rein to keep them from stampeding again. As the lead mules sniffed the body on the trail ahead, they started fighting the bits, but even without a whip the deputy managed to drive close enough. Then he set the brake and handed the reins to MacLeod, saying, "Don't let them have an inch of slack or you'll be on your way to wheresoever."

He climbed down and walked over to the body of the jehu. He didn't have to roll the old man over to see that he was dead. There was a gaping hole between the driver's shoulder blades. Longarm sighed, "Poor old bastard. You should have stopped, but I'm glad you didn't."

The door opened and the girl jumped down, asking, "Is there anything I can do?"

Longarm said, "Not for this one, ma'am. There's a man hit bad up in the boot who could use a woman's hand on his brow, if you have the belly for it."

Felicidad stared down at the dead man in the road and sighed, *"Ay, pobrecito!"* Then she turned and walked to the front of the coach. MacLeod reached a hand down to help her, but she ignored it and climbed up beside him without comment. Longarm noticed that she climbed proficiently for a woman in skirts. She placed a foot on a spoke of the near wheel and went up like a hand climbing the side of a corral one jump ahead of a rogue steer. He surmised that she sat a pony well, too.

Leaving the dead driver for the moment, Longarm walked a big circle in the dust, searching for sign. The bodies of the two ponies he had shot carried no brands and had been stripped of their gear. He spotted a hoofprint and muttered, "Son of a bitch. I thought so!"

Then he bent over, reholstered his gun, and dragged the body by its heels to the coach. The dead jehu was as limp as a dishrag, but a good deal heavier. It was a task getting him inside, but Longarm managed. He slammed the door and climbed up beside MacLeod and the girl, saying, "This other fellow might be more comfortable down there, too."

Felicidad shook her head and said, "He is dead. What do we do now?"

Longarm said, "For openers, one of us has to drive while another rides shotgun. You want to give her the shotgun, MacLeod?"

The young mine owner looked surprised, so Longarm explained, "I can see by the way you're holding that thing that you ain't a skeet shooter. Miss Felicidad, here, knows her country and moves like a lady who's used to traveling around it safe and quick. How about it, Miss Vallejo?"

The girl lowered her eyes and said, "I have hunted since I was six. If they intend to hit us again, it will be up past the next few bends, where the trail passes between high outcrops."

Longarm laughed and said, "There you go, MacLeod. Give the lady the scattergun. If you're any good with that .38, move back along the deck and keep an eye on the brush on either side. They'll hit us low if they don't hit us high."

MacLeod did as he was told, and once everyone was in place, Longarm swung the team around once more and yelled, "Heeeyah!!"

As they lurched forward, Felicidad asked, "Are we pressing on? I thought you'd head back to Sacramento for another driver."

Longarm said, "We've got a driver. Me. I've been trying for a week to get to the damned old mine, and it's getting tedious as hell."

MacLeod called forward, "I'm for that. My wife will worry if we're late. Did you find anything back there, Deputy?"

Longarm said, "Yeah. A hoof print. U.S. army issue. I thought one of the rascals was riding my gelding and shooting my old Winchester at us. Lucky he didn't know its windage is a hair off to the right."

"Jesus! You mean those rascals had the horse you say Constable Lovejoy took from you?"

"I do. It'll be interesting as hell to see what Lovejoy has to say about it. He'd best have one good story, and his stay on this earth depends on whether I believe it or not."

Chapter 3

A stagecoach got its name, of course, because it got where it was going by stages. Calaveras County lay a good forty miles from Sacramento, mostly uphill, and a good team can sustain a ten- or twelve-mile-an-hour trot for little more than two hours. So the coach had to stop for a fresh team every twenty miles. Like other lines, Wells Fargo maintained a cross-country network of roadside corrals with comfort stations and, occasionally, kitchens for the passengers. So Longarm hauled in eighteen miles out of Sacramento for a change of teams—and to get rid of the bodies before they started bloating.

They told the Wells Fargo crew what had happened and the telegrapher put it on the wire. So all stage crews, of any company in the area, would be watching for road agents. The man in charge of the station seemed to think Longarm should let him have his company's stagecoach back. He said that they'd send for another crew and that the three survivors should wait awhile. Longarm said he was commandeering the coach for U.S. government business. When the Wells Fargo agent said he'd have to check with his headquarters, Longarm told him to do anything he liked as long as Longarm, MacLeod, and the girl didn't have to hang around.

They were still arguing—or rather, the agent was arguing at Longarm—when the deputy whipped the fresh team into motion and left the bewildered man standing in the road, calling out, "Hey! Come back here with my coach, God damn it!"

Kevin MacLeod was roaring with laughter and, for the first time since he'd met her, the girl at Longarm's side reluctantly chuckled. She shifted the shotgun in her lap to cover an approaching grove of live oak and observed, "It's nice to see an Anglo screaming helplessly for a change. I didn't know you people were as highhanded with one another as you are with us."

Longarm grinned and said, "There was nothing personal meant by it when we stole California from you, Señorita. We'd just as likely have taken it had it belonged to anyone else."

She no longer looked amused as she nodded and said, "I believe you. You people are natural bullies. You seem to have understood the survival of the strong long before Darwin published his outrageous book."

Longarm shrugged and said, "You'd best take that up with God, ma'am; He made the rules. Besides, we could have been even meaner, if you study on it. I'll allow that some of the forty-niners were a mite uncouth, and some of your people got the short end of the stick, but a lot of your Spanish grants were recognized by the U.S. government."

Her dark features took on an ironic cast. "I see. You think, because you only stole *half* of our land, that that makes it just."

"Not as just as it might have been, but a better deal than you folks offered the Indians who owned all this land in the first place," Longarm said evenly. He saw that he'd scored a point and added, "How much land did Cortez let Montezuma keep?"

She flushed and said, "That's not the same!"

"Sure it is," he insisted. "You Spanish found a land filled with gold and Indians, so, being tougher than the original owners, you just up and took it. The forty-niners found a land full of gold and comfortable Spaniards and they were just as tough on the Spaniards as the Spaniards had been on the Indians. Like I said, it was nothing personal."

"We were not living under the tyranny of Castile," the girl objected. "California belonged to Mexico, a friendly democracy!"

"Mexico was friendly as hell at the Alamo," Long-arm countered, "and if you want to call Santa Ana's dictatorship a democracy— Well, what the hell, we've elected some funny folks ourselves, so you're likely right. I'd give California back if it was up to me, but it ain't, so let's talk about something else."

She smiled wryly, and replied, "It is a waste of time now, isn't it? Do you think those banditos are liable to come back?"

He shook his head and said, "Doubt it. I left two dismounted and we showed them we weren't school-marms. We're carrying some mail in the strongbox under the seat, but the agent says there's no gold aboard."

"Then why did they try to rob us in the first place?"

"Because we were aboard. There's usually a gold watch or a pretty gal aboard any stage. If that bunch is who I suspicion, they don't run to much common sense. You might say they rob folks on impulse."

"You know who they were?" the woman asked with a puzzled frown.

"Not for sure, but I think they're what's left of the Calico Kid's gang. The one who was riding my gelding looked like a rat-faced saddle tramp I met in Manzanita near the livery stable. Either Constable Lovejoy gave it to them or they stole it."

Felicidad's lip curled contemptuously. "I know this Lovejoy. My people call him *el stupido*."

He chuckled and replied, "Fair is fair. When you folks are right, you're right. Do you live in Manzanita, Señorita?"

"No. Our rancho is just outside of town. We will pass it on the way in and I will get off there. How soon do you think we will be there?"

"A couple of hours, the Lord willing and the creeks don't rise. You say your people know Lovejoy well enough to call him names. Can you tell me if they have any notions about those highgraders stealing from Mr. MacLeod back there?"

The girl shook her head and said, "We have heard of the robberies. We would like to think it was one of our people, but that is too much to hope for. Some of our vaqueros are sure it is the work of Joaquin Murietta, but that is just wishful thinking."

He frowned and said, "It'd have to be. Joaquin Murietta was shot and beheaded nearly thirty years ago!"

"I know. But some of our people still see him, late at night on a moonlit trail."

They dropped Felicidad off on a wooded path a mile outside of Manzanita. Then Longarm drove the stage to the Wells Fargo office, where MacLeod's wife was waiting with a buckboard and a worried look. Lottie MacLeod was a pretty little dishwater blonde in a sun bonnet two sizes too large for her little head. Longarm could see that her face had been freckled by the mountain sun in spite of the bonnet. He told the MacLeods he'd be up to visit them as soon as he found something to ride. As the MacLeods drove off, Longarm explained to the suspicious-eyed Wells Fargo men whose hands were resting casually on their sidearms that he hadn't really stolen the coach. They'd gotten some of the story by telephone, they said. Everybody but the U.S. government seemed to believe in the newfangled things. The station boss said the company had posted a reward on the rascals who'd shot their employees. Longarm said, "I ain't allowed to accept rewards, but it'll be my pleasure, anyway. One of the bastards was riding my horse."

Leaving the Wells Fargo men to figure out how they were going to move the stage a mile farther east, Longarm headed for the constable's office down the street. He walked in the shadows of the overhanging wooden awnings with his new gun in his hand. The few townies he passed looked at him suspiciously, but he paid them no mind. Until he knew how much pull Boss Buckley really had up here in the hills, he was going to make sure they didn't get the drop on him a second time.

Constable Lovejoy must have spotted him through the window and been spooked by the sight, for he waved a white handkerchief out the door and called out, "Put that fool gun away, Longarm! It was all a mistake!"

Longarm stopped within strategic range of a watering trough he could duck behind in two jumps and called in reply, "That's one thing we're agreed on, Lovejoy. Come on out and let's talk on it."

"You must think I'm loco! You're pointing a god-damned gun at me!"

"You bring out my own gun, my badge, and the other things you stole, and I'll put this one away. You'd best make your next move careful and slow. I've taken just about enough shit off you and my job gives me a certain amount of leeway about dealing with coyotes and other varmints."

Lovejoy stepped timidly outside, holding the white kerchief in one hand and a big paper bag in the other.

Longarm saw that he'd thought to leave his gunbelt where it couldn't get him in trouble, so he put his own gun away, but stayed near cover just the same. He was well within rifle range of the jailhouse window.

Lovejoy crossed over to him, saying, "I got all your stuff right here, Mister Long. Like I said, I've seen the error of my ways."

Longarm took the sack from him, saying, "I know you have a telephone line to the capital. I'll take your word for what's in this bag, for now, but it seems a mite light. You don't have my horse, Winchester, and saddlebags in here, I'll bet."

"Listen, Longarm. I got a nice pinto stud with a new Visalia stock saddle for you. Got a spanking new Remington rifle I'd be pleased to offer, too."

"I don't want your horse and gear. I want *mine*. What happened to them?"

Lovejoy licked his lips and said, "Honest, I just don't know. After you run off, I went to the livery to see if you'd left any clues in your possibles. That's when we noticed someone had sort of, well, *stole* them."

Longarm nodded and said, "A little rat-faced tramp in a hickory shirt and gunbarrel chaps. He just chased me on my own mount, shooting at me with my own rifle. You sure run this town sloppy, old son."

"We heard about them smoking up the stage. Some of the boys're out looking for the rascals right now. I can see I had you wrong, Longarm. I'll just bet the Calico Kid's gang has been behind this highgrading all the time."

He waited for Longarm to answer, got nervous waiting and tried to grin, saying, "But, hell, we're on the same side now, right?"

Longarm said, "Maybe. You were about to tell me who passed the word that I was to be kept away from the Lost Chinaman and such."

Lovejoy hesitated, then shrugged and said, "Hell, no sense in me trying to cover for folks who can't make up their own durned minds. It was the U.S. marshal in Sacramento. The same hombre just called to say we were to leave you the hell alone!"

Longarm nodded, but said, "I want a name to go with your tale. Was it the marshal himself or somebody farther down his totem pole?"

Lovejoy said, "It was a deputy named Harper. Sam Harper, I think his name was. He said you had no jurisdiction the first time he called. Now he says the case is all yours and he hopes you choke on it."

Longarm nodded again and said, "You can start breathing again, Constable. I don't aim to shoot you after all. Did that deputy of yours get over the little set-to we had over at the jail?"

Lovejoy smiled shakily and wiped his heavily perspiring brow with the white handkerchief. "Old Pete? He's all right. I got him out looking for them road agents with the others. He said he still can't figure out how you slickered him. Pete says you and that Injun started a row and the next he remembers is me standing over him with a pail of water. How did you do it, Longarm?"

"I've got magic powers. But tell me something else. When Bitter Water and I ran off, did you trail us as far as a saddleback ridge about eight or twelve miles to the southeast?"

"You must be funning! We knew you had a gun and the Injun who knew the country with you! Do I look like the sort of fool who'd ride into a bushwhacking with night coming on?"

Longarm was too polite to say what sort of a fool he thought Lovejoy looked like. Instead, he said, "I'll take you up on the loan of that pinto."

"Sure, Longarm. Where you headed, up to the mine?"

"Not right now. I've got to get my own horse and rifle back."

"But you said them road agents had them!"

"They do. I think I spotted the smoke from their hideout a few nights back, too."

"Jesus!" Lovejoy gasped. "I'll deputize some of the boys and we'll ride with you!"

But Longarm shook his head and said, "No thanks. I got enough on my plate facing the four of them. I don't like folks behind me holding guns unless I know them real well."

"Aw, hell, you still don't trust me, Longarm?"

"Not as far as I can spit, Constable."

It was almost dark in the canyon when one of the four men hunkered around the firepit looked up and said, "Listen! Did you hear that?"

One of the other road agents poked at the fire and replied, "Hear what, Slim? You been listening for ghosts again?"

The first man who'd spoken said, "I could swear I heard a pony nicker, just now."

His companion glanced over at the two tethered to a live oak and said, "Of course you did, you durned fool. The two we got left are lonesome."

Another owlhoot nodded morosely and observed, "Thanks to your fool idea about that stage, we're riding double these days."

"Hell, how was I to know they had some sort of durned old sharpshooter aboard?" Slim protested. "I picked off that shotgun rider neat as anything, just like I said I would."

"Sure you did. Then some other son of a bitch blew two ponies out from under us and left us in the dust feeling foolish. Did any of you boys get a look at the jasper? We owe him, if we ever meet up again."

Slim said, "All I seen was some hombre in a brown suit. He was one shooting son of a bitch, whoever he was."

A smaller, rat-faced youth in gunbarrel chaps frowned thoughtfully and said, "The cuss who shot Calico was dressed in brown tweed. You reckon it could have been that lawman, Longarm?"

Slim said, "Shit, they threw that one in jail for shooting old Calico. Must have been somebody else."

A new voice in the canyon said soberly, "You're wrong, Slim. It *was* me."

The four owlhoots stiffened as Longarm stepped out of the underbrush, his gun in his hand and trained on them. Slim dropped a hand to the gun at his side and the .44 in the lawman's hand spoke once. Slim went over backward, wetting his jeans as he died with a soft sigh.

Longarm asked mildly, "Any other takers?"

Rat Face gasped, "Please, mister! You got the drop on us!"

Longarm said, "I know. I want the three of you on your feet and grabbing sky, but be sure you get up like the little gents your mothers always said you were. I still owe one of you to the ghosts of that stage crew, and I ain't particular who I shoot next."

The trio rose from the fire slowly, their hands raised. Longarm nodded to the one in the checkered shirt and said, "You first. Bring your hands down slow and unbuckle that gunbelt."

The owlhoot dropped his hands to his middle. Longarm fired and the outlaw jackknifed with a scream as the bullet tore his guts apart. As he went down, Longarm fired again and blew away the side of his head. The body lay limp in a spreading pool of dusty blood as

Longarm said, "Damn it, when I say slow, I mean *slow*."

One of the two survivors gasped, "Are you crazy, mister?" and made the mistake of moving a step. So Longarm put a bullet in his chest. The man's hands flew reflexively to cover the gaping bullet hole. Blood spurted from between his fingers as his eyes rolled backward and he crumpled heavily to the dust.

The lone survivor in the gunbarrel chaps screamed like the frightened animal he was and fell to his knees, babbling, "Please, mister! You can't just shoot me like a dog!"

Longarm grimaced and said, "I can do anything I want to, you sniveling little pissant! What did you think this was, a game for schoolboys? You gave up any rights you had to life when you first strapped on those guns and started scaring folks."

"Oh, Jesus, I don't want to die!"

"Not many folks do," Longarm agreed. "Those men you shot today likely didn't enjoy it much, either."

He saw the trickle running down the inside of the terrified owlhoot's thigh and said, "Unbuckle that gunbelt or *draw*, you shithead!"

The rat-faced youth fumbled hysterically with his buckle, got it open, and let the gunbelt fall from his hips as he knelt in the dust, pissing in his pants. Longarm said, "That's better. Now we can talk. Your continued existence depends on how *well* you talk. What's your name, shithead?"

"Carson, sir. They call me Buck."

"No they don't. They call you shithead. We know you tried to rob the Wells Fargo, so let's not waste time on that. What do you know about that ore that's been disappearing off the narrow-gauge between here and Sacramento, shithead?"

"Ore, mister? We heard something about some high-grading, but that wasn't us, honest to God."

"How long have you boys been skulking about out here in the brush?"

"You mean here in Calaveras County, mister? About a month. We rode up from the Santa Monica Mountains with the Calico Kid about a month ago."

"You get one point for something that agrees with what I knew already. I'm cheered a mite more by seeing that you've taken good care of my gelding over there. You keep singing the right tune and I just might take you in alive."

"Anything, mister! I'll tell you anything you want to know!" Carson said with great enthusiasm.

"All right. If you boys have been roaming around out here, looking for a chance to steal, you must know the territory pretty well after a month. I'm interested in railroad properties. You know the tracks to the low country?"

"Sure, we've rode over 'em plenty of times."

"You ever notice a siding? Maybe a spur line running off into the trees or some old mine tunnel?"

Carson shook his head and said, "No sir. Not that I remember, and I'm thinking hard as anything."

Longarm nodded and said, "Let's try another one. You boys have likely been keeping your eyes open for strangers on the horizon line. Have you seen any others playing your same game?"

"You mean another gang, mister? I don't think so. We've spied greasers working cows a few times, and once we spotted an Injun squaw picking nuts, but she got away."

"Lucky for her, I reckon. But I'd say if you stumbled over Diggers you were moving pretty slick. You'd likely have noticed white riders if they were about. So the highgrading has to be an inside job. I want you to study on my next question before you lie to me, boy. I noticed you and the Calico Kid had the freedom to roam the streets of Manzanita. Can you enlighten me on how the law felt about that?"

"Hell, mister, there ain't no wanted posters out on us."

"There are now; Wells Fargo just posted them. What I'm aiming at is how the Kid happened to be on such friendly terms with Constable Lovejoy and the sheriff's department."

Carson shrugged and said, "He was just scared of Calico, I reckon. He was a pretty hard case and Lovejoy has a wife and kids."

"What about the county sheriff?"

"Never met up with him. Calico said not to steal nothing near the county seat."

Longarm thought this over. Then he nodded and said, "I can't think of anything else you might have to say, so we'd best get on with it."

Then he put his revolver in its holster and said, "I figure I've got one bullet left. Your gun is within easy reach when you've a mind to go for it."

Carson gasped, "Oh, no, I ain't about to try! You got to give me a break!"

Longarm stood with his hands out to his sides as he said, "I *am* giving you a break. It's against my nature even to step on a bug without giving it a chance."

"I can't fight *you!* You said you'd carry me in alive!"

"I said *maybe.* Your trial would be a needless expense to the taxpayers, since we both know you shot that old man and the hunchback."

"Slim shot the guard! Brown, there, killed the old man! I've never shot it out with nobody!"

"It might be a good time to start trying; I ain't got all night. I can see you've started to reconsider the error of your ways, and if you and I were the only folks I had to worry about, I'd be tempted to let you go, for I don't have time to trifle in a case I ain't assigned to. But you see, sonny, there're other folks out there that you might run into, and I'd hate to have a six-year-old kid on my conscience when and if you start feeling tough again."

The owlhoot started to cry.

Longarm said, "Come on, you've got at least five rounds in your gun and I cross-draw, so you have an edge on me."

"Oh, please, please, I'm so damn scared!"

"It doesn't feel so good to be on the receiving end, does it? Didn't you think anyone was ever going to call your play when you decided to be a big bad cuss?"

"Mister, I just want to go home to my poor old momma! I swear, if you let me live, I'll never wear a gun again!"

Longarm shook his head and said, "I'm counting to three, and then I'm going to draw. You do whatever you want to about it."

"Oh, no! You got to let me live!"

"One!"

"I'll be good! I swear I'll never do it again!"

"Two!"

"No, no, I don't want it this way!"

And then Longarm said, "Three!" and reached across his waist for the .44. The owlhoot screamed and dove for his gun as the deputy fired. The bullet hit Carson just under his nose, drilled through his skull, and blew his brains out the back of his head. His body didn't even twitch as it went limp and keeled over on its side.

Longarm stood silently, looking down at the four bodies as he reloaded. Then he swallowed the funny taste in his mouth and muttered, "I must have eaten something that didn't agree with me. Likely the chili I had in Sacramento."

He knew he'd done the only sensible thing; it wasn't as if they'd have treated him differently. So it surprised him a bit, as he walked over to reclaim his horse, that he suddenly gagged and had to lean against a tree trunk to throw up.

Chapter 4

By the time Longarm got back to Manzanita, leading the two other ponies and riding the army remount gelding he'd reclaimed, the posse looking for the road agents in other parts had ridden in too, bone-weary and out of ideas.

Longarm told Lovejoy he'd had a shootout with the rascals and added that the constable was welcome to the reward if he and his boys would ride up to the canyon and pack the bodies out, so Lovejoy didn't press him for details.

It was getting dark by then. Lovejoy asked if Longarm had a place to stay the night in town and he answered, "Nope. It's taken me a while, but I'm riding up to the damned mine."

He left them celebrating their good fortune and headed up the slope along the wagon trace that they said led to the Lost Chinaman. The mine was said to be only a couple of miles away. He'd gone maybe a quarter of the distance when he heard hoofbeats behind him, approaching fast, so he reined in just off the road and sat his mount quietly in the inky shade of a canyon oak.

It was Sylvia Baxter and a man he didn't know. They saw his outline at about the same time and reined in. The man called out, "Who's there? I see you, my good fellow."

Longarm saw that things were getting tense and called back, "It's all right, folks. I'm the law. 'Evening, Miss Sylvia."

"Is that you, Custis?" she asked, squinting into the darkness.

"Yes, ma'am. You had me spooked, too. It was dumb of me only to hide halfway till I took your measure."

Sylvia laughed and said, "Ralph, dear, this is the man I was telling you about—Marshal Long."

Her brother sniffed and said, "I daresay," and Longarm wondered just how much she'd told him.

Ralph Baxter was twice as snooty as his sister, but not as pretty. He had muttonchop sideburns and a pouty mouth. He was wearing a little sissy hat and English jodhpur boots under too-tight whipcord breeches. Longarm wondered how he posted, trotting in that rented stock saddle. The only thing anyone could take seriously about the dude was the Webley revolver riding butt forward on his left hip. Longarm knew that most men who didn't know too much about riding armed favored fancier border rigs that looked mean enough until you had to draw quickly from the saddle. He couldn't see well enough in this light to be sure, but the black hard-rubber grips of the big pistol had a no-nonsense look to them that said Ralph had paid a good gunsmith to fit them to his palm. He wondered why a man who looked like a sissy was armed like a hired gunslick.

He asked where they were headed, and Sylvia said the Lost Chinaman. Longarm smiled and said, "We'll ride together, then. I met MacLeod and his woman earlier. I hope they don't keep early hours."

Ralph Baxter said, "My sister and I were *invited* to join them this evening. Do you make a habit of these rather informal social visits?"

Longarm clucked his mount out from under the

tree and got them all started again before he said, "I don't pay too many what you'd call social visits, Mr. Baxter. I'll just let you folks sip tea with the MacLeods while I have a look around the diggings."

Before Ralph could think of a suitable snotty retort, Sylvia cut between them. "We heard about the attack on the stage, and I was so worried about your poor hurt head."

Ralph added, "Sylvia told me how she nursed you back from the grave. My sister has always had this sensitivity for those born less fortunate than she."

Longarm growled, "Let's back off a mite, Baxter. You can say what you like about me, but you're carrying this close enough to my kinfolks to rate my saving a dance for you, and I ain't talking about the waltz."

Ralph laughed and said, "You're really not good at veiled threats, Deputy."

"Hell, old son, there's nothing veiled about it. You keep sniping at me and we're headed straight to Fist City! What's wrong with you, anyway? We've never laid eyes on one another, and you're acting like I ran off with your silverware."

"My silverware isn't what I'm concerned about at the moment."

Longarm didn't answer. If he knew, he knew, and there was nothing he could say right now that wouldn't get them to rolling on the ground, if not shooting at one another. What was wrong with women, anyway? To hear them let on, you'd think they'd slash their wrists in front of stampeding buffalo to hide what they called their shame. Yet it seemed that half the times he'd had a little fun with a gal, she managed to let the whole blamed world know about it!

As if she knew what he was thinking, Sylvia tried to smooth things over. "Don't mind my brother, Custis. He's miffed because he's been stuck out here for months trying to close a deal, and the boys in town have been teasing him."

That seemed reasonable enough. Longarm said, "I don't tease folks much. MacLeod told me you'd been sent out here to buy his mine, Ralph."

"Would you mind calling me Mr. Baxter?"

"I'll call you the Prince of Wales if you'll tell me a mite about the Lost Chinaman."

Baxter said, "You'll see it soon enough. It's only a hole in the ground. The idiot seems to think he's found El Dorado."

"And you don't agree?"

"Oh, it's not a bad little strike, given a bit more science and some capital to put it on a paying basis. He's trying to run it with a crew of shiftless, unskilled Mexicans, digging the hard way, with hand tools."

"It doesn't take all that much digging, if it's high-grade ore, does it?"

Warming to the subject, Baxter said, "It's not high-grade. I'd say it assays at less than a thousand dollars a ton."

"Then you've been down the shaft and seen the gold?"

"Of course not. You don't *see* gold in medium-grade ore. The grains are microscopic."

"Then how do you know there's any gold at all?"

Baxter snorted and asked, "What do you take me for, an idiot? The man has an assay office report, and besides that, I've tested it for color myself."

"Do tell? How do you test for gold you can't see?"

"With aqua regia, of course. The acid dissolves any gold in the rock and leaves a deposit in your test tube." Baxter frowned. "What are you suggesting, a salted mine?"

"The thought's crossed my mind," Longarm admitted. "I can't think of any way on earth they could be switching so much ore in bulk on the fly. But if they were loading barren rock on the train in the first place, there'd be no mystery at all."

To his credit, Ralph Baxter thought for a moment before he shook his head and said, "That wouldn't make sense. MacLeod is losing money every time he loses a shipment, and he's been supervising the whole operation. How in blue blazes could it profit the man to rob himself? It's his gold in the first place!"

"Maybe. I'll take your word that he's got a real gold mine, for now. But I'd be obliged if you showed me how you test for gold, before they send another load down."

Sylvia said, "Of course he will. But just what are you planning to look for, Custis?"

Longarm said, "Gold, of course. I'm making it my business to ride down the mountain aboard the next trainload of ore. Before I do, I aim to make sure that what they put aboard is real ore. Then I'm going to be interested as all get-out to see if anyone tries to switch it with me sitting smack-dab on the pile!"

They could see lights through the trees ahead, now. Ralph Baxter's tone was almost friendly as he asked, "Just what did you mean about a salted mine, Deputy? I'll confess you've made me thoughtful. My company just authorized me to offer more than we've been bidding up till now."

Longarm said, "I figured they might. I don't know about microscopic grains, but many a mining claim has been sold to unsuspecting folks by a smart jasper firing gold birdshot into a rock face with a shotgun. I'll go along with you that MacLeod seems like a tolerable cuss, but we live and learn. If I was you, I'd hold off till we test the next shipment and see if it gets through."

They were within sight of the mining property now, so Longarm dropped the conversation. He could see the MacLeods' cabin, off to one side of the diggings. The operation itself was a lunar landscape of torn-up earth. A high loading tipple built of logs hung over a narrow-gauge railroad siding. The whole area was illuminated by torches, and Longarm saw cotton-clad workmen loading a couple of small, tubby ore cars. A dog started to bark and Kevin MacLeod appeared at the cabin door as they rode in. He waved amicably, even though he hadn't expected Longarm.

As the three of them dismounted, Longarm said to MacLeod, "You folks just visit away. I came up here for a look-see. You got anybody who could show me through the diggings?"

MacLeod called out, "Vallejo?" and one of the Mexicans came over to join them. Before he reached earshot, Longarm asked quietly, "Is this fellow related to that gal on the stage, MacLeod?"

The mine owner laughed and said, "You know, I never made the connection? Half the Mexicans in this county seem to be named Vallejo. The rest are named Garcia or Castro."

The foreman was too close to discuss it further, so MacLeod introduced them and told Vallejo to show Longarm anything he wanted to see.

The foreman was a man of about thirty, with a friendly, open smile. He was either innocent of guile or a damned good poker player. As Longarm walked away from the cabin with him, he asked, "Are you any kin to Felicidad Vallejo?"

The Mexican answered, "We are distant cousins, unfortunately. She is *muy linda,* no?"

"I'll go along with that. I'm unfortunate, too. She doesn't like gringos much."

Vallejo laughed and said, "That side of the family was very rich before you people came. I come from a less fortunate branch of the family, so I've made out all right. Señor MacLeod is *muy simpatico.*"

"Have you been working for him long?"

"Since he and his wife bought the mine. The last owners refused to hire greasers. What was it you wished to see?"

"Well, I was thinking of going down the shaft, but I hear it's a waste of time for a man without a degree in chemistry. When do you aim to ship those cars you're loading?"

"The engine is coming for them in the morning. That is why we are working overtime. If you don't wish to go down in the shaft, what can I show you?"

Longarm walked over to the siding. Grabbing a hand iron, he pulled himself up to the lip of an ore car, saying, "I ain't stealing. I'll put it all back in a while."

Then he reached in at random and selected three lumps of the salmon-colored quartz they'd been loading. He got down, went to the rear car, and did the same. Then he put the ore samples in his coat pocket and asked Vallejo, "Do you have a guard posted over this siding at night?"

The Mexican nodded and said, "Of course. We are not at all pleased by what has been happening."

Longarm thanked him and walked quickly back to the cabin. He went in without knocking, found Sylvia and her brother seated in front of a fireplace sipping tea with the MacLeods, and said, "Baxter, I'd like you to aqua-whatever these rocks."

Baxter said, "Oh, for God's sake." But MacLeod smiled a bit thinly, and said, "We've been talking about your suspicions, Longarm. It's all right with me, Ralph."

Baxter shrugged and said, "Well, I do have my kit in my saddlebags, but I assure you, all this is none of my doing!"

MacLeod said, "I insist. I think I see what he's getting at, and frankly, I haven't been assaying the ore, once it's out of the mine!"

Muttering to himself, Baxter got up and went out to his tethered horse as Longarm followed. Sylvia followed too, and as she and Longarm waited on the porch she nudged him and asked, "Where are you staying tonight, darling?"

He answered, "Right here. If that's really gold ore in those cars, I ain't letting it out of my sight this side of Sacramento!"

"Damn it, Custis, I want you so badly I can taste it!"

Longarm nodded. "I know the feeling, but I wish you wouldn't call me Custis. Now hush or he'll hear us, and he's suspicious already."

Baxter came up the steps with an oilcloth bag. He said, "I have to have some light."

From the doorway, MacLeod called out, "You can use our kitchen table, Ralph."

Longarm wondered if MacLeod had heard Sylvia's somewhat forward statement, but he didn't know how to find out.

They all went inside. MacLeod led them back to a lean-to kitchen, and Baxter set up his testing gear on the redwood table as Longarm watched. Baxter asked for a sample and Longarm handed him a hunk of ore. Baxter said, "It's supposed to be crushed first, you moron," but he took out a pocket knife and, using the back of the blade, scraped a few grains off the surface. Longarm strolled over to a nearby window and folded his arms. He could see both the table and the men working outside from this vantage point.

Ralph Baxter put the sandy dust in a test tube and poured something from a little brown bottle into it, saying, "Aqua regia is a mixture of sulfuric and nitric acid. It's the only acid that dissolves noble metals."

He waited a few minutes and poured a few drops of

something else in the tube, holding it up to the light. The test tube started smoking like a lit cigar, and Longarm asked why. Baxter said, "I'm neutralizing the acid to precipitate any metal it's dissolved. Don't you know anything about basic chemistry?"

"Not much," Longarm said, "but I'm willing to learn. What does it look like?"

Ralph held the test tube out to him and said, "See for yourself. But be careful. Even with bicarb in the tube, it's been known to burn skin away. This is hardly a chemical lab and my field methods are a bit rough-shod."

Longarm took the test tube and held it up to the light, squinting at the muddy contents. He nodded and said, "Yeah, I can see the specks of gold in it. Are you sure it ain't fool's gold?"

"Iron pyrite? Don't be inane. Fool's gold settles a rusty red in the tube. I hope you're satisfied?"

Longarm took out another lump and said, "I will be, once you test them all. I gathered hunks from all over."

Baxter sighed and went back to work. It took him a half hour to satisfy Longarm, but in the end the deputy nodded at MacLeod and said, "I owe you an apology, sir. I'll allow that what you've just loaded must be the real thing."

MacLeod grinned boyishly and answered, "Oh, I don't know. I could have put a few chunks of pay dirt in with the dross to fool you."

Longarm said, "I know. That's why I sampled from both cars. To salt the load that rich, you'd have had to put enough aboard to make it worth shipping. So let's see if we can get those cars through to the mill."

MacLeod said, "We're shipping it in the morning. I suppose you want to come back early to ride herd on it?"

Longarm shook his head and said, "Nope. I'm staying put. I'm going out right now to climb aboard with my Winchester. Then I ain't getting down until the train reaches the Big Valley."

"Longarm, you'll freeze out there and it's not yet ten o'clock," MacLeod said.

"I never said I hankered to be comfortable. I just said I aim to watch it from this moment on. We just made sure the gold's aboard, and this time, by thunder, it's *staying* aboard unless somebody shoots me right off the top of it."

Kevin MacLeod had been right, but Longarm had already learned the hard way how cold the Sierra nights could be. The Mexican crew knocked off before midnight and, at Longarm's suggestion, took the torches with them. He didn't want to sit up on the piled ore like a big-assed bird outlined in torchlight to anyone in the surrounding brush. Vallejo had explained that most of the miners went home to their local farms downslope. The foreman and a couple of men who usually took turns as night watchmen stayed in a shack near the mine entrance on the other side of the tipple. Longarm had told them to stay well clear of his stakeout. He was sitting on the uncomfortable, jagged lumps of ore with his feet braced against the bulkhead of the rear car and the Winchester across his thighs. It would be a hell of a mistake for anyone to wander into range unless they had something serious in mind.

He had a round in the chamber, so he could fire without levering the action. He was dying for a smoke, and knew he'd want it even more before the sun rose, but you could see the lit end of a cheroot for almost a country mile on a moonless night in air as clear as this. The unwinking stars hung above him almost close enough to brush his hat, it seemed, as the planet slowly turned under him. The high country was the place to spend a night if one admired stars. The Milky Way arched overhead from horizon to horizon, and every few minutes there would be another sparkle of movement in the silent sky as another meteor burned itself to nothing.

The crickets serenaded him for the first hour or so, then it got too cold for them and they faded away to wherever crickets go between songs. It became so quiet he could hear his own pulse in his ears, and once he heard a hoot owl that he judged to be about a quarter of a mile away. Longarm shifted his weight, and the crunch of the glassy rock he sat on was almost loud enough to make him jump. Anyone trying to lift so much as a single lump from either car would be heard.

He'd climb up in the loading tipple before the crew left, to make certain it was empty. He'd noticed that the ladder rungs squeaked under his weight at the time, so he figured he could ignore the black mass he could just make out against the stars. There were no trees or bushes close to the track, and the open, dusty ground all around was light enough to outline anyone moving sneakily across it. He couldn't see how anyone could sneak anywhere near him, and since nobody did, his watch became as tedious as hell.

Longarm was an active man, and the dull routine that makes up so large a part of a lawman's life was hard to take. But like a good soldier, a good lawman knows that the secret is in lasting as long as most people can, then lasting just a minute more. The average criminal, like the average human being, lives by an average clock. Few crooks he'd met up with had been men of infinite patience. Men who are used to dull routine seldom take to a life of crime. The whole idea of being a crook is *easy* money.

Longarm knew most night prowlers made their moves between three and four in the morning, when most of the world would be sound asleep. But three o'clock came and went and a million years later it was four, and nothing happened.

Longarm thought about that. The highgraders had to be watching for another shipment. Anyone on a distant ridge could tell just by looking when the ore cars were loaded. But he'd climbed up here with the lights out. If they knew he was staked out, someone had told them.

Sylvia and her brother had left hours ago, of course. The MacLeods hadn't stirred from their cabin at all, and there were no wires running from the mine to anywhere else. Only the foreman and the few workers sleeping on the site knew he'd planned to guard the shipment. He'd asked Vallejo not to gossip about it much. On the other hand, every man who had been there that night knew he was law and might have figured out what he was up to. There were just too many suspects to work with right now. He could see that he was going to have to start whittling them down one at a time, and that meant more dull routine that could take weeks. He estimated that there were at least a dozen men in the Mexican crew. His job would be a lot easier if the highgraders just came out of the woods for a good old-fashioned fight.

Another million years dragged slowly by. The ice age came and went, and mankind had invented fire and built the pyramids by the time the sky grew lighter in the east. By the time Columbus discovered America, the birds were sassing him from the treeline and he started making out colors as well as the forms of daybreak. Off in the distance he heard a train whistle, and a few minutes later Vallejo came down from the bunkhouse with a pot of coffee and a tin cup. He handed them up to Longarm and asked if anything had happened. Longarm poured himself some coffee and said,

"Nope. I didn't even see the ghost of Joaquin Murietta."

Vallejo laughed and said, "You have heard of him, eh? I was only a child when he held up the stage over near Angel's Camp. At least, they say he held up that stage. Joaquin was very mysterious, even when he was alive. There are a dozen versions of who he was and what he did. Our people's stories have him all over the state at the same moment. There are even those who say he never existed."

Longarm sipped some coffee and said, "Well, they shot somebody they said was him, down in Kern County. Was that whistle I just heard what I hope it was?"

Vallejo nodded and said, "Yes. It will be here any minute."

Kevin MacLeod came down from the cabin with a Henry rifle cradled in an elbow and wearing a worried smile. As he joined them, Longarm said, "No, they didn't shoot me and steal this ore I'm sitting on."

MacLeod looked relieved and said, "Thank God. I'm riding down the line with you this morning. If this shipment doesn't get through, I'm going to be in a real fix."

He climbed up beside Longarm and explained, "I've barely got enough money left to meet my next payroll. I don't want to sell out to that damned Baxter, but he's got me by the short hairs and he knows it."

Longarm nodded, and asked, "Is he the only one who's made an offer?"

"For the mine? Yes. I've had a few ridiculous offers for the property, of course. I've filed on a full section of land, and apparently some of the local rancheros feel I'm sitting on enough grass to matter."

Longarm swept a thoughtful eye over the surrounding country. The mining claim was in rolling parkland. Most of the bigger trees had been cut long ago for pit props and lumber. The grazing looked like tolerable grass, but nothing to get excited about. He asked, "Do you pump your water, or is there a running spring on the spread?"

MacLeod said, "I thought of the water rights. I doubt if anyone's that serious about the brook cutting across one corner of the place, over beyond our cabin. These hills are well watered all around. Besides, the only serious offer was from Baxter's syndicate."

Before they could go into it at length, the narrow-gauge locomotive backed into view, the fireman waving to them from the cab. Longarm watched with interest as the little engine eased into the ore cars with a bump and they coupled up. The engineer called back, "Are you boys riding shotgun?" When Longarm nodded, he said, "Let's get cracking, then. I got a timetable to think about." He tooted his whistle and they started up with a jerk as Vallejo and another Mexican who'd just come down from the quarters waved goodbye.

Longarm saw MacLeod's wife waving at them from the cabin door and put a finger to his hat brim as her husband waved back. And then the ore train was in the trees around the bend and picking up speed.

The trip down the line was uneventful. The narrow-gauge tracks wound down the slopes in a series of hairpin curves. The train ducked through a few cuts and over a dozen bridges. Longarm and MacLeod sat back to back, rifles at the ready. But nothing seemed interested in them this morning. Longarm watched for an unmapped rail siding. He couldn't spot any. They crossed wagon traces where a Conestoga could move off with maybe a ton or so of ore, but there was no traffic on the dusty roads at this hour. They passed farms where kids ran over to the fence line to wave at them, and they chuffed through a couple of sleepy mountain towns where nobody paid any attention at all. Had he been asked to drive the train, Longarm would not have held the throttle as wide as the engineer did. But while the speed around a few drop-off curves was a bit hair-raising, it eliminated some possibilities from his mind. If they didn't get through this time, he was going to have to consider Joaquin Murietta's ghost as a suspect.

They got through. The train reached the flats of the Big Valley and tore out across it at thirty miles an hour. In what seemed no time at all they pulled into the yards behind a string of big wooden buildings. Even before the wheels stopped clicking under him, Longarm could feel the pulsing of the earth being pounded by the machinery of the stamping mills. They'd stopped near a tall chimney belching black smoke into the blue sky, and the sounds made by tortured rock set his teeth on edge.

A man came out on the platform with a sheaf of papers and waved up at them, shouting, "You from Lost Chinaman?"

When MacLeod nodded, the mill supervisor yelled, "Got to assay you before you unload. The boss is sore as hell about the worthless stuff you've been gumming up our machinery with!"

As he and Longarm climbed down, MacLeod explained that they'd come through with real ore this time. But the mill operator took random samples anyway and they followed him inside.

The noise wasn't quite as bad in there, but they still had to shout at one another to be heard, and Longarm wondered how the workers here could stand it day after day. Another man took the ore samples to a workbench and fed them into what looked like a big coffee grinder, operated by a leather belt feeding through the wall. The little crusher started chewing gritty quartz with a noise that made the boards tingle under their feet. The lab worker didn't seem to mind. He slid a tray filled with fine powder out from under the assay mill and put some in a glass jar. He poured aqua regia in as Longarm and the others watched. He seemed to follow the same routine Baxter had, but on a bigger scale.

After a time he shook his head and shouted above the general din, "Nothing! Not a sign of color! What the hell are you digging up there, MacLeod, a well?"

Kevin MacLeod paled and gasped, "Oh, shit! Not again!" He whirled on Longarm and added, "God damn you! You were supposed to be watching!"

At the assayer's words, Longarm had nearly bitten through the cheroot he was smoking. "I *was* watching!" he told MacLeod. "The stuff never left my sight!"

"But God damn it, it was gold ore when we loaded it!"

Longarm said, "I know. I saw the color myself." He scratched the back of his neck vigorously, then headed for the door. MacLeod followed him outside, bleating, "Where are you going? We have to figure this out!"

Longarm crossed the platform, picked out a few random samples of ore, and put them in his pocket, saying, "I've got to get on into town. I figure it's a half hour's walk if I don't shilly-shally."

"Can I come with you? Where are you going?"

"U.S. assay office. It's near the state house about two miles from here. You can come if you've a mind to."

"What about my ore?"

"Yeah, what about it?" Longarm asked rhetorically. "If I were you I'd sit tight right here and make sure it's all there when I come back."

"But they just told us it's worthless rock!" MacLeod protested.

"I know. I heard them. I'm aiming to get an opinion from somebody else."

MacLeod opened his mouth to ask something, then

blinked and lowered his voice to say, "Jesus! I never thought of that! I've delivered these people fourteen loads and never gotten paid for one of them!"

Longarm nodded grimly and said, "That's as good a reason as I can think of for asking Uncle Sam, personal, who's been lying. Because someone has been lying like a rug!"

It proved to be a long, dusty walk to a dead end. The men at the government assay office tested the samples Longarm brought them and came up with the same results. The federal assayer held his test tube up to the light and said, "It's the Mother Lode formation all right, but there's not enough gold in it to matter."

Longarm asked, "Is there any gold at all?" and the lab worker explained, "There's *some* gold in seawater. Probably in you and me. But you don't get rich processing anything but ore. It's simple economics. You have to spend less getting gold out of something than the gold is worth. Every few weeks some idiot comes running in here with a rock he's found somewhere and I have to go over it all again. There's still plenty of gold in the Mother Lode, but it's spread out between hell and breakfast. A pebble with a speck of color in it doesn't mean you have a strike. The metal has to be in one place before you can spend it. If you spend a thousand dollars refining a hundred dollars worth of gold, you're going to wind up busted. Folks keep finding that out the hard way, all over the West. Go down to skid row and you'll find a hundred old prospectors mumbling in their beards about a claim they have out in some neck of the woods, if only someone would grubstake them. The samples they'll show you have real color, too. A dollar's worth of color in a fist-sized rock makes a pretty paperweight."

Longarm nodded and asked, "Couldn't you show a profit by busting up the rock and panning it?"

"Sure," the assayer said, "but men don't crush their dreams. A few hand-picked samples from an otherwise worthless outcropping can make any man dream big. Over in the desert on the other side of the Sierra there are places where a man can pick up a burroload of fairly decent gold quartz in a couple of days. By the time they haul it out of the dry country, figuring a dollar a day for their time, they might break even. You have to have water, supplies, and plenty of money to make a profit even on a real strike."

Longarm said, "I understand that part. Let's stick to this shit I brought in here today. You say it's worthless and I'll take your word for it. But just last night I saw it tested the same damned way, and there was maybe ten dollars' worth of color in the test tube."

The assayer shrugged. "Then someone switched samples on you."

"No. They couldn't have. I picked them myself, at random. If someone had salted two freight cars with enough real ore to fool me, there'd be enough aboard to be worth milling. Is there any way to fake that test?"

The government man thought and shook his head. He said, "Nothing but aqua regia, mercury, or cyanide will dissolve pure gold. What did the other chemist use?"

"He said aqua regia."

"I'd say he had no reason to lie. Cyanide's dangerous to carry around and you'd have known mercury on sight. If he got a real precipitate, the samples you had him test must have been rich."

Longarm frowned and asked, "Is there anything else in that rock he could have separated out? Maybe fool's gold or mica?"

The assayer said, "No. You don't find pyrite in

106

quartz. It's a sulphide of iron you find in shale or slate."

"Maybe brass or tin or something like that?"

The man was growing impatient. "Damn it, Deputy, I just told you there's not enough metal of any kind in this stuff to matter. Don't you think I know my own business?"

Longarm sighed and said, "You likely do, but I can see I don't know *mine* as well as I ought to!"

He went outside and caught a hackney cab back to the mill. He told the driver to wait and went back to the loading platform, where he called to MacLeod and explained, "I got us a ride to the stage line. We may as well get on back to Manzanita."

"You mean they did it again? God damn it! I owe the railroad for hauling it and the mill supervisor just told me there'd be a charge for unloading it on their tailings dump!"

"You have a hard row to hoe and that's the truth, MacLeod. But we surely won't catch any rascals hereabouts. The U.S. government backs what they said. There ain't enough color aboard those cars to pay for our ride and breakfast, but that's all right. I'm on an expense account and I'm feeding you as a material witness."

As they left the mill in the hackney, MacLeod said, "I'm too sick at heart even to think of breakfast. I'd like to go straight home."

But Longarm insisted, "We can't help matters by neglecting our innards. Besides, we've got plenty of time."

"Well, just a quick bite. What's our first move, once we get home?"

Longarm had been afraid MacLeod was going to ask that.

He had no answer.

Chapter 5

Longarm rode up to the ranch house and tethered his gelding to the hitching post. As he climbed the steps, a suspicious-looking Mexican with a shotgun opened the door and snapped, *"Que pasa, señor?"*

Longarm said, "I'm looking for Señorita Felicidad, amigo. Is she at home?"

"For why do you wish to see La Doña Felicidad? She has no business with your kind, Americano!"

Longarm didn't think it would please the lady to have her employee shot on her doorstep, so he tried to figure out some politer way to get past him.

Then Felicidad herself appeared in the doorway behind the man with the gun and murmured something softly in Spanish. The man shrugged and went off.

The girl led him into a baronial living room and indicated a chair by the fireplace. Longarm sat down. He saw she had no intention of offering him any of the coffee she'd been drinking from a cup that sat on a little table beside her chair, so he took out a cheroot and asked permission to smoke. She nodded a bit sullenly, and he lit up, placing his hat beside him on another table.

She asked what he wanted and he said, "I understand you offered Kevin MacLeod a thousand dollars for his mining claim, ma'am."

The girl shrugged and said, "It was Vallejo land in the first place, but I see no other way to get it back."

"Ain't that a sort of miserly offer for a gold mine?"

Her smile was bitter as she answered, "Who cares about the gold? It is the land, Vallejo land, I want." Then she added, "I would offer more, if I had it. My late husband did not leave me enough to be imprudent."

"I didn't know you were a widow, ma'am. I'm purely sorry to hear it. Is Vallejo your married name?"

"Both my married name and my maiden name. We of the old aristocracy tend to marry cousins."

"Well, I never came to jaw about religion. MacLeod has another cousin of yours working for him. Do you know Tico Vallejo, ma'am?"

"I do not speak to him. He has become an Americano."

"Forgive me, ma'am, but since you're both American citizens and have been for a good long time, it doesn't strike me as such a foolish notion on his part." He smiled and added, "You couldn't have been born yet when California changed hands back in '48."

"Just the same," she said, "I shall never be an Americana. But we are wasting time discussing such matters. You still have not told me what you want."

Longarm smiled self-effacingly. "Well, you might say I'm sort of fishing. I know us lawmen can be a bother asking all sorts of fool questions, but it's the only way we can work things out. You heard the MacLeods got robbed again?"

She smiled the sort of smile he had seen on the faces of Apaches. It chilled him slightly. She said, "Yes. My vaqueros were laughing about it just before you came."

"I believe you. How many hands have you got working for you, ma'am?"

"Eight vaqueros, the house servant you just met, and

a stable boy. I take it you don't suspect the chicas I have for cooking and cleaning?"

"I didn't see a man or a woman of any kind anywhere near that last shipment of ore they somehow got away with from under my . . . whatever. Let's get back to your real estate notions. A thousand is way low for a gold mine, but a mite high for a section of rough grazing. Half the spread is all torn up from the mining. What's left under the sod ain't worth a thousand dollars."

She shrugged again and said, "Once I have reclaimed what is rightfully mine I intend to have the men fill in the pits with the spoil and plant alfalfa. In time, the scars will heal."

He took a long drag on the cheroot, examined the lit end thoughtfully, then said, "I can see you're more interested in just owning it again than in any profit you might ever show."

"We may seem quixotic to you pragmatic Anglos. But what of it? I made an honest offer. Does this make me a suspect? How do you think I stole the gold?"

"I don't know. I was hoping you'd tell me."

She laughed a trifle wildly, and said, "We have the ghost of Murietta riding for us, didn't you know? I have the gold hidden under the house. Would you like to have me show you through the wine cellar?"

Longarm nodded and said, "Sure."

"You are joking, of course?"

"Maybe. Don't you have a wine cellar?"

"Certainly I have a wine cellar, but what do you think I have hidden down there?"

"You're the one who mentioned it. If you don't want to show it to me, well, I don't have a search warrant."

She rose to her feet and snapped, "Come. I insist you see it, now."

"Hell, honey, I was just funning you. You're acting like you've got red ants in your nevermind. I just rode over to ask some routine questions."

"You suspect me of being a thief and I won't have it!" she said angrily. "I insist that you search the whole house!"

He got up and said, "All right, I'll take you up on it. I can play stiff-necked stubborn, too."

She led him through an arched passage and into a hallway. There she opened a thick door under a staircase and said, "Be careful. The steps are steep."

She struck a match as he followed her down into the musty, cobwebbed darkness. Felicidad lit a candle stub on an empty barrel and waved expansively, saying, "Behold the vaults of Monte Cristo! You can see they are a maze of treasure-filled caverns!"

He looked around the tiny hole and observed, "Looks more like a root cellar to me. Do you make your own wine, or are those barrels empty?"

"They are empty. We've made no wine since my grandfather passed away." She chuckled theatrically before adding, "It is just as well for you, señor. We sinister Spaniards are well known as poisoners."

He mulled that over as he followed her back upstairs. She was touchy as hell about being a Mexican, he thought.

She conducted him through the kitchen, insisting that he look in the beehive oven for the missing gold ore. He had a sudden thought as she led him through another room. He asked, "Your people make these 'dobe bricks by mixing clay and straw with sand, gravel, rocks, and such, right?"

"Of course." She turned to him, one eyebrow cocked. "Are you suggesting the missing high-grade ore has been built into the walls of my house?"

"Not hardly. Not this house. But I mean to sniff

around the county for new construction. No trace of the missing ore's turned up, but ore is bulky stuff to hide. Building a wall or a barn with it and just leaving it there until the search wore off might not be a bad notion."

"My God," she said with amazement, "you have a lively imagination. Do you want to know what I think? I think there is no gold at all. My people owned the land the mine stands on for generations. If there had been gold they would have known it."

"You're wrong, ma'am. You folks had California for generations, like you said, but you never knew the gold was up here in these hills. It was a gringo who found the first nugget at Sutter's Mill. Your folks were cowboys, not prospectors, so they likely never *looked* for color. I'm a jump ahead of you on the Lost China-man. I checked the records down in Sacramento. It's a real mine. They shipped over a million dollars' worth of color to the mint in one year alone, back in the seventies."

"Perhaps, but it has been closed for years. MacLeod and his wife are fools. They should have accepted my offer."

They were in a bedroom now. Longarm said, "Mac-Leod's turned down bigger offers than yours, ma'am. Besides that, I saw the stuff he's digging tested and it was real. You see——"

Then he noticed the way she was standing there, looking up at him with her eyes limpid and confused. It seemed the most natural thing in the world to just reach out, haul her in, and kiss her full on her trembling lips.

For a moment she responded, running a hot tongue between his firmer lips. Then she stiffened and tried to pull away, murmuring, "What is happening? I don't want you to touch me! I hate you and everything you stand for!"

He said, "Sure you do," and kissed her again before drawing her closer to the bed and running his hand down her back. She wore no corset under the black lace and her buttocks were quivering like a nervous colt's. He pressed her closer to him. Her feeble struggles threw them off balance, so he rode with gravity and let it deposit them across the mattress of the old fourposter. They wound up with her half under him. He had a hand between her thighs, now. She churned her knees and one of her slippers flew across the rug to a corner as she gasped against his lips, "We have to stop! You're acting like a monster!"

But he noticed she had her arms around his neck, so he didn't answer. He unbuckled his gunbelt before he started inching her skirt up a fold at a time. She was kissing him with a fervor to match his own, but every time they came up for air she told him how much she hated him, so he decided it might not work if he took time to get undressed. He got her skirt up around her waist and she tried to cross her naked thighs as he slid his hand between them. But he was too strong, or she wasn't trying as hard to stop him as she was pretending. She was wearing no knickers under the skirt. Her sex was as moist as a ripe, sliced-open fig. He fingered her and kissed her until she started moving to meet his thrusting hand. Then he braced a boot on the rug, lifted himself up and over her, and unbuttoned his trousers. The respite gave her time to twist her head away, wild-eyed, and moan, "Please don't. I am not that kind of woman!" But she opened her thighs wide to him as he plunged into her.

He pinned her to the mattress with his pelvis and stayed like that long enough to rid himself of his frock coat. And then, as he started moving, she sighed, "Oh, you *are* a monster!" and dropping the maidenly notions, started pumping back.

She wrapped her legs around him and groaned, "Oh, *querido,* it's been so long since I felt this way!"

He said, "Can't we get out of these duds? This tweed must itch you some."

"Don't stop. I like it. You feel like a big, woolly bear and I'll never forgive you, but, *Madre de Dios,* don't stop! It's happening!"

For a woman who hated him, Felicidad nonetheless seemed to be taking great pleasure from this encounter as she heaved, plunged, and bucked beneath him. When their movements quieted for a moment after their first climax, Longarm was surprised to notice that they had managed to get fully undressed. Her hips began to gyrate under him once again before his erection had had a chance to wilt very much. He felt himself growing hard again. He felt purely sorry for her poor husband, dying young with so much to live for, but one man's misfortune was another man's bliss. As he stopped to get his breath back after a second climax she said, "You are a terrible man and I hate you. But as long as you've defiled me—" Then she started kissing her way down his moist chest and belly on her way to further glory. They made love for a good two hours before she lay quietly in his arms, her lips against his chest, and murmured, "If you tell anyone about this, I will kill you before I kill myself."

He patted her bare back and said, "I ain't given to talking about such things. Your secret is safe with me."

"You must think I am a terrible slut. I suppose you'd laugh if I told you there has been no one in me like that since my husband died?"

"Hell, I believe you. I could tell you'd been saving yourself for me."

She laughed in spite of herself, and asked, "How

could you tell? I didn't know how much I needed that, myself."

"I know. That's likely what had you acting so ornery. Maybe some day gals will be allowed to admit that they get just as randy as us men."

She giggled and snuggled closer, saying, "I thought I hated you that first day on the stage. But you were so brave about those bandits. You moved like such a beautiful big cat and you were so much braver than any man I'd ever known. I started feeling butterflies inside me, in a most indecent place for butterflies to be, and I told myself I was overexcited because of the shooting. You knew, even then, didn't you?"

"To tell you the truth," he said, "I was thinking more about not getting shot. You likely think I came out here with this in mind, but I really wasn't expecting to make love to you."

She smiled. "I am glad. It would shame me to think I'd been so transparent. But why did you seduce me, if you never planned it?"

"Honey, if I knew the reasons for half the things I do, I likely wouldn't do them. I did what I did because you're pretty as a picture and, well, because I could read the smoke signals in your big brown eyes."

"What are we to tell everyone?"

He frowned and said, "I just heard you ask me not to tell anyone at all."

"I wasn't thinking. If you are going to stay with me, the servants must be told something."

He'd been afraid she'd say something like that. He knew what she'd say if he explained that he wasn't the marrying kind, too. So he just said, "We have to keep it a secret for your own protection, Felicidad. I wouldn't want the men I'm after thinking they could get back at me through my woman."

She gasped with pleasure and said, "Oh, *mi cabal-*

lero! You are so gallant, but I am not afraid to share your dangers."

"You may not be scared, but I sure am. We're up against somebody who's as slick as goose grease. I'd fight hell and high water for you if I knew who or what was likely to come at us. But I can't do my job and guard your pretty little body at the same time. So we'll have to play-act that we're only friends until I catch the rascals."

"I understand. And after you catch them, *querido*, I shall never let you out of my sight again!"

The county seat of San Andreas was a lot closer than Sacramento, but still a long ride from Manzanita. There was a library near the San Andreas courthouse, and it was stocked with more books on mining than Longarm cared to read. The librarian was a little sparrowlike woman, but she had a sweet smile and he noticed her well-turned ankle when she climbed up a ladder to reach him down some books.

He took them to a table and started reading. Every time he looked up, the librarian was staring at him. Immediately, she'd duck her head and pretend she hadn't been looking. *The womenfolk in Calaveras County sure are friendly,* Longarm thought.

He skimmed through local history without finding out much except that there had never been a frog-jumping contest in the county before Mark Twain made that story up. Some of Bret Harte's tales of the forty-niners, however, turned out to be true. Calaveras had really been a humdinger in the gold rush days. Now it was withering on the vine as the mines played out. People here were raising cows and cutting timber for a living, for the most part, and it was hard-scrabble living at that. The country was pretty enough, but you can't feed scenery to cows and what timber was left was mostly second growth or tough old twisted oaks that had been passed over in the first place. Canyon oak burned well, but it didn't mill worth a damn.

He looked for someone opening a new mine more recently than the Lost Chinaman. He couldn't find one, so there went one good idea. He'd thought some tricky cuss might have thought to sell the stolen high-grade as his own, using a dummy mine as a front. But it didn't pan out. The nearby mine being operated by George Hearst shipped ore of the wrong composition. He intended to stop off at Sheep Ranch on the way back to Manzanita, but it was likely to prove a waste of time.

He cracked open a high school chemistry book and boned up on aqua regia. The book, like everyone else, said it was nasty stuff to spill on your pants and that it dissolved gold. He already knew alkali neutralized acid, so it was easy to see how the test worked. The acid picked up the invisible molecules of gold and they floated around in it until you poured in alkali, which turned the acid to some sort of brine that wouldn't hold the gold in solution any more. So it formed heavy crystals of pure gold and sank to the bottom along with other sludge it wouldn't mix with. Being heavier than lead, the gold settled faster than any other crystals. That accounted for the color he'd seen—the color that hadn't been there when the ore reached Sacramento. The damned book didn't make any mention of the part where the gold disappears without a trace. Once again, the possibilities flitted through his mind. Could he have dozed off? Could he have been knocked out somehow for a spell without his knowing?

It's impossible, he thought. *But so is stealing a carload of ore out from under a man with a Winchester, damn it!*

He walked back over to the desk and asked the librarian if she had any books on magic tricks.

She had a couple, and this time when she climbed the ladder he got to see even more of her legs. He wondered if she was doing that on purpose, and decided not to find out.

He sat down and started reading about false bottoms, mirrors, black silk strings and such. He found out how to make a rabbit come out of his hat, but not a clue to the shell game the highgraders had played with at least four ore cars, with him watching.

He was about to give up when he stopped to go back over a paragraph he'd skimmed: "Misdirection is the basis of most good stage magic. It is hard to perform before children because they allow their eyes to wander. Adults can be counted on to keep their eyes fixed where the skilled magician directs them. If one is certain everyone is watching one part of the stage, many things can be done with impunity in full view of the audience. Those watching know they are being tricked, therefore they are so intent on watching the magician's more *obvious* moves that they are oblivious to less subtle happenings, often in plain view."

Longarm nodded and muttered, "That's for damn sure."

The librarian smiled over at him and called, "Did you want something else, sir?"

He shook his head and thanked her. She looked disappointed. As he carried the books up to her counter, she asked, "Are you coming to the dance tonight, Marshal?"

He said, "I'd have asked you to save a dance for me if I was, ma'am. But I've got other chores."

She blushed from her hairline to her lace collar, but grinned like the Cheshire cat. He hoped he had made her day a bit brighter. He thanked her and went out into the bright sunlight.

As he walked out to his gelding, a hard-eyed,

thoughtful-looking fellow leaned away from the awning post he'd been holding up with his shoulder and asked, "Are you Longarm?"

"I've been called worse. What's your pleasure, pilgrim?"

"The sheriff wants to see you. Over by the courthouse."

Longarm nodded and said, "I've been meaning to see him, too. Just lead the way."

The stranger pointed down the street with his chin, his thumbs hooked in his gunbelt, and said, "His office is just past that church steeple yonder. You can't miss it."

Longarm decided to walk, since it was less than a city block and there was no sense fooling with the gelding's reins twice more than he had to. He nodded and started toward the steeple. Then he remembered he'd ridden in from the other direction, and remembered what he'd seen down the other way. He crabbed sideways, going for his gun as a bullet buzzed through the air he'd just been walking through!

Longarm reversed his direction with a firmly dug-in heel and whirled about, gun in hand, as the man who had tried to set him up fired a second time. The misdirected slug went through the space the gunman had thought Longarm was headed for. Then the deputy fired.

The stranger was apparently not experienced enough to take on an old hand like Longarm. He stood in one place as he pumped lead. Longarm's first round took him just under the belt buckle and folded him up neatly as it knocked him down. Longarm saw that he'd dropped his weapon, so he held his fire and walked slowly back, covering the man he'd shot and keeping wary on all sides. The librarian came out, saw the man lying almost at her feet, and screamed. Other people boiled out of other doorways, ran halfway over, then stopped uncertainly as Longarm stood over the groaning gunslick.

Longarm kicked the man in the ribs to gain his undivided attention and asked, "All right, old son. Who are you working for?"

The gutshot gunman groaned and said, "Fuck you."

A man wearing a tin star and a worried look came down the center of the dirt street with a shotgun. He saw that Longarm was keeping his sixgun trained in a neighborly fashion at the dirt, so he called out, "What's going on?"

Longarm said, "Don't know. I'm a deputy U.S. marshal and this jasper just tried to shoot me in the back."

The man came closer, staring down at the wounded gunslick, and said, "He's a stranger to me, too. I'm Sheriff Marvin. My office is just up the street."

"I know. He told me you wanted to see me, but he pointed the wrong way. I don't know if it was ignorance or a better field of fire for him. Lucky for me I passed your sign riding in and remembered in time to ponder his words."

The sheriff frowned and said, "I never sent for anybody. Hell, I don't even know you!"

"I figured as much. I'm Custis Long."

"The one who shot the Calico Kid and his gang? Jesus, I want to buy you a drink, son!"

"I'll buy you one too, as soon as we figure out why this son of a bitch was gunning for me."

He kicked the downed man again as the sheriff walked over and picked up the revolver the man had dropped in the dust. He said, "Sonny, if you ain't aiming to die, you'd best tell me the facts of life and I'll see about a doctor."

The gunslick groaned and said, "Stuff it up your ass, lawman."

Longarm said, "Suit yourself, but it's going to smart like hell when the first shock wears off."

A man wearing a white apron had been watching and listening from the crowd. He came forward and said, "I served him in my saloon one night. He said he was with the Calico Kid."

Sheriff Marvin grinned and said, "There you go, Marshal. He was one of the gang you missed before, but now it looks like you've made a clean sweep of the rascals!"

Longarm swore softly and said, "Damn! I was hoping he was somebody important. I ain't got time to trifle with saddle tramps."

The sheriff said, "Just the same, you did the county a favor and the drinks are on me." Marvin pointed to a pair of town loafers and called out, "Luke, you and old Bill drag this skunk over to the jailhouse and send for Doc Cunningham. Mind you don't put him on a bunk. I don't want blood on my furniture."

Then the sheriff slapped Longarm on the back and, together with the bartender, they crossed over to the saloon, where half the town seemed bent on getting Longarm drunk.

As they bellied up to the bar, Longarm told the sheriff of his misadventures. Marvin knew about the high-grading over in Manzanita, but had no suggestions. The only thing Longarm learned was that he might owe other local lawmen an apology or two. Both the sheriff's department and the California marshals had gone over much the same ground before abandoning the case as embarrassing as well as impossible to crack. His notion of guarding the train from loading to delivery had been tried before, with the same results.

Longarm said, "We've missed something. I was just reading about the way magicians trick folks. The high-graders are doing something we just ain't thought of."

Marvin said, "Hell, tell me something I don't know! You know what they did to me? It was purely spooky. I had a man watching every likely suspect—and I had a long-list, too. I put two deputies aboard the cars; I staked out every Mex who works at the mine; I threw a cordon around the whole durned spread, then sat on MacLeod's porch with my own gun handy till the train pulled out with a load of ore. None of us saw even a pack rat near that ore. But it got stole just the same. Ain't that a bitch?"

Longarm nodded, his lips twisted in a wry smile. "Yep. I know the feeling. How come you gave up, though?"

"Hell, Marshal, it's an election year, and it gets tedious looking like an idiot. Besides, I only have so many men and it's a big county. While we were wasting time watching the Lost Chinaman, some rascals ran off thirty head of cattle up by Murphy. When they told me the government was sending in a man, I just thanked the Lord and handed it back to you folks."

Longarm regarded the sheriff for a moment, then downed his shot of Maryland rye in one throw. "I see," he said. "Well, I've only got one man. Me. Old Lovejoy over in Manzanita is a crook, and—"

Marvin cut in, "He's not a crook. Just dumb. I heard about the set-to you had with him. The way I hear tell, the marshals in Sacramento were a mite peeved at the government for not trusting them."

As the bartender poured him another shot, Longarm asked, "What can you tell me about George Hearst, over at Sheep Ranch?"

Marvin frowned. "Nothing. Hearst just owns that mine and a lot of others. He's a big hoorah down in Frisco and over in Virginia City circles. He don't dig his gold personally."

"What about the folks working for him, then?"

Marvin sipped his beer and said, "Eye-talians. A whole colony of Eye-talians who come over the mountains together from some town in Italy. They talk funny, but they never give us no trouble. I know what you might suspicion, but it won't wash. There's only one mule track between Sheep Ranch and Manzanita, and we been over it again and again looking for sign. No freight wagons could make it, even empty. Besides, the Sheep Ranch ore is another kind of rock."

Longarm shrugged and said, "I'll have a look-see anyway. Was that mining engineer, Ralph Baxter, one of the folks you had staked out when it was your turn to look foolish?"

Marvin shook his head and said, "He hadn't come up here yet. He wasn't in the county, as far as I know, when the robberies first started."

Longarm grunted, "He's here now, and he's offered a million for Lost Chinaman."

The sheriff's mouth fell open. "Jesus, I'd take it if I was MacLeod. He ain't making anything on the mine now, the way they've been robbing him. It's a wonder anybody wants to buy it at any price. There's no way to show a profit till we find out who's highgrading it, and make the rascals stop!"

Longarm nodded and said, "Yeah. Makes you wonder if Baxter thinks he can stop it any time he wants to, doesn't it?"

"Hot damn! You reckon that prissy dude is behind all this?"

"It's sure starting to look that way. On the other hand, some slick son of a bitch might just be wanting it to look that way. I'll know better when I catch him." Longarm tossed back his drink, thanked the sheriff for his hospitality, and strode out through the batwings into the brightness of the street.

Chapter 6

Longarm never found out why they'd named the little town Sheep Ranch. Nobody there knew. There was a billy goat grazing atop the town dump as he rode in, but not a sign of a sheep. Of course, he hadn't seen any disoriented Orientals over at the Lost Chinaman and he doubted that Angel's Camp had been built by celestial beings.

Sheep Ranch had a big frame hotel with a built-in taproom. The miners lived in less imposing accommodations—shacks that lined the single street, which was only a wider stretch of county road. The mine works were surrounded by a barbed wire fence. The fence was posted against trespassers with the additional warning that survivors would be prosecuted. So he went to the hotel bar and told the bartender he wanted to meet up with someone who could answer questions about mining.

The bartender said, "That'd be Herc Romero. He'll be here in a little while. They're about to change shifts."

Longarm said, "Romero, huh?" and the bartender snapped, "Do you know who the last man who saw Custer alive was?"

"Some Indian scout, wasn't it?" the deputy guessed.

"No. Custer sent his bugler, Trooper Martin, with a

message for Terry, just before the Sioux wiped out the Seventh Cav."

Longarm was puzzled. "That's interesting as hell, but what's the point of your yarn?" he asked.

"Trooper Martin's real name was Martini. He came from Palermo, damn it!"

Longarm blinked, surprised at the intensity of the bartender's response.

"Well, don't get your balls in an uproar. Everybody has to come from some damn place."

"Palermo is in Sicily. Martini was an Italian. Herc Romero is an Italian. And I, God damn it, am Italian!"

"I don't aim to dispute your words, old son. I just don't savvy what you're getting at," Longarm said, pushing his hat back from his forehead.

Slightly mollified, the bartender said, "My folks came across the prairies and deserts in a covered wagon. Everybody seems to think that's funny as hell. You Irishmen weren't the only people who won the West, you know."

"That's for damn sure," Longarm agreed, "but I ain't Irish. Ain't an Indian, either, and they were here before damn near anybody else."

The bartender nodded and said, "Just wanted to set the record straight. They buried a Yankee over in Dorado for calling somebody a dago last year. Folks in this part of the county are just as Western and mean as anybody else."

Two men came through the swinging doors and the bartender called out, "Hey, Herc. Lawman here wants to talk with you. He sounds like he's all right."

Herc Romero was a bearish man of about forty with a red bandanna around his neck and rock flour in his hair. He came over to Longarm and offered his hand. He said, "I'll drink with you, but I'm wore out answering questions about the Lost Chinaman. I've never seen the damned mine."

The deputy smiled amicably. "I'll take your word for it. But Kevin MacLeod over there said someone working for the same boss as you rode over for a look-see a while back. MacLeod said he took the Hearst man through his diggings. Do you have any idea who it might have been?"

Romero shook his head and said, "Nobody working under me. The way I hear it, our ore is higher grade, and even that's not anything to get excited about. The Mother Lode is playing out. We'll be shutting down here in just a few more years."

Longarm frowned, wondering who in thunder *had* visited MacLeod. But he knew Romero couldn't—or wouldn't—tell him. So he asked, "If I was to ask you, would you ride over there with me right now?"

The foreman considered this briefly, then said, "Maybe. If you can give me two good reasons."

"One reason is that you ain't on duty," the lawman offered.

"My wife's expecting me for supper."

"The second is that you'll be helping the U.S. government. I want a man I can trust to have a look at a few things over there for me."

Romero smiled and asked, "How do you know you can trust me? You never met me before."

Longarm chuckled. "Sure I have. You've been married up with the same gal for nigh twenty years, you were cited for bravery in the Battle of Cold Harbor, and you've never been sued or arrested since you stole those watermelons when you were twelve."

Romero and his friend looked startled, and the mine foreman asked, "How in hell did you find out so much in the short time you've been here?"

Longarm said, "I didn't find it out here. I've been over to the county seat. I've read your whole record."

"Damn it, I don't have no record!" Romero protested.

"Sure you do," Longarm said. "Everybody does. Every time a man gets hitched, serves his country, or gets dragged before a judge for any reason whatsoever, there's a record kept. Since you've lived in this county most of your life, except for five years in the War, I know all I need to about you. I need an honest man to back my next play, too. Will you do it?"

The bartender said, "I'll be damned, you never told us you got a medal in the War, Herc."

The foreman shrugged and said, "It wasn't much. What do you want me to do over at the Lost Chinaman, Deputy?"

"Answer questions as I think them up. I'm going through the diggings from top to bottom and I need a hard-rock mining man I can trust as a guide."

Romero nodded and said, "You got one. Just let me tell my woman. Do you suppose I'm going to need a gun?"

Longarm said, "Don't know. If you've got one, you'd best bring it along. The folks we're after are pretty slick, and they might start playing rough if we get near pay dirt."

Kevin MacLeod's wife said her husband had gone down to Sacramento to see about another bank loan. But Tico Vallejo said he'd show Longarm and Romero through the mine.

As they moved down the gentle slope inside the entrance, walking between the tracks with Vallejo holding a lantern, Longarm held back and let the two other men talk. He knew Romero was likely to ask more sensible questions about the operation than he was. So he just listened.

Vallejo seemed friendly and at ease with the burly Italian. Romero was friendly too, but he'd been filled in during the ride over, and was asking more questions than the usual guided tour might call for.

Romero rapped a pit prop with a knuckle and asked, "How come you have live oak instead of cedar, Tico? Didn't you know oak gives all at once, without warning?"

"I think some of these tunnels were dug before my time. The hills hereabouts are thick with oak. Isn't oak stronger than cedar?"

"Sure it is, but cedar groans like a sick cat for at least a few minutes before it gives. If this mountain ever decides to sit down on you boys over here, it'll happen with no warning."

Vallejo looked morosely up at the hanging wall and said, "Well, we're solid rock, and it's lasted this long."

Romero grunted, "It always lasts *this* long. By the time you can say it lasted *that* long, it's too late. You folks are operating on a shoestring over here!"

Vallejo nodded and said, "There's no argument about that, Herc. Señor MacLeod says if the bank turns down his application for another loan he's going to have to close or sell out."

A workman was leading a burro hitched to a little ore car up the slope toward them, and the three men squeezed back against the wall to let it pass. Longarm reached out and snagged a lump of rock from the cart, but Vallejo laughed and said, "Save yourself the trouble. It's overburden."

Romero started to explain, "You have to dig ten tons of nothing much to get at a ton of high-grade ore," but Longarm cut him short, saying, "I've been in a few mines before."

Vallejo led them farther down the slope to a point where the main shaft ended in a lopsided T. As they turned to the left, Romero ran a finger along the standing wall and said, "Metamorphic quartz, sure enough. I can see where they followed the vein as she pinched out."

Vallejo said, "It opens up again a bit farther on. We're almost there."

He held his lantern high as they approached a wet dead end of glittering rock. Though hardly a geologist, Longarm could see how the pinkish, glassy quartz ran in wavy bands through darker, duller rock. He asked, "What are the middlings—quartzite?"

Vallejo sighed, "Yes, it's tough as a bitch to shatter. Takes twice as much dynamite to shave the face as it ought to."

Longarm could see the shallow craters from the last blast running in neat rows across the mine face like the stars in the American flag. Romero bent to pick up a loose lump of quartz and put it in his pocket.

Longarm followed suit with another sample, holding it up to the flickering light of Vallejo's lantern before putting it in his pocket. If there was gold in it, it couldn't be seen with the naked eye. Romero asked Vallejo for the lantern and held it close to the wet rock face. He ran his free hand over the rock and tasted his fingertips. He grimaced and said, "Metallic, all right. Sulphur, too. Are there any hot springs in the neighborhood, Vallejo?"

The Mexican shook his head and replied, "Not that I know of. Why?"

Romero said, "If the temperature starts rising down here, run like hell. You might be digging your way into a hot spring."

Vallejo muttered, *"Madre!"* but before they could

get into a geology lesson, Longarm asked Romero, "What do you think, Herc?"

Romero said, "Looks like a gold mine. Tastes like a gold mine. I'll know better in a minute."

He squatted on an empty dynamite box and took a pocket-size kit from his loose wool trousers. He uncorked a small bottle, placed a shallow glass dish on one knee, held his ore sample over it with one hand, and dribbled some acid over the sample from a thin glass tube he had dipped in the bottle. As he corked the little vial of acid and opened another small bottle, Longarm observed, "That's a right cunning little outfit. Do you carry it all the time?"

"Sure," Romero replied, "when I'm working. It gets tedious digging worthless rock, and all this durned quartz looks the same."

"They say you have another kind of quartz over at Sheep Ranch," Longarm said.

Romero shook his head. "A deeper shade, is all. Ours has more iron in it. Gold is gold no matter what the rest looks like."

Romero dripped alkali into the little basin, put the glass tube away, and swished the dish around like a tiny prospector's pan. He asked Romero to hold the light closer. Then he held the dish up, peered at the muddy contents, and nodded. "Medium-high grade. Our stuff at Sheep Ranch is richer, but this rock's well worth digging."

Vallejo said, "I don't understand what you're trying to prove, Señor Longarm. We have told you from the first we were digging gold ore here."

Longarm nodded and said, "Just wanted to be sure."

The Mexican insisted, "Sure of what? Why on earth would we be working so hard if there was nothing down here worth our efforts?"

Longarm held up a cautioning hand. "I never said I doubted anyone's word, Vallejo, but somebody is tricking the shit out of us and I'm eliminating as many angles as I can think of."

"Damn it," Vallejo said, "we are digging real gold and loading real gold and shipping real gold. You were the one who was supposed to be guarding it. None of my crew were near you when you let the highgraders steal it!"

Longarm said placatingly, "Now don't get your balls in an uproar. If you weren't so sensitive you'd see we just gave you and your men an alibi."

Vallejo simmered down and said sheepishly, "Oh."

Longarm explained. "That's how I aim to find our culprit—by figuring out who *didn't* do it, till I whittle down to the only ones who *could* have." He ticked off possibilities on the fingers of his large, calloused hand. "So far, I know *I* never stole the gold. I don't think Herc stole it, and it looks like you and your men are home free."

Vallejo sighed deeply and nodded. "I understand. Forgive my outburst. One becomes a bit sensitive after being called a greaser a few times. Who else have you eliminated from your list of suspects?"

"Nobody. And there's a lot of folks in Calaveras County, too. Let's go topside. Maybe I can start crossing off a few more names."

Vallejo led the way with the lantern and they followed him back to the main shaft. Romero asked where the other miners were. The Mexican explained that the three of them had come down at the end of the shift. He added, "We are only working one shift a day now. Señor MacLeod is having difficulty raising more working capital."

Romero said, "I can see you're running a shoestring mine with semiskilled labor, no offense intended. If I was MacLeod, I'd sell out. He sounds like a stubborn cuss."

Vallejo said, "He is. This mine means much to him. He says he put a lot of time and effort into finding his first decent strike and has no intention of letting others get rich from it."

They started up the slope. Vallejo was in the lead, with Romero in the middle and Longarm bringing up the rear. Longarm neither heard nor felt anything unusual until Romero suddenly whirled around and pushed him, yelling, "Run! Run like hell, and cut around the corner!"

Wondering why, but willing to learn, Longarm tore after Romero as the burly Italian raced down the pitch-blackness of the shaft. He could hear it now. Something was chasing them!

He reached the end of the entrance shaft in the darkness and ran full-tilt into the hard, wet standing wall. A hand reached out and hauled him into the side tunnel as an ore car, with an explosive, earth-shaking crash, slammed into the space he'd just been occupying. Longarm was hit in the back with a chunk of flying rock. A wooden plank slapped him across the behind like an initiation paddle wielded by a school bully who'd eaten gunpowder for breakfast. Longarm and Romero sprawled together on the sloping, muddy floor as things tinkled and shuddered into dead silence. Then Longarm got off Romero and helped him up, saying, "Thanks. You have damn good ears!"

Romero lit a match, saying, "I felt the air pressure building. A hard-rock man gets to where he can feel things before they happen, under a mountain."

He raised the little light over their heads and took a gingerly few steps back the way they'd come, muttering, "Jesus!"

The ore car that had chased them down the track

was a pile of shattered debris against the standing wall at the bottom of the slope. The rock it had been filled with lay in a spread-out pile. A lantern lay on its side among the lumps of ore, its chimney shattered and its flame snuffed out. Romero's match went out, but he lit another, picked up the lantern, and lit the wick, saying, "This thing's warm. I think it was Vallejo's."

As he held the lantern up, Longarm pointed with his chin at a trickle of blood running out from under the piled rock and wreckage and said, "He came down the tracks with the car! He's under all that shit!"

Romero put the lantern down as he dropped to his knees and started lifting rocks, saying, "*Help* me, damn it!"

But Longarm was running up the slope, his drawn Colt in his hand, as he called back, "There's no way he's *alive* under there, but the son of a bitch who killed him can't be far!"

He boiled up out of the ground, dodged to one side as he left the overhang of the mine entrance, and took cover behind another ore wagon sitting quietly on a siding as he scanned the sunlit surroundings.

He seemed to have the mine head to himself. He'd come up out of the darkness so suddenly that the sun hurt his eyes. But he could see to the treeline all around, and it was just dusty and dead-looking in the late-afternoon light. There wasn't even a wisp of hanging dust to hint at anyone's presence.

The back door of MacLeod's cabin opened and the owner's freckled little wife stepped out. Longarm shouted, "Get back inside!" and then, as he saw she was just standing there like a big dumb bird, he swore and ran over to her, grabbing her as he whipped them both inside, slammed the kitchen door, and peered out the dusty kitchen window.

Lottie MacLeod gasped, "What's wrong? What happened?"

Longarm said, "They just killed Vallejo and damn near killed me and that other fellow. Have you been working in this kitchen, ma'am?"

"Of course. Kevin will be home any minute and it's getting on to supper time."

Longarm nodded at the pot of beans simmering on the kitchen stove and asked, "Did you see anybody moving about out there, just now?"

The girl shook her head and said, "Not since the men knocked off a few minutes ago."

"Did they all leave directly, or did some of them sort of hang back?"

"Heavens, I wasn't paying that much attention." She thought for a moment, then shook her head again and said, "I just don't know. I'm so used to seeing men come and go up there by the diggings, I never notice who comes or goes."

He saw Romero in the mine entrance now. He went to the door again and called the husky Italian over, covering Romero's back as the big man dog-trotted to the cabin. As Romero joined them, he told Longarm, "You were right. They're going to have to carry him out in a sack." Romero saw the horror in Lottie's eyes and quickly added, "Sorry, ma'am. But facts is facts."

She gasped, "What happened down there—a cave-in?"

Longarm said, "Runaway ore car, ma'am. Romero, is there any chance at all it was an accident?"

The Italian shook his head and said, "The shift was over. I noticed the other cars were on a siding sloping *away* from the entrance. They've led the burros off, too. Somebody pushed that car in on us the hard way. From the speed it came down, I'd say they followed it a ways, still pushing."

"Could one man do it, or would it take more?"

Romero shrugged and said, "One man could have moved her if he really put his back into it. Once he had her headed downhill, of course, he was just pushing to be ornery."

Longarm nodded, looked out the window again, and said, "Whoever it was seems to be long gone. We'd best get you headed back home while it's still light, and I thank you for your help." He turned to Mrs. MacLeod. "When's your man due back, ma'am?"

She said, "His stage is due before sundown. He left his pony at the livery in Manzanita. Why?"

"I ain't sure it's safe to leave you up here alone. By the way, didn't a dog yap at us when we rode in?"

Lottie looked around at the floor and replied, "Rex? He was here just a minute ago."

"He ain't here now," Longarm observed. "He should have been sounding off about all the excitement we've just had."

Lottie said, "That's funny. He usually does bark at strangers."

She went to the back door and called out, "Rex? Here, boy!" a couple of times. No dog appeared.

Longarm glanced at Romero and said, "Stay with her a minute, will you?"

The miner nodded and put a casual hand on the grips of his sixgun.

Longarm stepped outside and walked over to the untrodden earth at the edge of the dust surrounding the cabin and mine works. He worked the grassy edge for tracks, but there was too much sign to read a pattern. He found rabbit tracks and deer scat along with plenty of prints that he assumed had been left by Rex. The dog had probably patrolled the grounds thoroughly and pissed on nearly every tree and bush.

There were human tracks too. Too many human

tracks. The workmen lived in every direction and had walked home every damned way. So Longarm started looking for hoofprints.

He circled the whole site, crossing the road and the rail siding without spotting anything worth following up. He cut back toward the cabin, holding his gun loosely at his side as he walked. As he passed the mine entrance again, he wondered who he was going to send to break the news to the dead man's kin. They were probably waiting supper on him right this minute. He passed an ore car parked near the tipple. A flash of chestnut caught his eye between the wheels and he stopped. He walked over to the car, bent over, and muttered, "Oh, damn!"

The dog, Rex, lay under the car on his side. A blue-bottle fly was crawling over his open eye and others were sipping at the bloody edges of his bared fangs. Someone had smashed the dog's head in with a club or a rock. The poor brute had died defending the property as best he knew how.

Longarm walked slowly back to the cabin. That woman was going to cry some when he told her. They were going to have to take her with them when they left. It wasn't safe to leave her up here alone.

Longarm had a sudden thought and stopped in his tracks, muttering, "Wait a minute!" Then he turned and moved back the way he'd come. The dead Vallejo had mentioned night watchmen. Sure. Nobody was waiting supper on Vallejo—he lived with two other workmen in that little shack just up the rise beyond the tipple!

Longarm cautiously approached the bunkhouse. The plank door was ajar a slit, but when he called out there was no answer.

He moved in carefully, kicked open the door, and stepped inside. There were two Mexicans in the bunkhouse. One lay on the floor and the other was sprawled across his bunk, staring up at the ceiling. The bunkhouse was filled with the smell of bitter almonds and both dead men had cherry-red faces, as if they'd blushed themselves to death.

Longarm had seen Death wearing this expression before. He knew cyanide was used in gold mining, so there was no mystery as to how they had died.

He stepped over to the body on the bunk and felt its cheek. The corpse was lukewarm. They'd died at about the same time as the dog, while he and the others had been down in the mine.

A bottle lay on the floor near the other corpse. Longarm picked it up and sniffed. The bottle was one-quarter full of red wine with just a hint of bitter almond to its bouquet. The dead men hadn't been fussy drinkers, but they'd probably known the man who had given them the free wine. That didn't tell him a damned thing. He already knew it was someone in Calaveras County.

Lottie MacLeod had been right about the stage. It arrived just before sundown and she was with Longarm when her husband got down from it. She threw herself against him and started to weep loudly as Longarm filled him in on what had happened up at his mine. He added that the bodies had been hauled into town and handed over to their kin for burial. MacLeod said, "Damn it, just as I get another bank loan, they start killing us!"

Longarm said, "Yeah, I'll be at the Manzanita Inn later, if you have any ideas. Constable Lovejoy's posted some deputies up at your diggings with orders not to drink any wine. So it's likely safe for you two to go home when you've a mind to. I've got work to do."

He'd noticed the stage crew ducking into the saloon across the street while the team was being changed for the next trot up to Angel's Camp. So he left the Mac-Leods to sort things out and moseyed over after them. He introduced himself to the jehu leaning on the bar and asked, "What time did you boys pull out of Sacramento this afternoon? I've got good reasons for asking."

The driver shrugged and said, "I never looked at my watch, but we've been on the road a good five or six hours. Why?"

"I'll pay for your drinks. You just saved me a ride in to Sacramento to talk with some bankers."

He placed a coin on the bar and went outside. He'd eliminated MacLeod as well as himself and Romero. That wasn't much, but every little bit helped.

He saw that the MacLeods had left. Constable Lovejoy had been in his office when Longarm and Romero had carried Lottie MacLeod and the news to town, but that meant nothing. The Baxters were staying in Longarm's hotel, but when he'd knocked on their door he had gotten no answer. Their horses were in the livery and nobody in town knew where they might have gone on foot.

He went to the Manzanita Inn and asked the desk clerk if they'd come back. The desk clerk said no, so he went upstairs. His own room was just down the hall from the suite Sylvia and her brother had rented. He knocked softly on Ralph Baxter's door, got no answer, and hit it a few hard licks. Then he took out his penknife and quietly opened the latch.

The room was empty, as he'd hoped. Knowing the room clerk was right under him, Longarm moved quietly on the balls of his feet as he gave the room a casual search, not sure what he was looking for.

Baxter's clothes were hanging in a closet. Longarm found a carpetbag under the bed, opened it, and found it filled with nothing incriminating or even interesting.

The engineer's chemistry kit was in a dresser drawer. He uncorked every bottle and sniffed for bitter almonds. Some of the stuff smelled godawful, but he found no cyanide. He remembered that Baxter had said he was afraid of the stuff.

There was a sheaf of envelopes and papers in the same drawer. They seemed to be assay reports and a telegram. Longarm read, ONE AND A HALF MILLION IS FINAL OFFER STOP WHATS HOLDING UP THE PARADE STOP MORRISON.

He folded the telegram and put it back the way he'd found it.

Wondering where in thunder the two of them could have gone, Longarm eased over to the connecting door between their rooms and tried the knob. The door wasn't locked. He opened it. Then he froze in the doorway.

They were in Sylvia's bed—asleep or dead, he couldn't tell which. They'd tossed the sheets aside to cool off. He imagined they'd been having a lively time. They were both naked. Baxter lay spread-eagled on his back with Sylvia cuddled against him. She was still wearing her black stockings and frilly garters, but nothing else. They didn't look as if they'd been poisoned.

As Longarm studied them for signs of life, Sylvia opened her eyes. Longarm stepped back and softly closed the door. He was halfway to his own room when Sylvia caught up with him and clutched at his sleeve. She'd slipped on a robe. She said, "You have to let me explain, darling."

Longarm opened the door to his own room and she followed him inside as he said wryly, "There's no need, ma'am. Incest ain't a federal offense, lucky for lots of folks."

"Damn it," she said, "he's not my brother. He's my husband."

"Adultery ain't a federal crime either, Mrs. Baxter. I wasn't prying into your personal habits. The high-graders have started killing folks and I was worried about you. I can see you're alive and healthy, so what the hell."

"Listen, Ralph understands my needs, darling. He knows I hold advanced views about sex."

"I figured that was why he's been so testy with me. But what's your play, Sylvia? How come you two are posing as brother and sister if you ain't?"

"We're a team," she explained. "We're fronting for a financial syndicate and, well, sometimes it gives us an edge if I'm free to have a romance or two along the way."

"The two of you are out to fuck folks either way, huh?"

"Don't be brutal. What happened on the steamboat was not in the line of duty. I let you make love to me simply because I wanted you."

"Maybe. Have you had Kevin MacLeod in your pants, too?"

"Of course not," she said righteously. "He's happily married."

Longarm noticed she had shut the door behind them and was already out of her robe. He asked, "If Ralph didn't sic you on me and you're not out to seduce MacLeod, why are you up here in the Mother Lode?"

"Why? He's my husband, of course. Don't you think poor Ralph has needs and feelings too?"

"He's got them under better control than most gents, I imagine. You'd best get back to him before he starts getting desperate again, Sylvia."

She smiled lewdly and said, "Ralph's done for the day. But I'm a warm-natured woman."

As she dropped to her knees and started to unbutton

him, he shook his head and said, "I noticed that on the steamboat. But I'll pass, this time around."

She fumbled for him. As he backed away she followed him on her knees, protesting, "Pooh, you know you want me."

He bent over and pulled her to her feet, saying, "Put on your damn robe and git, girl. Aside from my delicate feelings, I've got work to do."

"You can't discard me like some used toy, damn it! The two of us are lovers."

"You mean we were," he corrected her. "I ain't any toy, either. If Ralph can't keep you satisfied, the saloon is filled with horny cowhands almost every night. So, like I said, I'm out of the game."

She shrugged and bent to pick up her robe, saying, "You'll be sorry, the next time you wake up with a hard-on. Ralph's left me more than once. But he always comes crawling back for more."

"Some men are like that. I ain't."

"Pooh, you men are all such hypocrites. There's not one of you who doesn't fool around on his woman, but when one of us acts the same, you act like you're shocked silly."

"You're probably right, ma'am. I reckon we ought to be horsewhipped for being like that, but that's the way we come."

"I'll bet you have somebody else lined up, right?"

He grinned and said, "Maybe."

She laughed and said, "I knew it." She put her and on the doorknob and added, "Well, if it doesn't work out, don't go to strangers. Meanwhile, good hunting, darling."

She left. Longarm sat on the bed and lit a cheroot, wondering how Ralph was going to take her odd views on free love this time. He puffed furiously on the cheroot as he ran the day's events through his head.

At least he supposed he could scratch the Baxters off his list of suspects. He wouldn't take Sylvia's word for it that the sky was blue, but the room clerk had told him he hadn't seen the couple for hours, and for now, Longarm was willing to go with the assumption that they had been exactly where he had found them. He was stuck for ideas. It was too dark to look for sign and he reckoned the murderers hadn't left any anyway.

For some reason he found himself thinking about the pretty little librarian over at the county seat. He shook his head to clear it. That was crazy. He had enough of that kind of trouble on his plate. There was a jealous husband just down the hall and a Mexican gal waiting for him who'd likely pull a knife on him if he looked at another woman. He frowned, blew a smoke ring, and thought, *Misdirection. That's what the book said. I ain't been looking at the right places. While I'm checking out a mine everybody says is all right, the rascals kill three men and a dog and damned nearly me, too.*

MacLeod would have his ore cars filled again in a day or so, since he had plenty of ore in the tipple at the mine head. Should he sniff around up there some more? No. That was what he would be expected to do. Check out the bank to see if MacLeod had told the truth about making another loan? That was also an obvious move. The stage crew had said MacLeod had really come up from Sacramento. What about wiring headquarters for a rundown on the Baxters? The girl's story jibed with what MacLeod had told him about their fronting for people who wanted to buy the mine. The telegram wasn't likely to be a plant. He doubted that they'd expected him to find them in bed like that. On the other hand, it was a neat alibi for folks to appear to have no shame. Ralph could have slipped out the back way. But what was his game? To crush MacLeod financially so he would sell the mine cheap? It was possible. But the snooty Bostonian couldn't move tons of ore all by himself, even with Sylvia helping. You'd need a whole crew to shovel all that ore and hide it. A man masterminding others didn't have to stage a bedroom farce; he'd just sic some side-kicks on you.

Had that gunslick over at the county seat really been just a pal of the Calico Kid's, or was that a set-up too? Wheels within wheels.

Misdirection, he told himself. *Nothing really matters but the way they've been stealing that ore. Find out how they work that one slick trick and you'll have the rest of it on a platter!*

He snuffed out the cheroot and checked his sidearm's ammunition. Guarding the shipments by sitting on top of the ore was useless; it hadn't worked for any law-man who'd tried it. There had to be something else he should be watching instead.

But what in thunder was it? They weren't switching the ore before it was loaded. They weren't switching it at the stamping mill. And he'd been sitting on it every-where between. What they were doing appeared to be plain impossible. But they'd done it, over and over.

"Secret trapdoors?" He asked the .44 in his hand. Then he shook his head. If they'd been sneaking the ore out the bottom of the cars as they rolled, he'd have noticed because he'd have gone down through the trap-door with it. If they'd somehow switched moving cars, in a tunnel, say, he'd have been switched as well. But another shipment would be leaving and he knew if he didn't figure it out, the ore would never arrive at the stamping mill. MacLeod would go bankrupt and have to sell to that snooty Baxter. . . . *Back off. I've been down that trail and it doesn't lead anywhere I ain't thought of.*

He put the gun in its holster and rose to his feet. He knew where he'd be spending the night, and that part was just fine. He had a while to figure how to guard the next shipment. Meanwhile, Felicidad was waiting.

Longarm lay in the fourposter, smoking in the dark with Felicidad's head on his naked shoulder. She murmured, "That was lovely, *querido*. But I can sense you are troubled. Is it about poor Tico and those other muchachos?"

He said, "They tried to kill Romero and me, too. Romero has a wife and kids. I've been thinking of magic tricks. I'm usually tolerably good at spotting a cardsharp dealing funny. I've never been taken by the shell game. So, if nobody can shift a card or a pea without my noticing, how do they move two loaded freight cars out from under my big behind?"

"I like your behind," she purred. "It is solid as a rock and you are so good at moving it. When you finish that smoke, can we make love again?"

He nodded and stroked her naked shoulder fondly though a bit distractedly as he ran every move of the past few days through his mind. Damn, that little librarian had a nice pair of legs. The gunslick who had thrown down on him had probably recognized his gelding tied up out in front of the library. He hadn't told the librarian his name, so she hadn't been in on it. She was just a lonesome little thing who liked tall men. She didn't look like a gal who went all the way. He thought it was likely she'd want to take him home to meet her folks.

Felicidad broke into his reverie, asking, "When will you be riding with the next shipment?"

He said, "Don't aim to," wondering why she'd asked. Then he decided it was a natural enough question. He was in a line of work that made men suspicious by nature. Felicidad had bid on the mine property, but her offer wasn't even under consideration. If she was fronting for some local Mexican outfit who wanted the land back, they were certainly being clumsy. MacLeod wouldn't be their main worry now. The Baxters were offering over a million for the Lost Chinaman. Anyone else who was after it should have taken a shot at Ralph by now. Once his syndicate got control, there would be plenty of working capital to hire a whole squad of Pinkertons.

He reached out to snuff the cheroot and Felicidad said, "Let me get on top this time."

She rolled over on him and started fondling him, asking, "Is something wrong? You are not responding, *mi querido*."

He started running his hands over her body to help focus his attention and she leaned forward to pass her nipples over his lips. That helped a lot.

She murmured, "Oh, you have such a lovely body, and there is so much of it," as she slid her thighs up on either side of his chest. She raised her knees and braced a foot in each of his armpits, still jackknifed forward. It opened her so wide he could have gotten in soft, but he wasn't soft anymore. He closed his eyes and pictured the little library gal in the same position. Why was it a man always wanted what he couldn't have? He knew that if he was wrestling with the librarian somewhere, he'd be wondering what that Mexican girl back in Manzanita was like.

He started moving up to meet her as she rode him like a trotting horse, but his mind was up at the mine. Lottie MacLeod was pretty, too. But that wasn't the answer. Everyone expected him to be riding shotgun on the next shipment. What could he do that they wouldn't be expecting?

Felicidad said, *"Ay, que chihuahua!"* as he absently

nibbled her breast. He saw she was about ready. So he rolled her over, braced both of his feet on the rug, and started plunging deeply into her with her ankles locked around his neck. She screamed aloud in pleasure and raked his back with her nails as she sobbed, "Yes, yes, all of it, all the way!"

He gave her what she was pleading for. That was easy. But the thinking part of him kept chewing like a bone on the next shipment.

Going through the same motions over and over wasn't as tedious in bed as it was in his job. But he and those other lawmen had just been jerking off at the highgraders. Billy Vail had sent him all the way from Denver to screw them *right!*

His anger at his own frustrated investigations added what the girl took for passion to his thrusts and she gasped, "Oh, my God, I love you! No man has ever made me feel like this before!"

She was making him feel like a shit, but he didn't say so. She was pretty and had her own land, and many men would have jumped at the chance to keep her permanently. How was he to make her understand that he wasn't one of them?

He'd met more than one woman in his time with whom he could have stayed. His badge, his gun, and the enemies he'd made kept Longarm moving on. Many a gunslick without the sand in his craw to come at him face to face would jump at the chance to hurt a lawman's wife or kids. He couldn't be married to a woman and do his job at the same time. He'd comforted too many lawmen's widows in his day even to think of it.

But he still felt guilty as the girl cried out and climaxed under him. He pumped her down from heaven and rolled off as she sighed, "Oh, I can't get enough of you, *querido.*"

He murmured, "Me neither. My back gives out

ahead of the parts that count. That ornery little rascal would rut us both to death if I let him."

She laughed and said, "I'd hardly call him little. Do either of you love me, just a bit?"

"More like a lot," he lied. "But let's just be still while I slow my pump down and catch my breath."

If he told everyone he was giving up and let them send the ore down with some of Lovejoy's men guarding it, that would leave him free to skulk about a bit himself.

It hardly mattered whether or not Lovejoy could be trusted. He knew nobody on the train was going to see anything. But he wondered what *he* might see, watching from the sidelines.

Felicidad said, "I shall miss you so when you leave me, *querido*."

He blinked and asked, "Did I say I was going somewhere?"

She said, "You didn't have to. I have come to know the sort of man you are."

"Listen, Felicidad, it ain't like I'm not fond of you. You're the prettiest little thing I've ever met, and—"

"Hush, *querido*. No lies between friends. I shall never forget you. I shall probably always be at least a little in love with you. But I am not a stupid woman."

"I never said I thought you were. Does this mean you don't want me to come back any more?"

"You will always be welcome in my bed as well as my heart, my darling. I have tortured myself trying to think of some way to make you stay with me. I even thought of saying I was in trouble, but you must have heard that many times before, eh?"

He had, but he didn't say so.

His thoughts returned to the Lost Chinaman with an almost audible snap. He couldn't follow the next gold shipment on horseback. It wasn't possible to stake out every mile of the track. And if he *could* watch from the side, what was he likely to see? There wasn't a better view than right aboard the damned train in any case; anyone could see that. He frowned and muttered, "Yeah, and that's what everyone's been doing! We've all been watching the magician's waving hand!"

Felicidad asked what he was talking about. He pulled her closer, cocking his right leg over her thigh. She laughed and asked, "Do you want to do it *again?*" and Longarm answered, "Yes ma'am, this time it'll be my pleasure."

"You mean you didn't enjoy it the last time?"

"Hell, you know I did," he lied, adding, "but I just thought myself out of a box and I'm feeling bright-eyed and bushy-tailed as hell!"

Chapter 7

He left Felicidad's before dawn, but as he rode across her spread toward Manzanita, he noticed a couple of her vaqueros topping a rise to his right. They didn't seem to be coming at him, so he waved and rode on. They didn't wave back. They didn't act as though they'd seen him at all.

He thought of a phrase from an old song: "All the boys on the rancho are wild about poor Pancho's widow!" But if he was stepping on any toes, it was their own blamed fault. Felicidad's husband had been dead for some time and they'd left the poor little woman playing with herself all alone in that big house long past what common courtesy dictated.

He cut through a grove of live oaks to put some of his new plan into action. As he'd anticipated, the telephone line to Sacramento followed the ridge beyond the grove, strung on ponderosa poles.

He dismounted, tethered the gelding to an oak, and shinnied up a pole in the gray light to cut the wire before he rode on.

When he got back to the hotel, the room clerk told him the Baxters had started earlier for Sacramento. Their key was in the box and they had said they would be back that afternoon. So Longarm went upstairs, forced their door, and started quietly messing things up, grinning like a polecat in a henhouse.

He pulled the mattresses off both beds and slashed them open with his pocket knife, scattering feathers all over. He took Ralph's extra coat from the closet and tossed it on the floor with its pockets turned inside out.

There was a hatbox under Sylvia's bed. He opened it and dumped the contents on her slashed mattress. He noted with interest that she took care of herself with a fancy French douche bag of India rubber.

He opened all the drawers he could find. He stole all the papers and messages. He opened the chemistry kit, and because he didn't really want to do enough damage to hurt the innocent owners of the hotel, he put the acid bottles in his pocket, hoping they wouldn't leak as he scattered the rest of the glassware on the rug and planted a boot heel on it. Some of the stuff fizzed and the rest stank like hell.

He went to his own room and messed it up also, but a bit more gently. Then he went downstairs and yelled angrily at the startled clerk, "Someone's been in my room! It's been searched and torn up. I thought you said you run a first-class hotel here!"

The clerk followed him upstairs and clucked over the signs of forced entry. He didn't enter the Baxters' suite, of course, but when they complained, Longarm knew the clerk could be counted on to tell them the deputy's room had been burgled too. Longarm accepted the man's apology and confusion in good grace, saying nothing had been stolen, and went to have breakfast while the hotel's staff cleaned up the mess.

Some teamsters were having breakfast in the greasy spoon near the jailhouse, so Longarm struck up a conversation with them and explained that he was about to pack it in. He said, "One man can't do it all by himself. I figure I'll hand that highgrading back to old Lovejoy, at least until I can get a whole posse of federal men up here to search every canyon and abandoned mine shaft all at once."

One of the teamsters nodded and said, "We've been jawing about that highgrading some, Deputy. Us mule-skinners know nigh every road and byway in these parts, but none of us have cut sign where strange freight wagons have been."

Longarm said, "That ain't the problem. Anyone could hide his wheel marks just by dragging a branch of canyon oak tied to his rear axle. The problem is that there are so many trails. I've been in all the likely hideouts, but that doesn't mean much. One rider can only be in one place at a time and I think they've been playing a razzle-dazzle, shell-gaming the poor, lone lawman by moving about like spit on a hot stove."

The teamster frowned and said, "All that ore, Deputy? Meaning no disrespect, I haul stuff for a living. This is right rough country to be scooting all over the map with tons and tons of rock!"

"Hell," Longarm swore, "they've likely dumped the ore down any of a hundred canyons. You can scoot tolerably with empty wagons, even big ones."

The two teamsters exchanged glances. Then the one farthest down the counter chimed in, "That don't make sense! Why would anyone want to highgrade the Lost Chinaman only to dump the ore down a fool canyon? Ain't the ore no good?"

Longarm nodded and said, "It tests out as fair ore, but it looks like any other rock. Dumped down a hill-side or in a creek, it wouldn't attract notice from any-one passing, who'd just think it was the same old country rock you see all over, hereabouts."

"Well, sure," the third teamster admitted. "But

what's the infernal point? You can't spend gold that's just laying in a creekbed, can you?"

"Not right away. But after the search dies down, say in a year or more, you could just come back, start loading up, and say—if anyone asks—that you just found a new placer. Hell, if they've dumped it all in the same place, they could file a mining claim on it and no one would be the wiser!"

The teamsters gaped at him in dawning understanding and one of them said, "Jesus H. Christ! I suspicion it would *work!*"

His companion added, "Sure it would! That's a right smart answer to how them highgraders have been getting away with the stolen ore! Everybody's been trying to figure how they've hauled it out of the county over the mountains, but if they've been dumping it nearby— Why don't you just form up a posse and start looking for it, Deputy?"

Longarm shook his head and said morosely, "It'd take too long. Like I said, it's just rock to the eye. We'd have to prospect every pile of loose rock with chemicals and such. It'd take forever even with a hundred men. Besides that, I might be wrong. Nope, I'm packing it in for now. If the treasury boys want their gold so bad, they can just start looking for it themselves. Justice is handing them back their hot potato."

He finished his ham and eggs and left, knowing the teamsters would gossip. With any luck, he'd just started a gold rush. Every man in Calaveras County who had nothing better to do would be poking around in any brush-filled canyon or abandoned mine shaft he could think of, with no intention of reporting anything he might find, for it was finders, keepers when it came to color lying about in the open.

He moseyed over to the jailhouse and went in. He found Constable Lovejoy tinkering with the telephone on his desk. He said, " 'Morning, Lovejoy. I've got a favor to ask."

Lovejoy said, "I can't get this infernal machine to work. What can I do for you?"

"Well, I don't want to play with your talking telegraph. I never thought it was a practical notion anyhow. Kevin MacLeod will be shipping again by this time tomorrow morning. I was wondering if you could lend him a couple of deputies to ride the train with him."

"Reckon I could, but where do *you* aim to be?"

"Halfway back to Denver, Lord willing. I'm as stuck for answers as the rest of you boys."

Lovejoy grinned and said, "So you're giving up too, eh? I thought you was supposed to be such a smart, sassy detective from the big city!"

"Don't rub it in, old son. I'll allow the rascals are slicker than I reckoned on."

"I thought you had a rep for never giving up on a case," Lovejoy needled him.

"James Butler Hickok had a rep for never getting shot, too. 'There was never a pony that couldn't be rode, and never a rider that couldn't be throwed,' like the song says."

Lovejoy looked unaccountably pleased as he said, "Well, I ain't thanking you for giving this can of worms back to me. But I could have told you it was too big a boo for any one man. Me and the boys will just have to muddle through until they slip up, or until they steal every ounce of gold in the Lost Chinaman and retire for life."

Longarm said, "You just do the best you know how. I'm wiring my boss for permission to crawfish out of here. I'll probably be around town for a while, so feel free to call on me if you come up with anything before I get clearance."

Lovejoy said, "It's too bad this here telephone is out of order. I could have saved you a trip to the Western Union office at the county seat if the blamed thing was working right."

Longarm said, "I know. But I'll just mosey over to San Andreas. To tell the truth, I figure Marshal Vail's going to ream my ass for failing him, so I ain't in such an all-fired hurry to give him the news."

He departed, leaving Lovejoy grinning from ear to ear, and mounted up to ride out. Before heading for the county seat, he walked the gelding up the trail to the Lost Chinaman, where he found Kevin MacLeod supervising his men as they hauled rock from the mine. Longarm didn't dismount as he smiled sadly down at MacLeod and explained that he was cashing in his chips.

MacLeod said, "You can't be serious! I'm shipping these cars down in less than twenty-four hours!"

Longarm said, "I know. Lovejoy says he'll have some deputies riding shotgun for you."

"Damn it, Longarm," MacLeod protested, "those townies don't have the sense to spit! If they hit me again I'm a goner! My men are asking for higher wages, since Vallejo and those other two got killed. I don't have enough to stay in operation. The ore *has* to get through this time!"

Longarm shrugged and said, "Ralph Baxter's in Sacramento right now, doubtless wiring for permission to up the ante. You and Lottie could live right nicely with over a million by way of consolation."

MacLeod shook his head and said, "I don't want to be just rich. I want to die *stinking* rich. I've lost nearly a million in bullion since they started highgrading me! Do you have any notion what it feels like to be starving on bread and beans on top of your very own gold mine?"

"Pretty frustrating, I imagine. But face it, MacLeod. The rascals are just too much for either of us. I will file a full report and see if I can get some treasury men up here. Meanwhile, having done all one man can do, I have to get back to my office."

As Longarm rode off, MacLeod shouted, "Damn it, come back here! I'll *pay* you to stay just one more day! I'll give you a quarter share of the gold I'll be shipping!"

But Longarm shook his head and rode on without looking back. He headed for the trail to San Andreas, but as soon as he was well clear of the neighborhood he cut upslope and rode into the mountains. He followed a game trail along a ridge until he came to a lookout point dominating the valley below, and there he dismounted.

He gathered dry twigs and used the papers he'd stolen from Ralph Baxter to start a fire. When it was burning properly, he slipped the saddle off his browsing mount and removed the saddle blanket.

He cut some green branches and threw them on the fire, sending up a billowing cloud of white smoke that smelled like medicine. He piled on more green brush and dropped the blanket across the smoldering mass, trying to remember how he'd seen a friendly Sioux do it, over on the other side of the Rockies.

As the smoke puffs rose in a series of balloon-shaped clouds, a voice behind him asked calmly, "Why are you doing that?"

Without turning, Longarm said, "Howdy, Bitter Water. Acorns any good this year?"

The Indian came out of the brush and squatted at his side, saying, "I have heard of smoke talk, but my people do not use it."

Longarm said, "I know. But lots of folks are ignorant. They'll be spotting this smoke talk about now from all over the county. I'm likely scaring the shit out of everybody down there, considering the Modoc war wasn't all that far back, or all that far away."

Bitter Water frowned and said, "My people are not on the warpath. There are no other bands in these hills. Who are you supposed to be signaling? What are you saying with that smoke?"

"Signaling nobody and saying nothing. A Sioux would likely laugh himself to death at me. But it's my hope that any white man who spots this smoke talk will get his womenfolk and kids inside and round up all his stock. I doubt if anyone will be out hunting deer today, either. When there's smoke talk against the sky-line, men don't ride out much unless they have a damned good reason."

Bitter Water pondered this as Longarm shook the dust and ashes from the blanket and sat down cross-legged next to the Indian, who finally nodded and said, "Heya! You intend to pin down all the innocent, un-important people around Manzanita, then see who still rides abroad on more serious business. It is a good trick—for you. But what of me and my people? Won't the soldiers come to hunt your wild Indians?"

"No. I'm riding over to the county seat to send some wires. I'll tell the officers who loaned me that gelding that you folks are working for me, but not to tell anyone else."

Longarm took two cheroots from his coat pocket and offered one to Bitter Water, who accepted it with a nod of thanks. The lawman lit the Miwok's cigar and then his own with a burning twig from the fire. They smoked in silence for a while until Bitter Water shook his head and said, "The soldiers may believe you, but I think it is a crazy story. What are we suppposed to be helping you to do?"

"Look for outlaws, of course. I'm deputizing your whole tribe."

Bitter Water laughed. "Now I know you are crazy. We Miwok are not lawmen. We stay as far from you people and your crazy laws as we can!"

"Just the same, I'm saying I've deputized your band. When you've a mind to, you can drop by the Indian agency and pick up the dollar a day I'm paying, oh, say thirty of you. I reckon the taxpayers owe you that much anyway, considering."

Bitter Water said, "You are generous, but crazy. If I were one of those outlaws I would see through your scheme. You grow weary with chasing them around in circles, waiting for them to make the next move. So now you are stirring up trouble to give *them* something to worry about!"

Longarm grinned and nodded, saying, "You'd make a tolerable lawman yourself, old son. I reckon the two of us had best be on our way now. You hear that distant tinkle?"

Bitter Water nodded and said, "Church bells. They ring the bells in the church at Manzanita when there is trouble."

"Right. They've spotted this smoke talk and someone's excited as all hell about it. If your band is anywhere near here, I'd take them over a few ridges pronto. They'll likely get everyone to cover and sit tight for our whooping attack, but in case anyone feels brave enough to ride up here before the army sends help . . ."

Bitter Water rose soberly to his feet and said, "We are going over the mountains where the Saltu have not yet cut the pinyons for mine props. It is well I found you. What if we had been caught unawares by your foolishness?"

"Hell, I spotted you watching me from that next ridge before I even lit the fire. In my time I've fought

Apache, so I know, better than most, where you folks can be found. I see by the polish on that boulder yonder that you've been using this peak as a lookout for a mighty long time."

Bitter Water laughed again and said, "Let us hope the others do not read sign as well as you do. I go with a glad heart. The money you offer will get us through another hungry winter."

Longarm said, "I figured it might. Listen, Bitter Water. Sooner or later you know you'll have to pack it in. You're a smart cuss. Why don't you lead your folks in to the agency and let them eat regular meals? It's late in the game for the old ways in these hills."

Bitter Water shrugged. "We shall last one more winter, thanks to you. Next spring the camus bulbs will be spread upon the table of the Great Spirit, the manzanita apples will ripen as always, and the acorns never fail us. I know what is in your heart, and you are a good person, but we were not put here to be the tolerated pets of your kind. We will live as we have always lived, or we will die, but we will die as real people. I have spoken."

As the Indian trudged away without looking back, Longarm saddled up and headed for San Andreas.

He rode down to the main road through a canyon, then cut to the north. He rode slowly. At the moment he was simply giving his quarry enough rope to hang themselves. As he passed through a road cut, he was thinking of the little librarian. He had no other serious plans for that evening. A bunch of poppies were growing from the rocky bank of the road cut. Longarm reined in and, leaning in his saddle, reached over for a bunch. A distant rifle snapped, and a high-powered bullet whizzed past his left ear like an angry hornet!

He was leaning anyway, so he just kept going,

snatching the Winchester from its boot as he dove headfirst off his spooked mount. The gelding ran off as Longarm hit the dirt on his side, rolled over on his gut in the dust behind a fallen boulder, and levered a .44-40 round into the chamber.

He spotted a drifting cloud of smoke amid the branches of an oak grove he'd just ridden past. The bushwhacker hadn't been laying for him there or he'd be dead right now. The jasper had followed him from Manzanita, seen him outlined nicely in the cut, and let fly.

Longarm had a clear field of fire into the oaks. He could see that there was little cover in the shade of the overhanging branches, except for the tree trunks themselves. The bushwhacker could be behind a trunk, but it hardly seemed likely. When a gent draws a bead on another man's back, and sees that he's missed, he either fires some more or runs away, and there had only been that one shot.

Longarm strained his ears for the sound of hoofbeats. His own gelding had run out the other side of the cut, but it was grazing now, in a patch of lush mountain meadow to the north. Longarm could hear it chomping wet sedge. It sounded like someone chewing celery. He could hear a distant redwing's doorbell cry, too. The cut he lay in was a natural ear horn. He should have been able to hear the bushwhacker's sounds, if the son of a bitch was making any. So he was either long gone or lying low.

Longarm felt like a fool, spread out on his belly like a lizard in the dust, with the bastard who'd shot at him already halfway home. On the other hand, he'd seen many a man catch a rifle ball between the eyebrows by raising his head too soon for a look-see. In his time, he'd put a few impatient jaspers in the ground himself. So he decided he'd just stay put for a spell.

It wasn't as though he had anything more important to do that afternoon than just to keep on breathing.

Longarm sniffed uncertainly as a stray current of breeze carried an ominous odor to his nostrils. *Smoke?*

That was a worrisome thought. The son of a bitch bushwhacker might have set fire to the brush to burn him out.

Longarm removed his trigger finger from the Winchester, leaving the gun braced and aimed at the oaks as his left hand grasped it by the forward grip. He wet his finger and held it up. Such breeze as there was came from the soggy meadow behind him. He was upwind of the oak grove, so the bushwhacker wasn't trying to smoke him out. He *couldn't* smoke him out. Even if he'd circled around and crossed the ridge this cut ran through, the meadow was watered by a meandering stream. *Jesus! You're getting old!* he warned himself, as he shot an anxious glance at the skyline to his left and right.

He was down between two rises. They'd told him in the army always to take to the high ground. If the bushwhacker was up on either ridge right now, he could be creeping in Apache-style. If he got to the top of either side of the cut, he could drop anything from piss to bullets on any fool lying spread out below.

Longarm shot one more pensive glance at the oak grove, decided it was the lesser danger, and started to get up.

Something stung him on the right hip. It felt like he had a pocketful of red ants or maybe a lit cigar in his britches!

Certain that he'd rolled on a scorpion in the dust, Longarm glanced down at his side as he started to climb the side of the cut. Blue tendrils of smoke were curling from the side pocket of his frock coat. He swore and started shucking out of the coat. Now he knew what he'd been smelling. It was the acid—the bottle of aqua regia he'd stolen from Baxter's kit. The goddamned bottle had broken when he had dived off the gelding!

Dropping the coat, Longarm kept going up, taking one emergency at a time. Some of the acid had soaked through to his longjohns. Baxter had said the stuff would dissolve pure gold, but a bullet tended to smart where it hit you, too.

There was no sense in sticking one's head over a rim where someone might be expecting company. So Longarm simply leaped over the top of the rise and crabbed to his left, training his Winchester down the length of the ridge. It was covered with cheat grass bleached tawny by the summer sun. The nice thing about cheat was that it only grew a few inches tall before going to seed and dying off. So there was no cover to worry about. The bushwhacker had fired a single shot and lit out, leaving the tall deputy with the ridge to himself and smoke pouring out of his right pants pocket.

Hoping nobody important was coming up or down the road from either direction, Longarm unbuckled his gunbelt and let it fall around his ankles. Holding the rifle in one hand, he started fumbling at his pants as he ran down the slope toward his grazing mount. The gelding shied and loped off a few yards, dragging its reins through the grass. But Longarm wasn't after the canteen hanging from the saddle. Not with a whole running brook right in front of him.

He had the trousers down around his thighs and had unbuttoned the longjohns by the time he ran the last few yards to the brook and ploppped down bare-assed, with his hide starting to smell like he'd just been roped, thrown and branded!

As the cooling mountain stream washed over him from the waist down, Longarm sat there with the Winchester across his knees and began to laugh like a jackass. He was aware of the ludicrous picture he presented—a grown man sitting bare-assed in the middle of a meadow in his shirtsleeves, vest, and Stetson, holding a rifle like a fishing pole. But he kept an eye on the treeline all around, just the same. Explaining what he was doing would be bad enough, if some carriage filled with womenfolk came along. If the bushwhacker was still skulking in the neighborhood, he might laugh too. Then again, he might not. Longarm knew he was a tempting target at the moment.

Gingerly, he rose far enough to survey the damage. The acid had burned through his tweed pants and cotton longjohns. He hoped it had lost some of its strength in digesting less important stuff than human hide. The burn wasn't all that bad. It looked and felt as if he had brushed against a hot stove. He'd been lucky. The bottle had broken and leaked out into his coat pocket as he lay face down in the cut, with the coattails spread out to his sides. Most of the acid had simply run into the dirt. What hadn't had ruined his duds and nearly ruined him, but he could buy new clothes and his rump would be all right.

He decided that the running water must have washed the acid away by now, so he pulled on his pants and got to his feet. As he squished back to where he'd left the coat, he explored his pockets. His jackknife was well oiled, so it wouldn't rust. His wallet and paper money were in the coat, on the dry side. He shook out the loose change that had been closest to the acid and whistled. Baxter had been right about the stuff being mean. A couple of silver dimes were stuck together and a penny had been gold-plated. A ten-dollar gold eagle was etched badly and silvered on one side from the dimes. He was glad he hadn't been lying right on top of the stuff.

His coat was still smoldering, so he held it out to one side as he emptied the pockets and carried it over to the brook to rinse it out. By the time he'd gotten it to stop smoking, it was a total loss. A few moth holes were allowable in an old tweed coat, but this was ridiculous. It looked like it had been attacked by wolves.

Longarm picked up his gunbelt and strapped it back on. Holding the rifle and the wet coat, he waltzed across the meadow after the skittish gelding, who seemed to think they were playing matador and bull.

Just as Longarm began seriously to consider shooting the gelding once and for all, it stopped dancing away and began to study a clump of wild onion as Longarm, swearing at it, lashed the wet coat to the saddle skirt, slid the rifle into its boot, and mounted up.

Wet from the waist down and sounding like an Indian squaw pounding her laundry on a rock, Longarm rode on. The thin mountain air was warm and dry, so by the time he got to San Andreas, his only wet clothes were his socks. He knew his boots would curl up like cardboard if he took them off to dry, so he left them on. The leather would mold to his feet and stay supple.

He stopped first at a drugstore. He went in, told the laconic old man behind the counter he'd sat in some aqua regia, and asked what the druggist suggested he do about it.

The old man led him into a back room and ordered him to drop his britches again. As he studied Longarm's rump, he said, "Only a first-degree burn. Lucky for you there was running water handy. I've got some camphorated bear grease we might try."

The deputy grimaced distastefully. "Ain't you got

anything that doesn't stink so bad, Doc? I was aiming to buy some new pants, and—"

"We'll just butter your ass a mite with spermaceti, then," the druggist said. "How does that suit you? Sperm whale oil smells sort of sweet."

"Yeah. I'd best spring for some cologne water, too. Every time I inhale, I smell burnt wool. You know, that fool acid smells like metal, even when you wash it away?"

"Metallic ions," said the druggist, as he started to paint Longarm's burn with a cotton swab dipped in the sweet-smelling oil. The old man muttered on about the way acids and alkalies worked, but Longarm was a bit weary of the subject by this time. He was annoyed at himself for ever having taken the stuff, and considered himself more of an expert on aqua regia than he'd ever intended to be.

Leaving the druggist, and smelling much better, Longarm rode the gelding to the livery and bedded it down. He took the ruined coat and walked back the way he'd just ridden, looking for a tailor shop he'd spotted before. He found the shop, and sure enough, the sign in the window said they sold ready-to-wear as well as tailor-made.

He went in to discuss his wardrobe. The tailor clucked over the acid burns and said he had a suit similar to the ruined one. Since Longarm never bought anything but ready-to-wear, this came as no great surprise.

The new coat was almost a perfect match for the tobacco-tweed vest. The pants were a little short, but Longarm said they'd do. A few holes in his longjohns weren't worth getting excited about in summer.

The tailor said, "You could use a new hat, too. I just got in a new line of Stetsons and you've been beating hell out of that one you have on."

Longarm took off his hat and regarded it soberly. Aside from the old bullet hole in the telescoped crown and a little wear and tear, he noticed a dime-sized hole in the brim. He fingered the charred edge. A drop of the acid must have spattered on it, probably when the bottle in his pocket first broke. He was glad it had missed the side of his head, or more importantly, his eyes. The acid had worn itself out eating felt and the hole was dry.

Longarm said he was in a line of work that hardly called for new hats. He paid for the new clothing with a government expense voucher, then he went out, feeling like a sissy and smelling of cologne and moth balls.

He went to the Drover's Rest Hotel and engaged a room, saying he intended to stay in town until he received orders to leave for Denver.

He'd told Lovejoy—and everyone else in Manzanita who'd listen—that he was giving up on the case. The constable had that telephone and would undoubtedly check around the county as soon as the wire was fixed. When he did, he'd find nothing putting Longarm anywhere near the Lost Chinaman or the next ore shipment. Longarm wondered if the Indian trouble would be enough of a distraction. He considered starting a forest fire, but decided it might not be neighborly. A forest fire would certainly distract pure Ned out of just about the whole county, but it was August and the California hills were tinder-dry as they waited for the healing winter rains from the Pacific. A wildfire this time of the year could get out of control and hurt innocent people. He figured at least half the citizens of Manzanita had to be innocent.

He went to the Western Union office. He was aware that the telegraphers were not allowed to divulge the contents of wired messages, but he knew that the pimply-faced kid who ran the office probably drank with Sheriff Marvin and everyone else in town. So, while it meant more time and trouble, he wrote his messages in code.

He sent one to an old friend in the War Department, telling him not to pay too much attention to any rumors he might hear about the bloodthirsty Digger Indians boiling down from the rimrock to rape the livestock and drive off the women.

The young telegrapher stared at the sheet of yellow flimsy and said, "I can't make head or tail of this, mister. This message looks like it was written in Greek, or maybe Chinese!"

Longarm said, "You just send it the way I wrote it, boy. I ain't paying you to understand it."

The youth looked at the address and said, "Oh, War Department stuff, huh? I'll bet you're telling them about the Miwok, right?"

"That's close enough," Longarm said. He'd been told that, to date, the U. S. army had spent over a thousand dollars for each and every Indian, friendly or otherwise, west of the Mississippi. Sooner or later he was going to have to explain his actions to Uncle Sam, and his expense account would hardly cover a fruitless military expedition.

He wet the tip of a pencil stub and composed a longer message to Marshal Billy Vail in the Denver office while the telegrapher sent his coded message to the War Department.

Longarm knew his boss wouldn't go along with half the notions he had in mind, but Vail had warned him not to go crazy anymore without a word of warning or at least some slight explanation. So Longarm brought his superiors up to date. He explained that he was pretending to back off, and then outlined what he intended to do next. He may have skimmed over some details, for he knew Vail was a worrier. That was the trouble with a lawman who worked behind a desk. Out in the field, a man did what he had to. Sitting in an office filled with books of rules and regulations, a man could lose sight of objectives. Longarm wasn't on this side of the High Sierra to enforce pettifogging regulations dreamed up by some idiot in Washington. He was here to find out who was highgrading Uncle Sam's gold, and to make the bastards stop.

It was that one word, *stop,* that caused Vail so much needless worry. The big boos in the Justice Department seemed to think Longarm's job was to build up water-tight cases that would hold up in court. But Longarm was not a lawyer. He knew his law well enough, he supposed. He knew how often some son of a bitch got off on a technicality, too. So he tended to settle his cases with more dispatch and permanency than Marshal Vail thought was decent.

He knew it would take his office time to receive and decode his message. So, after paying the confused Western Union clerk, he said he'd be back in the after-noon to see if there was an answer waiting for him. He didn't add that he had no intention of ever letting on he'd received one, if Vail told him not to overstep his authority again.

Longarm looked at his watch and saw that it was nearly noon. So he moseyed over to the library to catch up on his reading—and whatever.

The same librarian was on duty, so he sent her up the ladder after some more chemistry books. He noticed that her ankles were still as pretty as they had been before, so he sent her up again after a tome on ore recovery. The mining book was heavy and she lost her balance on the way down. Longarm caught her and said, "Steady on, ma'am."

The girl flushed as she turned her head away and said, "Oh, I'm so clumsy."

Longarm tended to agree, but it was nice to know she trusted him to catch her.

He said, "My name is Custis Long and, like I said the other day, I work for the Justice Department as a field deputy."

She handed him the book and smiled shyly, saying, "I'm Pru Sawyer, and I wish I worked just about anywhere else."

"Don't you like books, ma'am?"

She brushed a stray tendril of hair away from her face. "There's a limit to what you can get from books, and they start smelling musty, after a time."

She shot him an arch look as she added, "I notice you've put on some cologne since the last time."

"Had to," he said. "I was all stunk up with chemicals and water lilies."

They stood there smiling awkwardly for a few moments. Finally, her hands moved spasmodically, as if she didn't know where to put them, and she went back to her desk.

Longarm sat down too, and began to skim through the books while he felt her eyes burning holes in the back of his neck. Few people seemed to come in here. Her days here were undoubtedly boring for her.

He wondered idly why so many men were put off by educated women. He supposed it was because education gives a person a certain amount of independence, and most men didn't care much for that in women. He smiled at the idea that most men couldn't feel strong and smart except when they could measure themselves against someone weaker and stupider. Longarm was not a man in need of such reassurance. He thought of Nellie Bly, the young lady reporter he had met in the Indian Nation a while back, and remembered with a concealed grin that her intelligence, independence, and strength of will hadn't diminished one whit their enjoyment of each other.

With an effort, he turned his attention to the books before him. There wasn't a thing in them he hadn't already read or been told about. But he had time to kill. None of the professors who wrote about gold recovery had considered highgrading.

Most highgraders tended to be petty thieves who either took a job in a mine or trespassed in the diggings when folks weren't looking. Nine out of ten lumps of ore looked like nothing much before they were crushed and refined. If there was a glitter of color showing, the lump was worth stealing, even a rock at a time. The average highgrader simply filled his pockets with rich ore, carried it off, and did his own refining with a nine-pound sledge and a prospector's pan. A man could wash a few hundred dollars a day from stuff with visible color.

But the Lost Chinaman's missing ore wasn't rich enough to refine by such methods. A thief down in some canyon could work for a month of Sundays with running water and not pan out enough to make it pay much more than if he'd been washing dishes for money instead.

He looked up cyanide. The entry didn't tell him much. Cyanide melted or dissolved the metal from the quartz too, a bit better, although somewhat more slowly, than acid. He knew the highgraders had cyanide; he'd smelled it on the dead men's breath and in the wine they'd been tricked with. But every mine in the county undoubtedly had some cyanide handy, and half the local Mexicans made their own wine. That line of inquiry was too fuzzy to bother following up on.

Pru Sawyer came over from her desk and sat down beside him. They were alone in the place, so he wondered why she whispered as she said, "It's almost siesta time, Marshal. I'm afraid we have to close the library until three this afternoon."

He stretched and said, "I'm about done here, in any case. You folks hereabouts follow Mexican notions?"

"You mean about the siesta hours? I'm afraid we do. Nobody will be stirring in town until later this afternoon, when it starts to cool off." She looked down at her hands, which were tangled together in her lap, and added, "Most of us eat and then go home to take a little nap during the hotter part of the afternoon."

He said, "I know how siestas work. I ain't never been one for snoozing in broad daylight, but I'll find something to do. I have to wait for a telegram before I can ride out, anyway."

"Oh, you're leaving San Andreas? I mean, for good?" she asked with what Longarm was sure was a definite hint of disappointment.

He nodded soberly, and said, "I was starting to like it here, too. I'd, uh, offer to buy you a meal, but I reckon you'll have to go home to your folks, eh? I mean, I notice you ain't wearing a wedding band."

She didn't look up at him as she murmured, "I live alone. I'm not from this part of the country, Marshal."

He grinned and said, "You don't have to keep calling me Marshal; I ain't talking official business with you. Most people I'm friendly with call me Longarm."

She looked a little confused, then brightened and said, "Oh, I see. 'Long arm of the law,' and all that."

"Well," he continued, "seeing as we're both strangers in these parts, with nobody expecting us home for the siesta and all, I'd take it kindly if you'd have a bite with me, uh, before your nap or whatever." Before she could take that the wrong way, he quickly added, "If you know a restaurant that won't poison us too bad, I'm on an expense account and you can eat anything you've a mind to."

She hesitated, her hairline going pink like sunset along a high ridge before she said, "The only cafe near here serves dreadful food."

He closed the book he'd been reading with a snap of finality and said, "Well, you can't say I never offered, ma'am."

She looked up at him, her eyes moist and thoughtful as she asked, "Will you be by later, Longarm?"

"Doubt it. You're right about books. You can only get so much out of any book. After that, you have to go out in the real world for whatever you're after."

She said, "I know. Uh, we could sort of eat at my house, if you're not in too much of a hurry. I mean, I live just down the street, and—"

Longarm nodded and said, "That's right neighborly of you, ma'am."

Chapter 8

Somewhere a clock chime was tolling two o'clock. Longarm propped himself up on one elbow and muttered, "Got to get on over to the telegraph office." But the girl at his side on the rumpled bedding pleaded, "Don't go yet, darling. We have until three before I have to go back to that dusty old library!"

He smiled at her fondly and said, "I never said I wasn't coming back."

Pru Sawyer was a funny little gal. She'd refused to take her chemise off even after he'd gotten them in bed and down to serious loving after a bit of sparring about across her kitchen table. She made tolerable coffee and awful flapjacks, but he'd eaten four of the damned things. The scattered sunlight through the drawn lace curtains of her bedroom dappled her pale, nude rump and legs with golden spangles as she lay beside him on her belly, one arm across his waist. She said, "You told me about expecting a telegram from Denver, but can't it wait?"

He ran his free hand down her spine and fondled her firm little bottom, explaining, "If I get the authorization I need, I may have to ride into Sacramento. I want to get there before the banks and such close."

"Pooh, the banks close at three. You'd never make it even if you left right now."

"I don't aim to make any deposits or withdrawals, honey. The bankers won't be out of the building before six and I knock plenty loud."

"Are you staying there tonight? I wish you'd take me with you."

He ran his fingers between her buttocks absently and shook his head, saying, "No. I figure on a fast round trip. If you want, you can put a light in your window for me. I'll be back before too late for more of your cooking."

She giggled and said, "You knew from the first I was wild, didn't you?"

He said, "I was hoping so. You must get tired of reading all the time."

"I get tired of the sort of men I usually meet in that place, too."

Longarm thought it was ironic that mousy little gals who looked like butter wouldn't melt in their mouths were usually wilder than all hell in bed. Probably thinking about it all the time was what made them blush so much.

She arched her back and wriggled her bottom as he explored it, saying, "You're getting me all hot and bothered doing that."

He said, "Just getting to know you better. How come you keep that shimmy shirt on like that? It ain't civilized to make love with half your clothes on."

"I just couldn't let you see me naked in broad daylight," she told him.

"How come? It ain't like we were strangers."

"I know, dearest, but I just feel funny about it." Abruptly she turned over, spreading her legs and pulling him on top of her. She wrappped her naked arms and legs around him as he quickly entered her. The chemise annoyed him and he bent his head down to grab the cotton over one breast between his teeth. She giggled and gyrated as he started pulling it up between their bellies, a mouthful at a time. As their moist, bare bellies rubbed together, she suddenly reached down to grab the hem and pull the shift up over her breasts and beyond, gasping, "Oh, yes, it does feel ever so much nicer naked!"

Still moving inside her, he helped her get it all the way off and she threw it across the room.

By the time they were through, they were halfway on the floor. Her hair was brushing the carpet as she bounced her hips all over the bed. Longarm braced a foot against the wall, and put a palm on the floor to keep from diving out on his head. She was still talking about how good it had been while he pulled on his boots.

As he was buttoning his vest, Pru tried to unbutton his fly. He laughed and shoved her hand away, promising, "I'll be back before you cool off enough to mention, honey. But I've really got to git."

"Are you sure you're not just trifling with my emotions? I've heard about you love-'em-and-leave-'em cowboys!"

Longarm had little doubt that she had. She'd probably worn a few down to a nub, too. But he knew the rules of the game, so he said, "I ain't a cowboy, I'm a public servant. When I ride back this way, I aim to trifle hell out of your emotions and anything else I can get my hands on."

Then he strapped on his sixgun, donned his frock coat, and put his Stetson on, insisting, "Got to get cracking, honey. Leave that light in your window and, like the poet says, 'I'll come to thee at midnight, though hell should bar the way.'"

As he kissed her goodbye and left, she sighed, "Oh, you're so romantic . . . sort of."

177

Longarm let himself out the side door, but strode boldly out to the plank walk, for skulking out of a lady's home in broad daylight or any other time draws more attention than walking tall, as if he were perhaps a visiting minister, a door-to-door drummer, or whatever.

An older woman in a sun bonnet was coming up the walk as Longarm left Pru's gate. Longarm touched the brim of his Stetson with a friendly smile and said, "Howdy, ma'am. Nice day, ain't it?"

The old biddy sniffed and said, "Well! I never!"

Longarm hadn't asked her if she ever, for she was a bit long in the tooth and as homely as a chicken's ass. He and Pru had probably made her day for her. But it was no concern of his what the backyard gossips said about the new gal at the library. He'd been invited fair and square, and it was up to Pru to consider what her neighbors thought.

At the telegraph office he found Billy Vail's message waiting for him: HAVE YOU BEEN DRINKING STOP U S GOVERNMENT CANNOT BE PARTY TO YOUR LATEST INSANITY STOP YOU ARE OUT THERE TO CATCH CROOKS NOT TO DRIVE WHOLE STATE OF CALIFORNIA CRAZY STOP SUGGEST YOU STICK TO BOOK AND CONDUCT PROPER INVESTIGATION STOP VAIL U S MARSHAL DISTRICT COURT OF DENVER

Longarm swore softly, balled the telegram up, and threw it in the tin wastebasket. The adenoidal operator opined, "Whatever that coded message you sent him was, he didn't like it much, did he?"

Longarm didn't answer. He walked outside, went to the livery, and retrieved his mount. Then he lit out for Sacramento, riding fast.

The manager at the Crocker bank in Sacramento was an oldtimer who'd panned for color without much luck

178

in the rush of '49. So he knew about highgrading, claim jumping, and the other crooked notions gold brought out in people. He was bored with paperwork, too, so he was more than willing to converse with a deputy U.S. marshal on almost any subject.

They chewed on the highgrading of the Lost China-man until they had most of the juice out of it and the banker said he would go along with Longarm as far as the law allowed. He said some of what the lawman suggested was slightly unethical, but when Longarm pointed out that highgrading was unethical too, the banker laughed and sent a clerk for the account records.

Longarm spread the account books out on the banker's desk and pored over them. As he ran a finger down a line of figures, the banker said, "I didn't know you rootin', tootin' riders for Uncle Sam were interested in bookkeeping."

Longarm sighed and answered, "We don't get to root and toot all the time. Two-thirds of this fool job is just boring routine. Before we get to arrest most folks, we have to ask the same fool questions over and over, and most of the leads we follow wind up nowhere much."

"Ain't life a humdrum bitch? What are you looking for there, Longarm?"

"Lies, mostly. Everyone I've met so far out here has a plausible tale and an innocent reason for being wheresoever and doing whatsoever. At least one of them has to be a crook."

He found the last entry he was looking for, closed the book, and sat back, muttering, "Shit."

Then he took out a cheroot and put it between his teeth, neglecting to light it.

The banker asked what was wrong and Longarm explained, "Everyone's told the goddamned truth about their finances. Lucky for me you run the biggest bank in these parts, so everyone who has enough money to mention banks the same place. The Baxters have the credit rating they told me they have. Kevin MacLeod and his wife are almost as broke as they say they are, since their account is running thin. I see the Vallejo family has the wherewithal to lay out the thousand they offered for the land the mine is sitting on, and Constable Lovejoy has no more in his account than modest graft would call for. I notice you didn't show me the records of the mining company at Sheep Ranch."

The banker nodded firmly and said, "I don't intend to show you, either. Folks like the Hearsts, Stanfords, Ralstons, Hopkinses and such don't take kindly to having their finances bruited about."

"I could likely get a court order."

"From Justice Stephen Field? That's funny as hell. Look, you're a nice young fellow and I like you. But take my advice and back off asking about the big shots who own this state. You'll never in a million years hang a stolen nickel on old George Hearst or his friends."

"Even if I catch them stealing from the U.S. Mint?"

"Shit, Longarm, who do you think *owns* the U.S. Mint?"

"The taxpaying public, according to the U.S. Constitution."

"Son, the Constitution doesn't apply to folks as rich and powerful as those old boys. But aside from the danger to your job if you piss them off, I'd say you were way off base. No big outfit like the Sheep Ranch mine would be interested in stealing ore. They've *got* ore! I'll tell you—off the record—Hearst and Ralston own half of the Big Bonanza over in Virginia City. They've staked claims to the Black Hills ore that Custer got killed over. George Hearst has an interest in that new Anaconda outfit up in Butte, Montana. Hell, all the gold the highgraders have stolen from Kevin MacLeod wouldn't pay the salaries of old George's house niggers!"

Longarm said, "I never suggested that anyone as big as an owner might be highgrading. I don't suspect Huntington or Stanford of playing games with railroad switches, either. But you're right about lots of folks *working* for those big shots. Many a hard-working cuss has plenty of reasons for wanting a bigger slice of the pie. Don't the branch managers of mining properties work on commission?"

The banker frowned and said, "Now that you mention it, they might. You ain't as dumb as you look. Have you studied the men who run the refinery south of town? They get a bonus on the bullion they extract from ore, too!"

Longarm nodded and said, "I mean to have a talk with them later. I don't think they lied to MacLeod about the ore he's been delivering."

The banker narrowed his eyes and pursed his lips as he muttered, "I know this sounds pretty raw and obvious, but have you considered how easy it would be to give MacLeod a false assay? I mean, we don't know the so-called worthless rock never went through the stamping mill *later,* say around midnight."

Longarm grinned and said, "That was one of the first things I came up with, but it won't wash. I was there when they ran the assay. Later on, I sort of snooped around the rock piles down the track. You see, I took the liberty of marking a few lumps of MacLeod's ore when they told him it was worthless. It's still just lying there. Besides that, they've got too many workers at the refinery to play so rough a game on folks. I've added up such refined-out bullion as there could be in ore twice as rich, and I arrived at a figure for the gang."

"You know how many highgraders there are?" the banker asked.

"Nope. I know how many there might possibly be, though. We're dealing with sophisticated professional thieves, or they'd have been caught by the first lawmen who looked for them. Professionals don't steal pennies. Allowing each possible member of the outfit at least a few hundred dollars each time a shipment's diverted, there can't be more than two dozen or so in on it, counting payoffs to folks who just look the other way. There're just too many folks to pay off down here at the Sacramento end. The ones I want are operating out of Calaveras County."

"That still takes in a mess of folks, son."

Longarm rose from his chair as he said, "I know. And since I don't aim to arrest you, I'd best be on my way. I thank you kindly for cooperating with me as far as your regulations allow."

Leaving the Crocker bank, Longarm walked over to the land office for another visit.

The man who remembered Mark Twain, although not the celebrated Jumping Frog of Calaveras County, was not on duty that afternoon. This did not make the tall deputy at all unhappy, for he wanted to see if they always gave out the same tale to visiting lawmen.

They did. Longarm talked to an almost-pretty girl named Justine. She said she was a miner's widow and that she'd gotten the job on merit. It was amazing how many women were holding down men's jobs, these days. Likely it had something to do with Queen Victoria, Longarm thought. Back when he was a kid, before the War, he never saw women in offices with pencils stuck in their hair. Ever since the English had allowed a woman to be ruler of the British Empire, it was getting harder and harder to say no to a female applicant. Which was the way things should be, he supposed, but he found it difficult to do real business without cussing.

Justine took him back to her cubbyhole and told him

she knew all about the Spanish land grants he was interested in. As he sat down across from her, she started by correcting him. "Actually, the so-called old Spanish grants you hear about in California were never granted by the Spanish crown. When Mexico declared its independence in 1821, California was sparsely settled. Aside from the missions, they had a few military garrisons: the San Francisco Presidio, Monterey, and so forth."

Longarm smiled at her, wondering if she wore her hair in that tight little bun to look more down-to-business, or if she really had no notion of fashion. He asked, "Are you saying folks like the Vallejos are full of bull when they brag about all the wild mustard they used to own?"

Justine shook her head and said, "No. Mexico gave away vast tracts of land in hopes of filling up this part of the continent before we got around to claiming it as our manifest destiny. The Russians were moving down the West Coast from Alaska, too, and the Hudson Bay trappers must have worried Mexico City. I know the Vallejo grant. It was one of the big ones. But the family obtained it from Mexico, not Spain."

"Ain't we sort of picking nits, ma'am? I understand the conceit your California Mexicans have about being called Spanish. But I don't see how it matters all that much."

Justine sniffed and said, "It's rather pathetic, but most of the early settlers were Spanish or Mexican *soldados*. Male, of course. The distaff half of the old grandees tended to be Indian squaws. The last Mexican governor of California was a Negro."

"That's what I just said." He frowned. He wondered if she was so precise in bed, and if it would be worth finding out. The girl explained, "The treaty of '48 between our government and Mexico recognized the holdings of former Mexican nationals. A real Spanish grant would be meaningless unless it had been confirmed by Mexico before the Mexican War and the resultant treaty. Most of the mission lands, for instance, were taken from the Church by Mexico before we got here. So the missions are simply empty shells today."

"What happened to the mission Indians?"

"They, ah, lost out in the shuffle. People like the Vallejos, Irvines, and Castros had sense enough to hire good lawyers."

"I heard about the Irvine Ranch, down past Pueblo Los Angeles. They didn't lose so much as a quarter section, did they?"

"The Irvine holdings are huge, even by land grant standards," she averred. "The Scotsman who married into that family had a good lawyer."

"He was white, too. The way I hear it, how much land you got to keep depended a little on your complexion."

Justine looked pained and said, "That's not fair. Poor Sutter lost his mill and everything else, and he was as white as you or me. The land office is not prejudiced, as some Mexicans seem to think."

Longarm smiled crookedly and said, "Sure it ain't. I've no doubt that all the land that was grabbed was grabbed fair and square. But it's the Vallejo holdings I'm interested in. The Lost Chinaman mine sits smack-dab on land the Vallejos used to own. I'd like to know how come."

Justine said, "I can tell you that without looking it up. Old land grants have priority over homestead claims. Mining claims come before agriculture."

"You mean if I was to find a gold mine on any land at all—even if it was occupied—I could just up and *take* it?"

"Of course. You wouldn't need to strike gold. Copper, silver, or mercury would do as well. Once you'd staked out the limits of your find and registered it with the California Mining Commission, it would be all yours."

Longarm's eyebrows rose. "Back up, ma'am! You mean I could start a mine anywhere at all? Suppose someone had a house already built over it?"

She shrugged and said, "It's happened. It's led to messy gunfights, too. Few old land titles include the mineral rights, as poor old Sutter found out when they panned the soil out from under his mill and general store."

Longarm frowned and said, "That hardly seems fair, ma'am."

"I never said it was. But the men who wrote the California laws were mining men, and the law is the law."

Longarm whistled softly under his breath as he mulled her words over in his head. Then he said, "I can see how the Vallejos lost the land the Lost Chinaman sets on. Is there any legal way they can get it back?"

"Not as long as there's a viable mine site up there. The owner of a mine is the landlord of record. He can transfer the property, hold it for land speculation, or do just about anything he likes. The original owners have no say. The only way they could hope to recover the property would be by buying out the mineral rights. This happens too, occasionally."

Longarm shook his head and said, "Felicidad Vallejo ain't got the wherewithal to buy a going gold mine. But what if the mine was to play out and be abandoned?"

Justine pursed her lips. Longarm noticed that they pursed nicely. She said, "As I recall, the mine you speak of did pinch out a few years ago. But the owners hung on and sold it recently. I could look the new owners up for you, if you like."

"I know Kevin MacLeod and his wife, ma'am. The cud I'm chewing is the final outcome of the mess. Am I right in figuring that the Mexicans who used to own the property could get it back if the Lost Chinaman went out of business for keeps?"

Justine nodded and said, "If the mine shut down and nobody else put in a mineral claim."

He stroked his mustache pensively for a moment, then asked, "What if the mine went broke, but some other outfit was to buy it?"

"They'd own it, of course. As long as anyone is working a mine, or even sitting tight over a hole in the ground, the original property owners are simply out of luck."

He swore under his breath and said, "I can see I'm chasing my fool self smack down another blind alley, most likely. But I thank you kindly for lighting the way."

She smiled rather warmly, considering the severe way she wore her hair, and asked, "I take it you're working on a process of elimination, sir?"

"You can call me Longarm, ma'am, and I've eliminated myself out onto another durned limb. I've got maybe one more arrow in my fool quiver, and if that doesn't work, I've met up with some cuss who's too durned smart for me."

He started to rise. Then he thought better of it, since he faced a lonely night ride back to the county seat in the first place, and wasn't in all that great a hurry in the second.

He said, "I can see you're anxious to close, ma'am, since it's creeping up on four-thirty. Do you, uh, live around here?"

Justine nodded and said, "Just a few blocks over." Then she added, "With a very possessive gentleman."

He said, "Do tell? I didn't notice a wedding band, ma'am."

Her smile was smug when she nodded and told him, "I never said I was married. I suppose you might call me an emancipated woman."

He shot a wry, wistful grin at her and rose to his feet, saying, "I won't keep you from enjoying your constitutional rights, ma'am."

As he let himself out with a slightly mocking bow, she grinned up at him and said, "Nice try, cowboy."

He left, frowning. He didn't think he looked very much like a cowboy, and his "try" hadn't been much more than common courtesy. He'd seen no need to twist the knife like that.

Then, as he walked out into the sunlight, he began to laugh. It sure beat all how women kept surprising him, but wouldn't life get tedious if a man was right every time? He headed for a café across the street to put away some chili and maybe some apple pie, telling himself, *What the hell, old son, you can't win 'em all!*

The next twenty-four hours were enjoyable, but had little to do with the case, since he spent as many of them as he could with Pru Sawyer. By the time he said goodbye a second time, she'd gotten over any inhibitions she'd ever had about nudity or anything else. She told him she'd read all the books about such matters that were in the library, but that he'd shown her a few tricks they hadn't mentioned. It was good to know he'd helped a young lady's education; she obviously intended to put it to good use. He almost felt sorry for the next gent she snared with her downcast eyes and shy little smile.

Nobody shot at him as he rode back toward Manzanita. His smoke signals seemed to have left the roads in a deserted condition and nobody was expecting him.

He circled up through the trees behind the Lost Chinaman, tethered his mount in a brushy draw, and eased up to a ridge that offered him a clear view of the diggings.

He'd timed his arrival well. The ore cars had been hauled away.

MacLeod and Lovejoy's deputies were well on their way to the mill with the latest shipment. He watched, chewing an unlit cheroot. He wasn't sure just what he expected to see. But until now, everyone had been watching the ore shipments. That train pulling out was the misdirection the book had been talking about. He was watching the stage instead of the magician's flashing hands.

Nothing much seemed to be going on. Some workmen brought a car of ore up out of the mine. Lottie MacLeod walked over from the cabin and he could see that she was directing them to put it on the lift and load it in the tipple. He could have figured out where the ore should go, but MacLeod had said they were using unskilled help.

The woman went back to the cabin and the men walked slowly back to the mine entrance and disappeared. It was pretty uninteresting. A jay sassed Longarm from an overhead branch for a while. Then, getting no answer, it lost interest too, and flew off to bother someone else.

Lottie came out of the cabin again and began hanging up some wash to dry. Longarm scanned the treeline all around. There wasn't any movement. Nothing worth thinking about was happening down there. But Longarm kept watching. He had no idea what the magician's assistants might be up to as everyone watched where they were supposed to. But if he knew what he was supposed to be looking for, he wouldn't have to look.

He took out his Ingersoll watch and studied it. Mac-

Leod and the others would be on their way back from the refinery by this time. If they came by stage, they'd be back around sundown. If they got the railroad to give them a ride back on the empties, it would be sooner.

The afternoon wore on. Not a damned thing happened. He waited a good two hours, made himself sit there for one more, then grunted, "All right. Either that magic book was wrong, or the pea is under some other shell."

He crawled back to his horse and mounted up. He circled wide of the diggings and rode slowly into Manzanita. He tied the gelding in front of the saloon and went in. He bought a bottle of Maryland rye and took it to a corner table, where he sat with his back wedged in the corner. When a cowhand came in and started to walk over to the music box, Longarm asked him not to play "Garryowen." The cowhand shrugged and settled for a beer at the bar.

After a while Ralph Baxter came in. He sat down across from Longarm and said, "I saw your horse outside. I thought you were leaving."

Longarm said, "I did leave. Now I'm back. My office wants me to look into a few more angles before I'm relieved."

Baxter said, "Our rooms were searched while we were in Sacramento."

Longarm said, "I figured as much. Mine was too."

"The desk clerk told me. What on earth do you suppose they were looking for?"

"Don't know. What was taken?"

"Nothing. Nothing important. What are you missing?"

"The same. They were likely barking up the wrong tree. You say you went to Sacramento?"

"Yes. I've been authorized to offer two million for

189

the Lost Chinaman, but that's the end of it. If they won't sell at that price, they're welcome to any gold they can get out of there. Frankly, I'd have broken off negotiations at a hundred thousand. That fool hasn't made that much since he reopened the mine."

Longarm poured himself a drink, holding the bottle out to Baxter. The Bostonian sniffed and shook his head. So Longarm sipped at his own drink and said, "So far, nobody seems to want to let him. The bank draft you're offering MacLeod is from the Crocker Trust, right?"

Baxter nodded with a frown and said, "As a matter of fact, it is. How did you know?"

"I rode into Sacramento myself to discuss high finances yesterday afternoon. They tell me your outfit's been known to play rough, but their checks don't bounce. By the way, did you bring your, uh, sister or whatever back to Manzanita this time?"

Baxter flushed and snapped, "Don't be crude, God damn it. We both know what Sylvia is. She tends to gloat about it. The only reason I don't beat the tar out of you is simply that there's a long line ahead of you. I'd have time for little else if I intended to thrash every yokel she's known in the Biblical sense."

Longarm stared down at his glass and said, "Yeah. She is sort of Biblical, but you didn't say where she was at."

"I'm afraid you'll just have to make do with your little Mexican thing tonight. We heard there was Indian trouble up this way, so I left Sylvia in Sacramento. I assume she'll find something to occupy her time while I settle this more important matter."

Longarm didn't ask how the jasper knew about Felicidad. That was the trouble with small towns. He said, "You ain't scared of Indians, huh?"

Baxter grimaced and replied, "I simply want to buy

the damned property and get out of this stupid country. I have no intention of riding out into the hills where they can get at my scalp."

Longarm nodded, fished out a smoke, and lit up before he said, "There's one thing I don't understand about your offer or your outfit, Baxter. We both know there's more to worry about out here than a few Indians. That mine's been hit high and low and sideways by highgraders. Three men and a dog have been murdered and nobody has an educated guess as to who's behind it all. Yet you're willing to lay out good money for MacLeod's claim. Do you know something I might not, or were you just born foolish?"

Baxter said in a low voice, "If you haven't guessed, Sylvia and I are working on commission."

"You mean it's not your worry whether your syndicate can make money on the mine or not?"

"I've confirmed that the ore is worth digging. How they dig it out and get it to market is their worry. I assume, once a real mining outfit takes over, these highgraders will find it less easy to do whatever it is they have been doing."

"You have no idea how they've pulled it off?"

"Longarm, I don't even *care*. Every grain of the gold they've stolen so far belongs to Kevin MacLeod. It's none of my business. Once the mine changes ownership, it won't be my business either. I'll have collected my commission and been long gone from here before it can possibly happen again."

Longarm started to observe that he thought Baxter was a cold fish. Then he decided that a man would have to be to stay with Sylvia, so he said, "When I rode down to Sacramento, I dropped by the ore mill to swap some ideas. They tell me you've never been by once. You don't seem to be a very curious cuss, Baxter."

"Why on earth would I want to visit the refinery? I have no ore down there."

"I just sort of wondered if you ever thought to assay MacLeod's ore at that end."

Baxter laughed with characteristic unpleasantness. "Assay it? You must be joking. We all know the high-graders have been switching the shipments for worthless country rock. Are you suggesting that the refinery owners have been tricking MacLeod some way? It never occurred to me to question their assay." He stopped talking and blinked a few times. "But see here," he went on. "If they've been accepting good gold-bearing ore, but reporting it as worthless, that would explain everything!"

Longarm smiled thinly and said, "Well, not everything. We've still got some murders and a few nice tries to study on. The other day, I got shot at near here."

He grimaced, having reminded himself of his sore rump, and added, "By the way, I hope you've still got your assay kit handy."

Baxter said, "As a matter of fact, those scoundrels wrecked my old kit when they tore my room apart. I picked up more supplies in the capital, however."

Longarm nodded. Before he could ask his next question, a gun went off outside and a loud voice cried, "Waaaaahooooo!"

The two of them got up and walked over to the doorway. Out in the street, two men were running around in circles slapping everyone they passed on the back and laughing fit to bust. Constable Lovejoy ran down the walk, calling out to them, and one of them fired his revolver in the air again and yelled, "We made it! Got MacLeod and his gold through slick as a whistle! We was just too much for them pesky highgraders, this time!"

Lovejoy danced a little jig and then, as he spotted Longarm, called out, "You hear that, big federal man? The boys got through, and Manzanita is back on the map as a gold camp!"

Longarm waved them over and said, "In that case, the drinks are on me. I want to hear all about it!"

As Lovejoy, his deputies, and half the town crowded in past him, he asked, "Where's MacLeod?"

One of the deputies said, "Rode fast for his mine, to tell the little missus. He was excited as hell. You know what we think? We think we owe it to them skulking Injuns up in the rimrock. The highgraders must have been camped out there in the woods someplace and likely got kilt or run off by Miwok!"

Longarm followed the crowd inside, tossed a twenty-dollar gold piece on the bar, and told the bartender to keep serving till it was all used up. Lovejoy slapped him on the back and said, "God damn it, I like a good loser! I reckon we've seen the last of them highgraders after all, and my men rate the credit!"

Longarm nodded and said, "Maybe. Ain't you interested in catching them for the killings?"

Lovejoy waved the question away expansively. "Aw, shit, who cares about a few greasers? The important thing is that we got through with the gold this time! MacLeod won't have to sell out and it'll mean jobs and boom times for us all again!"

Longarm noticed that Baxter had slipped out. He shrugged and worked his way to one of the celebrating deputies, saying, "I want to hear the whole tale, pilgrim. Start with leaving the Lost Chinaman."

The deputy swallowed a shot of redeye, neat, and slammed the glass down for more before he said, "Shucks, there's nothing to tell. We rode the ore cars down uneventful. Kept an eye peeled for Indians as well, but nobody never come near us. We rolled into the mill yards and they took a couple of samples to be tested. Come out to say the ore was medium-high grade, for once. Then they wrote out a check for MacLeod. Oh, the check was what they called an advance. They said they'd have to see exactly how much the stuff runs to the ton before they paid him in full. But he left with a couple thousand, so his troubles is likely over. If he gets another couple of shipments through, and it seems likely, he might be able to get rid of them no-account greasers and hire white men like we told him he should. He said he'd study on it."

Longarm had heard enough. He went outside and mounted up. As he reached the Lost Chinaman, Ralph Baxter was tethering his own bay to the porch rail of the MacLeod cabin. Longarm rode in at a trot.

The door opened as he dismounted. Lottie MacLeod let them both in, but said her husband was up at the mine shaft. Ralph Baxter gave her an officious look and explained, "I have a bank draft for two million dollars here, Mrs. MacLeod. I know your husband got his ore to market this time, but it might have been a fluke. I seriously suggest that you sell before you're robbed again."

Lottie looked excited, but said, "You'll have to talk to Kevin about that, sir. He's in the mine at the moment, but he should be back any minute."

Baxter said, "I have to speak with him at once," and marched for the door. He saw Longarm tagging along behind him and asked, "Where do you think you're going, my good fellow?"

"I ain't your good fellow, but I'm headed the same place. It ought to be interesting to see if he'll sell out now."

They argued about it all the way up the slope and into the mine entrance. Baxter picked up a lantern near the entrance and lit it. As they started down the tracks,

Longarm noticed that none of the workmen were on duty. The last shift must have just ended.

With Baxter leading the way, they rounded the turn at the bottom. Longarm noticed that someone had whitewashed the bloodstained standing wall where Tico Vallejo had died. They'd hung up a wreath and the cut-out picture of a saint, too.

Baxter led them to the ore face. But MacLeod wasn't there. The Bostonian looked puzzled as Longarm stared at the wet wall and said, "He must be in the other tunnel. It branches like a T down here."

He stepped aside to let Baxter take the lead with the light. They came to the entrance slope, crossed it, and went down the other tunnel. They found Kevin MacLeod on his hands and knees against another rock face. The air was filled with the smell of chemicals. The mine owner had glass dishes and vials of acid spread out near his knees and he'd been hammering on a lump of ore. He turned to smile up at them.

MacLeod said, "The highgraders missed us this time. We got through with a whole load."

Longarm said, "I figured you might."

Baxter said, "See here, MacLeod. You still need working capital. Even if you *can* get your ore to market, I'm authorized to make you a damned fair offer."

MacLeod shook his head and said, "You must be crazy! Didn't you hear me say I *delivered?*"

"Yes, but what of it? It will take you years to make two million clear profit, even if you have no more trouble with those outlaws." He let that sink in before he added, "And that's not saying you won't! Deputy Long here tells me he still has no idea how they've been robbing you. Isn't that right, Longarm?"

Longarm nodded and said, "I've been shell-gamed pretty good, up till now. How come you're testing that rock, MacLeod? I thought they told you it was good in Sacramento."

MacLeod said, "I have two good reasons. I'd be a fool to accept another man's assay, for one thing. For another, they said it was richer than what we've been digging. I think we may have struck through to another vein of bonanza, but, as you see, it all looks the same."

Before Longarm could answer, the ground tingled under them and the air suddenly got heavier. MacLeod gasped, "Oh, *no!*" as the roar of cascading rock filled the mine!

They froze in place, all three holding their breaths as the roar grew louder still, then faded with a last few crashes of falling stones. MacLeod got up as Baxter raced back along the tunnel with the tall deputy following. Baxter stopped, holding the lantern high, and moaned, "Oh, Jesus Christ!"

Longarm joined him and said, "You can say that again."

The leg of the T was filled with dusty rocks and earth, all the way to the ceiling.

Longarm sniffed the air and said, "Smell those nitro fumes?"

Baxter gasped. "You mean someone dynamited the tunnel, with the three of us down here?"

Longarm said, "Wouldn't have been much point to it if we weren't. You don't have a rear door to this mine, do you, MacLeod?"

MacLeod said, "Don't be ridiculous! We're a quarter of a mile under the fucking mountain!"

Baxter put down his lantern and fell to his hands and knees, grasping at a jagged rock. MacLeod said, "Don't do that, you idiot! You'll bring more of it down that way!"

Longarm nodded and said, "Timbers, tracks, and such are likely wedged crossways up the slope, holding back some of the rock. No way we're going to dig our way out from this side!"

Baxter started to argue. Then he brightened and gasped, "MacLeod! Your wife knows we're down here and must have heard the blast!"

Longarm said, "There you go. She's likely running for help right now. We'll just sit tight till they muck out the tunnel." He turned to the ashen-faced MacLeod and asked, "How long do you figure it should take if Lottie doesn't waste time trying to do it herself?"

MacLeod frowned and said, "All night, if she's in town this very minute."

A drop of water ticked the brim of Longarm's hat. He asked if there was a drainage problem and MacLeod shook his head. "It would take a week for enough water to seep in to matter. But the air won't last that long."

Longarm had been afraid he was going to say that.

Chapter 9

Longarm sat in the blackness with his back against the damp wall. He had no idea what time it was. He felt like they'd been trapped since the decline and fall of Rome.

The lanterns were out to save air, but as it was, the air they were breathing was getting sort of gamy. MacLeod was filled with cheerful observations and had explained that it wasn't lack of oxygen that killed men trapped underground. It was the poisonous fumes of their own breathing that did the job long before every bit of oxygen was used up. Longarm sure wished Baxter hadn't put on all that infernal bay rum the last time he washed up. He was stinking up the darkness something fearsome.

The Bostonian asked again who Longarm thought had set off the charge. Longarm hadn't bothered to answer the first few times; it was a stupid question, even for Baxter. To shut him up, Longarm said, "Old son, if I'd had any idea someone was fixing to drop a mountain on my head, I'd have never come down here with you."

MacLeod said, "Listen! Do you hear that?"

Longarm answered, "Been hearing it for a while. It's

either the biggest gopher in the world or somebody digging on the other side of that crud."

Baxter started shouting, "Help! *Au secours!* We're down here!"

Longarm snorted and said, "Oh, shut up. They can't hear you for one thing, and if they didn't figure someone was down here, they wouldn't be digging us out!"

MacLeod said, "I just thought of something awful!"

Longarm said, "I figured you would. But go ahead."

"What if that digging we hear isn't a rescue party? What if it's the highgraders?"

"Ain't likely," Longarm answered. "We didn't hear much of a blast down here, with all that rock between us and the dynamite, but I *felt* the bump and it was a big one. The noise would have been louder on the other side, shooting out the side of the mountain like a big cannon shot. They'd have heard it in Manzanita and the town's already on the prod, between highgraders and Indians. Whoever set off that blast aimed to kill the three of us and light out."

He put a cheroot between his teeth and chewed it, dying for a smoke, while Baxter went on about who might have done it and why. He suspected everyone from the other miners over at Sheep Ranch to the Chinese Tongs in San Francisco, but he didn't have anything really sensible to hang his worries from.

MacLeod said, "What I can't figure is why the *entrance* was blasted. Now that I think on it, anyone doing it should have known we were safe enough around a right-angle turn. You're right about the noise carrying, too. Hell, it makes no sense. As a matter of fact, it was a dumb way to try and kill us!"

Longarm nodded and said, "Might have been a spur-of-the-moment thing. Might have been a right slick attempt to scare you into selling this mine quick."

Baxter gasped. "See here! That's a ridiculous suggestion, even from you, Longarm. You may not have noticed it, but I was standing right beside the two of you when the blast went off!"

"I know. And you said Sylvia was in Sacramento, too. Maybe someone else is figuring to top your offer. Or maybe you ain't as upset as you let on. The digging sounds are getting louder. I know *I'd* sit still in the dark for a few hours for the commission on a two-million-dollar deal."

Baxter made a gagging sound and said, "You're insane. Even if I went in for such dramatic methods of persuasion, how could Sylvia and I be sure I'd be safe down here? The blast might well have dropped the whole hanging wall!"

Longarm started to say Sylvia might not care, but he decided it wasn't right to talk about a lady with another man listening. The mention of wives seemed to jog something loose in MacLeod's brain and he suddenly blurted, "Oh, Jesus! I forgot all about Lottie!"

Longarm said, "I doubt if that's her I hear digging. It sounds more like six or eight men with picks and shovels. I can feel the rumble of ore cars with my poor sore behind. This wet, rocky floor leaves a lot to be desired as a place to sit all night."

"You don't understand," MacLeod insisted. "Lottie was up there alone when they hit us! My God, I'm such a selfish brute! I forgot all about her when it looked like we were done for!"

Longarm said, "That ain't as rare a feeling as it's supposed to be, old son. Most of us look out for our own hides when the chips are down."

"Do you think they might have hurt her?" MacLeod asked anxiously.

"Can't say, for sure. Every time I think I've got a line on the rascals, they pull something new on me.

Let's eat the apple a bite at a time, though. Does Lottie know anything important enough for whoever's behind all this to want her out of the way?"

MacLeod thought silently as Baxter comforted him: "We left her in the cabin, so it's unlikely she saw anyone. These scoundrels have been almost impossibly clever, up till now. No one has ever so much as had a glimpse of the highgraders. Surely, if they were ready to come out in the open and simply start killing people, they'd have done so before now."

Longarm said, "There you go, MacLeod. Once in a while this gent makes sense. Everything the murderous skunks have done has been done sneaky. I'd be surprised as anything if your pretty little gal isn't right as rain, even though she's likely worried sick right now."

A rock rolled down the pile in the blackness and a hoarse voice called hollowly, "Anybody breathing in there?"

Longarm shouted back, "Is that you, Herc? We're all right."

Romero called out, "We'll have you out in a minute. We rushed over as soon as we heard what'd happened. Found some half-assed Mexicans trying to get down to you with their bare hands, but I brought a crew of real hard-rockers. Somebody's sure as shit *mad* at you, Longarm!"

MacLeod crawled over to the pile and shouted up, "Is my wife all right?"

"I don't know. Who are you and who's your wife?"

"I'm Kevin MacLeod. My wife Lottie was up there in our cabin when the blast went off!"

There was a murmured consultation. Then Romero called down, "There's a Mexican lady up here. No other gals nearby. The Mex gal's vaqueros were helping your mine crew when we got here. Doing a piss-poor

202

job, but I'll admit they were willing. We put them to work hauling and mucking while we dug."

But MacLeod wasn't listening. He was on his knees hauling rocks from the pile when Longarm thumb-nailed the head of a match and relit a lantern. MacLeod was growling and cursing as he dug with his hands. A stream of broken rock and sand cascaded down over his knees and buried him to the waist, but he paid it no mind. Longarm got up, moved over to him, and pulled him back, saying, "This would be a dumb time to bury yourself alive."

"My wife! I have to find my wife!"

"Well, sure you do, MacLeod. But let's get out of here alive first."

Some more boulders and shattered mining timbers slid down the pile. Then Herc Romero grinned down at them through a hole near the overhead and said, "There you go, boys. Just let me widen this a mite and you can crawl up over the shit."

As the burly Italian crowbarred a slab of rock aside he observed, "The way I put it together, someone put a box of dynamite in an ore car, lit the fuse, and sent it down the tracks at you. Lucky for you, MacLeod, you run a shoestring operation here. The car jumped your crooked old tracks a third of the way down, hung up on a pit prop, and went off up the slope. If it had made it to the bottom the way it did when they killed Vallejo, we wouldn't be having this conversation."

MacLeod suddenly scrambled up the slope and shoved past Romero. Baxter turned to Longarm and sniffed, "I'd say you owe me an apology, sir. As you see, it was certainly an attempt to murder all three of us!"

Longarm coughed some rock dust out of his lungs, and said, "No, Baxter, just two of us—me and Mac-Leod. I don't think they cared about *you*, one way or the other. Let's get out and study on these interesting new developments."

Felicidad was waiting at the top of the tunnel. She sobbed as she threw herself in Longarm's arms. He hung on to her long enough to kiss her and comfort her a bit. But his mind was preoccupied and he untangled himself as soon as it seemed polite to do so.

The whole town seemed to be gathered around. Some fool was shooting a pistol off in the air as if it were the Fourth of July instead of the middle of August. All the mysterious doings of late had made the whole community skittish, but they'd somehow gotten a load of ore past the highgraders and now, when they saw that the murder attempt had gone sour, they were feeling good. Not a man in the valley had any idea who the highgraders were, or how they'd done their magic, but the spell was broken. The skunks didn't win *every* time, after all.

As Longarm untangled himself from Felicidad, Constable Lovejoy caught his sleeve. "God damn it, Longarm, for a man who thinks he's so all-fired smart, that was a dumb play you just made. Didn't you know the chance you were giving 'em by going down in that fool mine with nobody up here on guard?"

Longarm said, "If I had, I wouldn't have gone down there. Let go of my arm; I've got chores to attend to."

He elbowed his way through the crowd to MacLeod's cabin. He noticed that Felicidad was trotting after him, so he held the door open for her and let her come in with him. Baxter and MacLeod were already inside.

The young mine owner was seated at his kitchen table, signing papers as Baxter stood over him, not bothering not to gloat. MacLeod saw Longarm and the girl and said wearily, "I'm cashing in my chips. I'm whipped. You haven't seen my wife, have you?"

Longarm shook his head and said, "No. She must've gotten scared and run off. Your buckboard was out front when we rode in before. It ain't there now."

MacLeod said, "They must have kidnapped her. Baxter is paying us a lot for the claim. So if they ask for ransom, I'll have two million to pay them."

Longarm whistled and said, "You must want her back a lot."

"She's my *wife*, you idiot!"

Longarm nodded and said, "I doubt she's with the rascal who's been funning us. Kidnapping ain't his style."

Baxter snorted and observed, "Longarm, you don't know who it is or what his style might be! You keep looking smug and acting like you know so much, but he's been making a fool of you from the beginning. How do you know it's a *he*, in fact? I'd say it's more like a *they!*"

Longarm explained, "There can't be more than one or two people involved. I've been shot at and dynamited, and those other boys were poisoned, but that's not the way a gang works. I'd say it's a small operation. As to desperados holding a mine owner's wife for ransom, it's a mite late in the game for that, ain't it? If they intended to play that way, why didn't they just start out by kidnapping Lottie and making MacLeod hand over his gold, instead of playing all those foxy grandpa tricks?"

MacLeod said angrily, "Will the two of you shut up and let me sign these infernal deeds? Whatever's happened, my wife is missing and I have to find her!"

Longarm said, "You got a check from the refinery in Sacramento earlier today. Do you have it on you?"

MacLeod looked surprised. He got up from the table and rushed over to a green tin box on the kitchen counter. He opened it and swore.

Longarm said, "There you go. She's likely on her way to the Crocker bank in Sacramento to cash her own chips in. You're supposed to be dead at the bottom of the mine."

As MacLeod gaped at him in horror, Felicidad gasped, "*Querido*, what are you suggesting?"

Longarm finally lit the cheroot he'd been holding in his teeth, and said, "Ain't suggesting—saying. Lottie's a pretty little gal with her best years ahead of her. She's probably found living up here in this shack tedious as hell, but she knew sooner or later they'd sell out and she could be living higher on the hog, with someone else to do the laundry and rustle up the grub."

Baxter looked thunderstruck as he asked, "Do you mean Lottie MacLeod sent that car filled with dynamite down the shaft at us?"

"Hell, it wasn't filled. Romero said it was only a box. Tonight you told her you were willing to give them two million dollars for this claim, but MacLeod here was being stubborn about the sale. I reckon that riled her some."

MacLeod said, "I don't believe you! We've been married four years!"

Longarm's voice was sympathetic as he answered, "You believe me; you just don't want to *say* you do. I'm as sentimental as the next gent, but if I was a lady, I'd have to like someone an awful lot to go on washing socks for him with two million dollars hanging over me and him acting like he *enjoyed* the rustic life."

MacLeod stared at him in sick horror as Baxter asked, "Have you forgotten I was down there with the two of you? I could hardly sign a bank draft for any amount if I was dead, you know."

Longarm said, "I know. But some other jasper could have. You ain't buying the mine personally, Baxter; you're only working for an Eastern syndicate. Lottie never tried to wipe *those* rascals out—just her husband. The two of them have a joint account at the Crocker Trust, so she has enough to live on from the ore sale till they send your replacement out with the two million for her mine. She figures it's her mine now. Herc Romero wasn't supposed to find us alive."

Felicidad asked, "What are you waiting for, then, *querido*? Why are you not chasing the murderess?"

The deputy arched an eyebrow at her. "Forty miles in the dark, chasing a lady who's good at killing? It was her who killed Tico Vallejo and those other two, you know."

MacLeod sputtered, "You can't prove that!"

Longarm nodded and said, "It might be hard to prove in front of a jury, but she did it. It had to be her. You were in Sacramento. She mixed some of your assay chemicals in wine and gave it to them. Then, with them out of the way, she just rolled that car down at us. It missed Romero and me, but . . . "

Baxter said, "The poor woman must be mad! Are you suggesting that she was behind the highgrading of her own husband's mine?"

Longarm took a long drag on his cheroot, and exhaled a billowing cloud of blue smoke.

"Nope. She just helped out by killing folks who came too close to figuring out the game."

"Then you *are* saying she was in on it?" Baxter pressed.

"There had to be somebody watching this end of the operation. None of the Mexicans working here knew much about mining, but Vallejo was bright and learning, so he had to go."

MacLeod asked, "Have you forgotten they killed Lottie's dog that afternoon?"

The marshal regarded the glowing tip of his cigar as he said patiently, "She did that herself to draw suspicion away from her. She had no alibi to speak of, but who suspects a pretty little gal who's all cut up about her poor dog, Rex?"

MacLeod said incredulously, "I don't believe a word you're saying. If you thought for a minute that Lottie had done half the things you say, then Señorita Vallejo's right. You'd be after her this minute."

"Oh, I'll use Lovejoy's line to Sacramento in a few minutes to call the marshal down that way. They've been peeved at me for sticking my nose into their jurisdiction, anyway. I'll have them pick her up when the bank opens tomorrow morning. It'll make them feel good to be in on the capture."

MacLeod scribbled hastily on the last paper and stood up again, holding it out to Baxter, as he said, "All right. Give me the bank draft. I haven't got time to listen to this maniac! I have to find out where my wife is!"

To his credit, Baxter wasn't a complete fool. He looked quizzically at Longarm, who nodded and said, "Sure, give the man his money. That's what you came all the way out here to do."

Baxter bent over and endorsed the bank draft, muttering, "For a moment I expected you to accuse *him* of murder!"

Longarm smiled crookedly, and said, "Nope. He's got enough on his plate with one murderer in the family."

Baxter handed MacLeod the draft and the miner stuffed it in his shirt pocket, hardly looking at it, then stepped over to his gunbelt hanging from a peg on the wall, strapped the revolver on, and headed for the door.

Felicidad asked Longarm, "Aren't you going with him to help look for her?"

Longarm shook his head, walked over to the stove,

and picked up the coffeepot. He got three cups from the china cabinet, came back to the table, and poured coffee for Baxter, Felicidad, and himself, saying, "We might as well set a spell. I want to give him a good lead. He took a shot at me the other day, and he shoots tolerably well."

The other two gaped wide-eyed at him, ignoring the coffee as Longarm pulled up a chair and sat down. He said, "Come on, nobody's going to fuss at us for helping ourselves. Neither of them ever intend to come back here to this cabin."

Baxter sank down into a chair, obviously puzzled, and asked, "Just what in God's name is going on around here?"

Longarm took a sip of his coffee before answering, "He's likely going to kill her when he catches up with her. She wasn't supposed to double-cross him like that. In all modesty, I played a right neat trick on the two of them. They call it misdirection in the magic book I was reading over at the county seat."

Felicidad stared in horror at him as she asked, "You *want* him to kill his wife?"

Longarm said amiably, "Sure. I'd never in a million years get a jury to believe she was guilty. I'd have a hard row to hoe proving it was MacLeod who played all those games with the ore, too. This way I figure to get two birds with one stone. He's too blamed mad at her to think straight, and I'll sure as hell prove he shot his wife. I just have to give the rascal time, is all."

Baxter exploded, "The hell with his damned wife! You just said MacLeod was behind the highgrading, but damn it, it was *his* ore they were stealing!"

"Hell," Longarm said, "there never was any ore to steal. The Lost Chinaman was played out years ago.

MacLeod and Lottie bought it for a song, aiming to sell it to some pilgrim like yourself."

"That's impossible! Have you forgotten that I assayed the ore personally? You had me check it out the day you rode down the mountain on it with MacLeod."

"Yep, and when we got to the mill, it was worthless. That was even more impossible. I don't believe in spooks and my fool rump was holding the stuff down all the way to the mill. So somebody had to be a liar. I figured for a while it might be you, but there was just no way to make you fit. A man doesn't salt a mine to *buy* it. He salts a worthless mine to *sell* it."

He saw the stricken look on Baxter's face and said soothingly, "Don't feel so bad. They fooled Herc Romero too, and he's an experienced hard-rock miner. MacLeod was too slick just to blast gold birdshot into the rock. He dissolved maybe a hundred dollars' worth in aqua regia, then let it soak into the rock face and some sample lumps he left about for snoopy folks to pocket. Did you notice, when we were down in the mine before, that they weren't working that face at all? He had his greenhorn Mexican help digging pure quartz in the *other tunnel!*"

Baxter shook his head in confusion. "Never mind the mine itself. Damn it, we took random samples from two whole cars of what you claim was worthless rock. I tested them with my own aqua regia. You saw the gold that settled out."

"Sure I did. That was pretty slick on their part. You see, they switched bottles on you. There are a dozen ways they could have worked it, since all those little brown bottles look the same. Either one of them only needed a moment to open your kit while you weren't looking and . . . hell, you're a bright lad. Explain it yourself to the señorita here."

Baxter's mouth was hanging open as though he

were trying to catch flies, so Longarm told Felicidad, "Gold dissolves in aqua regia. It stays dissolved and invisible till you neutralize the acid with alkali. Then the gold settles out, no matter what else you may have put in the test tube. I read that in a book."

Baxter's face brightened as his confusion cleared. "Yes, by God, I can see how that would work! If my acid was contaminated with gold, it would assay almost anything as gold-bearing ore!"

Longarm said, "I know. I got a drop on my hat, and when it dried, I had a medium-high-grade Stetson. That was me who busted up your room, by the way. We call it misdirection, among us magicians. I found out about the gold in your acid when the bottle busted on me."

"Hah! I knew you were behind that mess! But you're missing something. They got through with two whole carloads of real ore, the last time!"

The deputy smiled slyly. "No, they never. That was misdirection, too. I asked the folks down at the mill to lie for me. They just *told* MacLeod he'd brought real ore this time. It must have surprised hell out of him. Did you notice that he was down there looking for a vein he hadn't known he really had?"

"But they *paid* him for the ore. Damn it, *I* just paid him, too! Oh, my God, if I just paid two million dollars for a salted mine . . ."

"Now don't go blubbering up on us, old son. The bank's agreed not to cash either check. I had a talk with the president of the bank and he thought it was a right good way to trap the two of them."

Felicidad said, "I still can't understand why she tried to murder her husband."

Longarm put down his cup, leaned back expansively, and said, "I figured I'd drive a wedge between them when I fooled MacLeod with the false assay at the mill. You can both see how hard it would be to prove any of this in court if they just stuck together. I was foolish to go down in the mine that way after seeing she was all riled that he was hesitating with their prize in sight. But I figured she'd argue with him some before she turned on him. Lottie was smarter than she let on. She must have figured I'd outfoxed them some way, and that he was playing into my hands. So, seeing she had us in a right convenient place, she just put a box of dynamite aboard a car, lit the fuse, and let her roll. She had no way of knowing we'd come out alive. She probably lit out before folks who might have heard the blast could ask pesky questions. She aims to hear the sad news in Sacramento, where she doubtless went to buy supplies or something. Her plan is to come back up, all sad-eyed, and sit tight until some other fool drops by with another bank draft."

Baxter said, "Ah, *that's* why you're sitting here so unconcerned! You expect her to return to the scene of the crime!"

"Not hardly. When she hears about the cave-in, she'll hear that the boys from Sheep Ranch dug us out, too. We'd best go out and take them down to the saloon, by the way. I'd say we owe those boys a drink."

Baxter looked at Longarm with new-found respect. "This time I'll pay. I'll even buy a drink for *you*, Longarm! But if you don't expect them back, shouldn't you be looking for them?"

Longarm looked at Felicidad and grinned, saying, "Later. I'm in no hurry to ride. At least not before sunrise."

Longarm made sweet love to Felicidad as the dawn light crept in on them through her bedroom window. But the woman was upset, knowing it was probably the last time they'd be together, even though Longarm lied and promised the way a gentleman was supposed to.

He was feeling a mite wistful, too. Felicidad was pretty as a picture, in or out of her dress, and he'd been right about one thing: she was better in bed than the librarian in San Andreas. Pru was wilder, but Felicidad was sweeter and warmer. He knew he was going to miss her, and that some night when he was all alone, he was going to think back to this moment and cuss himself for being such a tumbleweed.

Common sense told him a man was far better off with some sweet little gal waiting at home for him with his pipe and slippers, only Longarm didn't smoke a pipe and he owned no slippers. He was a hard-driving lawman with a job to do, and such pleasures as life handed out to him had to be enjoyed on the fly.

For the fifth or sixth time Felicidad pleaded, "Can't I come back to Denver with you, *querido?* There is nothing to keep me here. I promise not to get in your way."

He fingered her pert brown nipple absently and soothed, "We'll talk on it later. I have to ride down to Sacramento after the MacLeods in a few minutes, honey."

She sobbed, "You are never coming back this way. Your work here is finished!"

"I don't know," he equivocated. "My office might want me to clear up a few loose ends. It doesn't seem likely that anyone around here was in on that confidence game with them, but old Billy Vail might want me to make sure."

"Do you promise, then?"

He shook his head and said, "Don't ask for promises, honey. Many a gal has chased a man out of her corral by trying to brand him with promises just as he was starting to eat out of her hand. I said I'll be back if I can make it. Let's leave it at that."

He made love to her one last time, a bit annoyed that she didn't seem as pleasured this time, then he sat up and pulled on his clothes. As he stood in her doorway, she stood up, naked, and came over to kiss him goodbye. She was well worth remembering as she stood before him in the rosy light. He kissed her deeply and with meaning, then he turned away and walked off quickly, not looking back.

He saddled his gelding in the barn and rode out, cutting across the rolling fields of wild mustard in the mountain sunlight. The air was cool and the gelding was frisky, so he rode northwest at a lope, jumping rail fences and feeling sort of good.

He told himself, *You really are a shameless skunk with women.* But he was grinning like a kid stealing apples just the same.

He rode the forty-odd miles to Sacramento, taking most of the morning and leaving the horse lathered and not so sassy at the army remount station just outside of town.

The remount officer started to give him hell for treating government property that way with an Indian uprising brewing, so Longarm said, "You must not have gotten word from headquarters yet. There ain't any Indian uprising. Old Bitter Water is a friend of mine. We used to bust out of jail together all the time."

"What are you talking about? The boys up in Calaveras County report smoke talk from a hundred hills. Some livestock is missing, and—"

Longarm interrupted him. "Now don't get your balls in an uproar. There was only one fire. I was there. As for missing stock, there's always missing stock. Cows don't have a lick of sense."

The officer blinked and asked, "You were *with* the Miwok when they started sending those smoke signals?"

Longarm didn't know just what the army regulations had to say about white men sending Indian smoke signals, so he hedged a little and said, "I just told you Bitter Water is a friend of mine. He was signaling his band to gather for the acorn harvest or something. They're sort of like squirrels when it comes to gathering nuts for the winter. But like I said, it never meant anything."

"Damn it! They have half the county holed up with loaded rifles! They had no right to scare folks so!"

"I know," Longarm soothed him, adding, "I told them they should put on overalls and start looking for steady jobs. Bitter Water says he won't send up any more smoke signals. Meanwhile, if you'd see about shipping my saddle and possibles back to Denver, and tell me how I'm to get into town without a mount . . ."

"I think the mess officer has a buckboard going into Sacramento for supplies. If you leg it over to the gate in time, you'll be able to hitch a ride. I sure don't want to issue you another horse! You ride like a goddamned Sioux on the warpath!"

Longarm suppressed the desire to observe that this attitude might be the reason the army had so much trouble chasing Indians. He simply waved and started dogtrotting away from the corral, holding his holster in place with his left palm to keep it from slapping.

He reached the gate as the chuckwagon was pulling out. He yelled, ran after it, and jumped aboard.

They rode him in to the crowded streets of the city and he dropped off near the federal building, dodging a clanging streetcar as he crossed the street.

He went upstairs to a frosted glass door and introduced himself to a morose assistant marshal from the Sacramento district. He didn't know if this was the son

215

of a bitch who'd gotten him thrown in Lovejoy's jail by disputing his jurisdiction, but it was water under the bridge now. The older federal man had doubtless gotten the word that Longarm was being backed by Boss Buckley, so he was trying to be friendly.

He said, "We have a flier out on the MacLeods, and the Sacramento P.D. is cooperating. But so far, nobody's seen a trace of them."

Longarm brought his fellow employee up to date and the man sighed, "I don't know why you've been playing chess when the game is checkers, Longarm. I mean, you *had* Kevin MacLeod up there at the Lost Chinaman, but you simply sat there like a big-assed bird and let him get away!"

Longarm took out a cheroot, thumbed a matchhead, and lit up before he explained, "Lottie MacLeod took off after trapping us all in the mine. I figured if I arrested her husband on the spot, we might never see her again."

"Good riddance, I'd say. The husband is the one we want."

Longarm shook his head and said, "Nope. He's pretty slick, as we learned the hard way. But Lottie *kills* folks. She's a bitty little woman who looks helpless and harmless. A gal can change her dress and dye her hair to where a man who's bedded her might miss her in a crowd, too. I figure her husband has a better chance of catching up with her than anyone working on our side."

The older man fumbled with a pencil and growled, "Maybe. She ain't been to the bank to cash that check she stole."

Longarm said, "Hell, the news that we were rescued was in this morning's issue of the *Sacramento Bee*. She'd be a fool to try and cash it now. He'll know better than to try and spend the two million they paid him

216

after all the trouble the two of them went to. He must be mad as hell."

For the first time, the older lawman grinned sincerely as he nodded and said, "I'll allow that you really messed them up by getting the bank and the refinery to play along with you like that. But the two of them have a good twelve hours' start and there's no telling where in God's name either one of them has lit out for. We ran MacLeod through the wanted files; he has no paper on him at all."

Longarm nodded and said, "Meaning they were using a fictitious name. Everybody leaves a trail of paper behind as he passes through this wicked world."

"I know. But there's no army record. Nothing to point to a hometown back East that they might be running for."

"Hell, no slick owlhoot runs for home after the first time. MacLeod may be somebody else, but he's been on the dodge before. If we could find out who he was or where he came from, he knows we'd be looking for him there. After we find Lottie, I'll catch the steamer down to Frisco Bay. He'll figure on hopping a boat out, sure as hell."

"Are you crazy? There must be a dozen clippers putting out through the Golden Gate with every tide!"

Longarm nodded and said, "Yep. But like I said, the jasper is slick as well as ornery. He won't catch just any boat. He'll want one headed for some port that has no extradition treaty with Uncle Sam."

The other lawman looked sheepish as he admitted, "I, uh, have some fellows covering the Mexican and Canadian borders, Longarm."

Longarm shook his head and said, "Queen Victoria's Mounties are nosy as hell about strangers up their way. As for Mexico, they might wink at a cow thief or two. But murder is serious on either side of the border. Mac-

Leod would stand out down in the Baja like a sore thumb, and the rurales would nail him pronto."

The older man studied his pencil before he sighed and said, "You're likely right. I understand the Vallejo family is offering a reward for the murderers of their kinsman."

Longarm nodded, adding, "The Vallejos are sort of important folks, too. I know one who figures they'll be able to get back some of their old lands now, since the mine was a bust. But getting back to the wheresoevers —I don't figure MacLeod will try a run for it over the Sierra, since there ain't too many railroads for us to watch. So we're back to an escape by sea. We ought to be able to whittle the ships leaving for an owlhoot's likely ports of call down to a tolerable list."

"Shouldn't we get cracking, then? What's to stop MacLeod and his woman from being there right now, about to leave?"

Longarm said, "A couple of things. For one, a man traveling alone has a better chance. For another, she tried to kill him. She's a tolerable-looking gal with a nice figure, but he's likely feeling testy. She knows too much, too. If he was to get rid of her and make it out of the country . . ."

"I agree he has the motive to kill her twice over, damn it. But while we're sitting here jawing about it, the two of them are out there someplace and you still haven't told me where."

Longarm blew a smoke ring and explained, "Hell, if I knew where she was, I'd have arrested her already."

"Agreed, but what if MacLeod can't find her either?"

"We'll be in a hell of a fix, won't we?"

The Sacramento marshal drummed his pencil on the desk blotter and mused, "On the other hand, they've traveled and plotted together all this time. MacLeod should know his wife's habits—the sort of places she'd be apt to stay, the sort of stores she shops in. If she's in the habit of changing her appearance, he'd know that too, and what to look for."

Longarm said, "There you go. My plan ain't as dumb as it looks, once a person takes the time to study on it some."

As he rose to leave, the other lawman asked, "What if *she* nails *him?* We know she's tried once, and what you said about their knowing one another better than we do applies in her case as well, doesn't it?"

Longarm nodded. "Yeah. But I purely hope she doesn't get lucky. I know I can likely catch *him*. But I ain't ever been one for trailing after womenfolks."

The older man, who'd heard a lot about Longarm, grinned slyly and said, "Oh, I don't know. The way I hear tell, you sort of like to go after gals. You figure, after you catch her, she'll be in shape to stand trial?"

Longarm replied morosely, "I ain't ever loved a gal to death yet, and besides, Lottie is a mite more passionate than I care for. I'd be willing to let her *try* and screw me to death, but she doesn't fight fair and I've had all the chemistry lessons I need."

Longarm went to the bank, but his hopes failed to pan out. The bank manager gave him a cigar and explained his plans in case either of the missing MacLeods tried to cash their worthless checks. He sounded like he was enjoying the change from his usually somewhat dull routine. But while the armed guards out front in plain clothes were dramatic, it didn't seem likely that either of the MacLeods would turn up.

The banker mentioned that Herc Romero had been promoted by his boss, the enthusiastic tycoon George Hearst. The Hearst holdings had offered a substantial reward for the capture of the murderers, perhaps to butter up the local Mexicans.

Longarm said, "I got to wondering about the other mines shortly after I got to Calaveras County. Old Hearst is unpopular with the local folks, likely for being so rich. But I looked into it and saw that the Hearst holdings weren't robbed. That sort of struck me as strange, since robbing an unpopular absentee owner with a richer ore body looked a damned sight easier than whatever was going on."

The banker nodded and said, "Now that you've explained it, we should all be ashamed of ourselves for not seeing it right off. I mean, damn it, there wasn't any way to steal ore from a guarded moving train, was there?"

Longarm puffed on the banker's fine Havana tobacco, and said, "Don't fret about it. I thought they'd done it too, the first time it happened. I'll admit I wasted time thinking up all sorts of tricks, and I'll allow I had some thoughts on the late Joaquin Murietta's ghost. But it slowly sank into my thick skull that I didn't believe in spooks and that I'm likely as smart as any other old boy when it comes to stealing. In my line, you get to meet a mess of thieves, and in my time, I've probably heard of every way it can be done."

"In other words, if you simply couldn't see how they were stealing the ore, they simply couldn't be stealing it?"

"That's about the size of it. Modesty doesn't pay off worth mention."

"So now all you have to do is figure their next move?"

"Nope. I know MacLeod's next couple of moves. I just wish the son of a bitch would get cracking and figure it out himself!"

Chapter 10

At Sacramento police headquarters, Longarm introduced himself to the desk sergeant. He was led to a squad room where he sat down to converse with two plainclothesmen. The one who did all the talking was named Flynn. Longarm never caught the name of his small, skinny partner. The man was too busy chewing and spitting to have much to say.

Flynn explained that they'd searched high and low for both MacLeods or the remains of either. Then he added his considered opinion that they were not in Sacramento. He said, "If I were one of them, I'd be on a clipper headed for China about now."

Longarm said, "It's good to see that you agree with me about his wanting to get clear out of our jurisdiction. But he won't want to leave his woman behind for us to pick up. To us, he's just a nondescript cuss in worn pants and miner's boots, but she knows his real name and such. And it ain't like they're *friends* anymore."

"All right," Flynn said. "Let's try it this way. Say he's already found her, killed her, and lit out. There are a thousand places you could hide a body in these parts."

"Maybe," Longarm conceded, "but we know she had

a good lead on him. So if and when he caught up with her, it'd be daybreak, or too close to matter. They don't own property here in town. So he has no basement at his disposal to plant her in. Someone would have noticed, had he gunned her down on the streets. That means they have to be someplace private for whatever. And that means a *rented* someplace private."

Flynn nodded. "We have men out checking the shabbier parts of town. There are lots of nasty alleyways down near the tracks, and if he caught up with her in some whorehouse—"

"Back up," Longarm cut in. "Lottie MacLeod is too high-toned to hide out in the tenderloin. Not because she might not screw as well as poison, but because she'd stand out. I'd say she'd aim for a more respectable part of town—a medium-priced hotel or a respectable rooming house."

"I read your drift. She ain't such a needle in a haystack after all."

"Her husband would know that, too. There's no telling how much money they still have between them, but she likely has some left over from their last flimflam. She wouldn't rent a place by the month, but she might pay a week in advance. She'd avoid the kind of hotel frequented by whiskey drummers with an eye for an ankle on a woman alone, too. Most towns I know of have respectable boarding houses catering to women only. That's where I'd start looking for her."

Flynn made a notation on a slip of paper. He rang a bell on his table and a uniformed patrolman came in to take the note. As he read it, the policeman said, "That's funny, Sarge. A couple of the boys just answered a call at an all-female rooming house out on the north side."

Flynn asked, "What kind of a call?" The patrolman replied, "Dead woman. Found by her landlady just a few minutes ago. The woman came in to change the linens and—"

But Flynn was on his feet and moving, with Longarm and Flynn's silent partner right behind.

They ran out a side entrance and piled into a waiting police van. The uniformed driver clucked the team forward and they boiled out of the alley, with the van's bell clanging.

It only took them a few minutes to reach the scene. It was a mustard-yellow frame building with a mansard roof. The whole neighborhood had gathered out front, where a patrolman was comforting an hysterical fat lady on the postage stamp-sized lawn.

Flynn asked the cop where his partner was and was told, "Upstairs in the back, Sarge. This lady here says she's sure no men have been on the premises since she locked up last night."

The three of them edged past the fat lady as she protested loudly that she didn't run that sort of a rooming house.

They climbed the stairs as women peered out through slitted doors with worried looks.

He knew they were in the right place as soon as they got to the open doorway of Lottie MacLeod's rented room. A patrolman stood near the bed, taking notes and trying not to look as sick as he must have felt.

In life, Lottie had been pretty. Her death had been ugly. Uglier than Longarm had counted on, and he felt a tinge of guilt as he swallowed the bilious taste in his mouth. He stared down at the figure sprawled on the blood-soaked mattress, and said, "I'm purely sorry it had to end this way, ma'am, but you did have some ornery notions about killing folks."

Lottie MacLeod lay stark naked in a thickening, glutinous mass of blood and her own innards. She stared at the ceiling, smiling widely up at the gray, cracked plaster as if it had said something amusing. Her throat had been slit from ear to ear. Then her killer had run the knife down from her neck to her pubic bone, slicing her open like an overripe watermelon. Her still-shapely thighs were spread wide, as if her smile were meant as an invitation to a lusty lover. But while she lay spread-eagled and naked, there was little in the way of obscene exposure. Her blood-smeared breasts were visible, but her torn-out guts covered her private parts like some gory apron of tangled wet coils.

Flynn's partner went to the window, opened it, and spit a stream of tobacco juice out into the sunlight. Flynn said, "They don't grin like that until they've been dead about three hours, right?"

Longarm nodded and said, "Found an old boy the Apache had left on an ant pile once. *He* was grinning like he enjoyed it, too."

Longarm spotted a slip of paper on the rug and bent to pick it up as the detective said, "Of course, we can't prove it was MacLeod without witnesses."

Longarm held out the paper and said, "This was part of the rubber check I had the refinery pay him for his worthless gold. They likely had words, with her taunting him some, before he went sort of crazy."

Flynn frowned and said, "I thought *she* had a worthless check."

"She did. You ain't listening. If both checks were here in this room when she died so messy, this scrap of paper puts him in here with her. Let's see what else we can find."

As Longarm found a woman's carpetbag and began to go through it, Flynn said, "You're right. I wasn't thinking. But what's this you say about her taunting him? How do you know he didn't just bust in and go for her with that knife?"

Longarm pointed with his chin at a nightgown

draped over a chair in one corner of the room. He said, "Not many gals sleep naked when they're alone. The landlady said she didn't hear anything, and the door wasn't forced. She let him in."

Flynn gulped. "Jesus! Knowing he was going to kill her?"

"Not hardly. I'd say that part came as a surprise. Most women feel they have certain powers over a man, spread out naked. If they didn't meet outside, he likely came here and signaled. They were good at signals other folks weren't supposed to know about. I'll let him fill in the blank spaces after I catch him."

Flynn stared down at the grotesquely mutilated body and said, "Yeah. She must have thought he wanted to screw her, and for all we know, she let him. But what was that about her taunting him?"

Longarm took a glass vial from Lottie's bag, sniffed it, and said, "Cyanide. Gals are funny that way. You'd think they'd learn that the last thing a man wants to hear right after some good loving is how dumb he is. But it does seem that they always pick just that time to let us have it."

Flynn smiled wryly and said, "Say no more. I'm a married man myself. I can see how it must have happened. They got back together and started to make up. But she was still sore at him and—"

"She was buying time, hoping for a chance to poison him. Only she said the wrong thing, or maybe he was just smarter than she'd counted on. Anyhow, she's out of the way, so we don't have to worry about some fool jury letting her off just for being so pretty and helpless."

"And now?"

"Now I'd best get cracking after MacLeod. I was worried some about presenting my case to a judge and jury, seeing how complicated it was and how little I could really prove."

He stared thoughtfully down at the mangled cadaver before he suggested, "It might be a good idea to get a photographer up here to take some pictures. He may try to brazen through his story about his highgrading confidence scheme, but no lawyer born of mortal woman is going to get him off for doing this!"

Flynn observed, "You sound pretty confident, considering the lead he has on you, Longarm."

Longarm put a cheroot in his mouth, chewed it, and said, "Hell, he can't have gone that far, poor bastard."

A foghorn moaned through the morning fog of San Francisco as Longarm lounged between two stacks of redwood lumber. The tall three-master moored to the end of the quay had finished loading and would be leaving with the next tide, bound for Australia. The gangplank was still down and he could hear the sounds of crewmen as they went about their chores on the ship's deck. He couldn't see them at this distance in the fog.

Longarm stiffened, gun in hand, as he heard the grating of shoe leather on wet cobblestones. He peered out between the stacks of lumber and saw a seaman moving toward the gangplank with a duffle bag on his shoulder. The man didn't look his way. It was just as well. Longarm didn't want to have to explain why he was skulking about with a .44 in his fist at this hour.

He took out his watch and consulted it by the dim gray light. The clipper would be leaving soon. He was probably wrong. He'd been wrong about the last two ships he'd come down to see off. Could the idiot be dumb enough to make a run back East with only three railroads to choose from and U.S. deputies watching every one?

The trouble with being a tricky knave was that it narrowed a man's options. Longarm wouldn't have known where to start looking for a wilder sort who simply cut and run. But MacLeod was shifty as hell and seven times smarter than he ought to be, so he could be counted on to do the smartest thing. He'd undoubtedly fooled a lot of people in his day. By now he might have figured out how he'd been flustered. He was probably pretty angry about it, too.

The sound of footsteps was coming down the quay again. Longarm glanced out, saw another dim figure toting a sailor's duffle, and began to back off. Then he noticed that the man was wearing miner's boots.

Longarm cocked his .44 and stepped out, calling, "Just freeze right where you are, MacLeod. I won't say it twice!"

The figure stopped and slowly turned. Then he suddenly dropped the bulky bag and fell behind it on the cobbles! A flash of orange winked at Longarm, and the lawman fired. A piece of redwood slapped the side of Longarm's cheek and his own bullet exploded socks and underwear out of the ripped-open duffle. Longarm dropped and crabbed sideways as MacLeod put another round where his head had just been. He knew he was invisible in his space between the lumber, so he fired once for effect, then turned and ran back. He grunted himself through a slit at the rear of the piled lumber, moved down two stacks, then holstered the gun and climbed to the top.

He crawled across the damp boards to the forward edge, drew his gun again, and peered over. From his new vantage point, he had a bird's-eye view of MacLeod behind his improvised cover.

He called out, "Give it up, old son. I've got you cold."

MacLeod rolled wildly and fired up at him. The bullet hit the wood just under Longarm's gun hand, driving a big splinter into the heel of his palm and knocking the Colt from his grasp!

"Aw, shit," he muttered, as the gun clattered to the paving below. Then MacLeod was up and running as Longarm rolled off his gut and fumbled the derringer from his vest pocket. He aimed the little brass pistol in his blood-slicked hand and got off a shot as MacLeod was running up the gangplank. Naturally, the shot missed at that range.

Longarm got down off the lumber and picked up his Colt with his left hand as he put the derringer away and sucked at his injured right hand. He took out a kerchief, bound it around his injury, and shifted the .44 back to his right hand as he walked slowly toward the gangplank.

A crewman up in the rigging called down, "What's going on down there?"

Longarm called back, "I'm a deputy U.S. marshal chasing a murderer. Did you see where he went?"

"Everyone on deck's took cover, Marshal. I don't see *nobody* down there."

There was the sound of a shot and the crew member yelped, swinging himself behind the thick pine mast as he yelled, "He just took a shot at me from the poop deck! He's down behind the skylight, for'd the wheelhouse!"

Longarm ran to the gangplank and moved up it, ducking his head as he reached the well deck. He dropped behind a pair of lifeboats on a hatch cover before risking a cautious peek aft.

There was nothing much to see. The railing of the higher poop deck was silhouetted against the skyline of San Francisco. MacLeod was too slick to have his head in view there.

There was a ladder leading up on either side, near

the rails. Longarm figured MacLeod would have them both covered. So he decided not even to consider getting there that way.

He called out, "Damn it, MacLeod, you're just making things complicated for no good reason! This ship ain't about to carry you to Australia or anywhere else!"

A voice called back, "I'll stand pat, you son of a bitch! How'd you know where to find me?"

"I figured you'd want to get someplace out of my jurisdiction. You're too smart to book passage on just any ship. So I had a talk with the harbormaster. This clipper stops at Valparaiso on its way to down under, and we don't have an extradition treaty with Chile, so— Hey, why don't you pack it in, and I'll explain it all as I take you to the federal building."

"You'll never take me alive, you bastard! What did you do to turn Lottie against me?"

"You did that yourself by being too greedy. Did you really think you'd somehow bought a real gold mine?"

"I've figured out how you tricked me with that false assay, God damn your eyes. You want me, come and take me!"

Longarm noticed that a member of the crew was staring out at him through a doorway leading to the quarters under the poop deck. He motioned the man back, even though MacLeod couldn't see him from up on top.

He knew MacLeod had no line of sight on his position either, so he broke cover and ran to the doorway, shoving the crewman inside.

He found that they were in a low-beamed corridor, running toward the stern. He whispered to the crewman, "Show me where the helm is, quick!"

The sailor led him back, muttering, "No way you can get at him without getting your head blown off, friend. There's a couple of hatches leading topside, but he's got everything for'd the wheelhouse under his gun!"

They moved back to a wardroom and Longarm saw the skylight overhead. He moved along the shadows of the port bulkhead as he kept his muzzle trained on the glass. There was nothing staring back at him but gray sky and, way up, a gliding seagull.

The wardroom ended, aft, in two more doorways on either side of what looked like a big wooden chimney. He pointed at it with his chin and asked, "Is that where the chains from your wheel run down to the rudder?"

The crewman nodded, but said, "You can't get inside. Wouldn't do no good if you could. The wheelhouse sits smack-dab on top."

Longarm thumbed the spent shells from his .44 and reached into his coat pocket for spare ammunition. The crewman whispered, "You're bleeding."

Longarm muttered, "I know I'm bleeding. Keep your voice down and get back out of my way."

He reloaded his revolver as, overhead, MacLeod called out, "God damn you, Longarm! Come out and fight like a man!"

Longarm raised the muzzle of his .44 above the level of his own head, aiming at the ceiling.

He waited until MacLeod called out again and he heard an overhead board creak. Then Longarm fired four times in rapid succession.

The sound was deafening in the low-ceilinged wardroom, but he could hear MacLeod yelp like a coyote being run over by a train, so he fired once more, directly up at the sound.

Up on deck, propelled by flying splinters and a .44 slug directly up his rectum, Kevin MacLeod took off for the sky!

He didn't get there. His froglike leap shot him out over the skylight, screaming in agony. Then he belly-flopped down on the panes of glass and just kept

230

coming as Longarm and the startled sailor moved back out of the way.

MacLeod landed face down on the wardroom floor in a windfall of shattered glass. He rolled on his side in agony and drew his knees to his chest, his gun hand pinned to the blood-spattered flooring as he glared with hate-filled eyes at the tall figure looming above him in the blue haze of gunsmoke filling the room.

Longarm muttered, "Aw, shit," and stepped forward to kick the gun out of MacLeod's hand. It banged against the far bulkhead, out of reach, so Longarm knelt beside the gutshot killer and said, "I'll bet that smarts. I'll send for a doc, old son."

MacLeod coughed blood, licked his lips, and said, "You've killed me, you son of a bitch! I might have known you'd pull another of your dumb tricks!"

Longarm said, "For a man with a bullet up his ass you sure have a poor opinion of everyone else. I'd say you were right about one thing, though. You're dying, sure as hell."

He started reloading his .44 as he added, "Before you go, would you mind confessing a few things in front of me and this witness?"

"You can go to hell."

"Thanks just the same, but I had Denver in mind. With you and Lottie both dead, a few loose ends hardly matter, seeing as how neither of you has to stand trial."

Other crewman were coming out of the woodwork to admire Longarm's handiwork. A man with the four stripes of a captain on his sleeve asked, "What's this all about, Marshal?"

Longarm said, "I ain't a marshal, just a deputy. And my tale is too long to be told before I have to catch the ferry back to Oakland and hop the C.P. back to Denver. Let's just say this poor cuss here was too smart for his own good."

He looked down at the dying man as he said, "You and Lottie should have ridden out your pat hand, MacLeod. You know I never could have proven my notions in any court of law, don't you?"

"The bitch tried to kill me. So I paid her back good. *That* was your doing too, wasn't it?"

"Yep. It's called 'divide and conquer.' "

He looked up at the captain and asked, "Do you mind sending one of your men for a doctor and the local P.D.?"

The captain said, "I already did, as soon as it was safe to move. They'll be here any minute."

Longarm nodded and told MacLeod, "There you go, old son. Just rest easy and we'll see how bad you're hurt."

MacLeod didn't answer. He couldn't. Longarm felt the side of his neck as a crewman said, "Jesus, I think he's dead!"

Longarm said, "You're right. He did say something about me killing him. First time the bastard's told me the truth since I met up with him."

The San Francisco police asked a lot of tedious questions, considering how simple it all was. But in the end they said it was all right for a federal marshal to shoot wanted killers on the waterfront, so Longarm went down Market Street and caught the ferry across the bay to Oakland.

He thought he'd probably missed the train to Cheyenne, and he'd already seen what there was of Oakland. So he hurried to the depot, hoping he was wrong.

As he stepped through the glass doors, he thanked his lucky stars for blessing him with good eyesight.

Felicidad Vallejo was standing by the ticket counter, as if she were expecting to meet someone.

A few feet farther on, standing with her arms crossed

and tapping her pretty little foot on the cement, he noticed Pru Sawyer.

Neither woman knew the other, and Longarm surmised that it might be a good idea to keep it that way. So he crawfished backward out the door before either girl could spot him. He didn't consider himself a coward, but there is such a thing as pure common sense, and he'd rather have faced an armed band of Apache than get into a hair-pulling contest between two jealous females!

He circled the big brick depot and found a board fence separating the yards from the carriage road. He put his hands up and hauled himself over the top.

He landed inside on the gritty cinders and started legging it across the yards. The dusty maroon sides of the eastbound express were just starting to pull away from the platform, so Longarm started running.

A yard bull saw him and yelled out, "Hey, you ain't supposed to be in here, cowboy!"

But Longarm paid the bull no heed as he chased the train. He ran down the tracks after it, slowly gaining on the rear platform as the train moved out through the yards. A girl in a big hat and a pinch-waisted dress was staring at him from the platform as he slowly caught up with her and the express.

Longarm reached forward, grabbed the brass railing, and was almost dragged before he could get an instep on the rear coupler and haul himself aboard, saying, "Howdy, ma'am."

The girl said, "Well, hello! Do you always board trains that way?"

He climbed over the rail, grinning sheepishly, and answered, "Only when they try to leave without me, ma'am. My name is Custis Long and I work for Uncle Sam."

She laughed a pretty skylark laugh and said, "I'm

Melony Evans and I don't. Are you going all the way? To Cheyenne, I mean."

He said, "Cheyenne and then some. I've got to get back to Denver before payday."

"How interesting. I'm on my way to Denver myself. We live on Sherman Avenue."

"We, ma'am? You don't seem to be wearing a ring."

"I'm not married. I live with my aunt and uncle in Denver."

"Oh," he said. "Well, I'd best go in and see if the conductor has a compartment he'll rent me. I purely hate trying to sleep sitting up in a day coach, and I figure at least two nights aboard this fool train."

As he eased past her, Melony said, "Perhaps we'll meet later, in the club car. You can let me know if they have a sleeping compartment for you."

He started to ask if she had one, but considered it a mite early to be so forward, so he just grinned and said, "I'll do that, ma'am. I'm sure I'll find someplace or other to spend the next couple of nights."

SPECIAL PREVIEW

Here are the opening scenes
from

LONGARM AND THE NESTERS

eighth novel in the bold new
LONGARM series from Jove/HBJ

Chapter 1

Longarm didn't wait to see where the shot had come from. He knew the sound of a rifle from its whiplash crack, and his reflexes sent him rolling out of his saddle before whoever had fired it could pump a second cartridge into the chamber. The yellow dust raised by the slug that had plowed into the ground between his horse's hooves was still settling when Longarm landed on his feet and crouched behind the animal. He stood near the roan's hindquarters, where its rear legs and haunches would give him the greatest protection, and bent forward to keep his head from becoming a target while he waited for a second shot to follow the first.

Enough seconds ticked by to give Longarm time to think about trying to grab for his own rifle, but the .44-40 Winchester was resting snugly in its boot on the wrong side of the horse. There was no way he could reach it without exposing his head, arm, and shoulder.

Seconds dragged into minutes, but the shot he was waiting for still didn't come. Longarm credited the bushwhacker with enough intelligence not to waste ammunition on an invisible target. He wondered how long it would take the shooter to think of the obvious next step. He got ready to drop to the ground in case the bushwhacker brought down his horse in an effort to strip him of his protective cover.

Instead of another shot, though, a man's voice, not too far distant, shouted, "A varning it vas I give you, *nesakonnley!* I see you turn off from the train track and ride this way. Now, I tell you to go back! You put your hands on my fence, then it don't be the ground I shoot at next time! I kill you dead!"

Frowning, Longarm tried to riddle out the strange accent that colored the man's speech. Billy Vail had explained that there would be a lot of foreigners involved in the assignment that had brought Longarm to southern Kansas, but the chief marshal had been somewhat vague as to the country of their origin. The accent was one Longarm hadn't encountered before, even though he'd run into representatives of most of the European nationalities that were part of the population of the West of the 1880's. It seemed to him sometimes that the whole damned world was moving into the wide-open, unsettled prairies and mountains on the sunset side of the Mississippi. There wasn't much time for him to think about that at the moment, though. From the sound of the bushwhacker's voice, the unknown man was edging up on him a little bit at a time.

He called to the still-unseen rifleman, "You've got me mixed up with somebody else, mister! My name ain't Connolly. I'm Custis Long, a deputy U.S. marshal, and I ain't a damned bit interested in your fence, except maybe to look at it!"

"You say to me you don't ride for Clem Hawkins?"

"I never heard that name either, any more'n I know this fellow Connolly."

"Is not somebody, *nesakonnley*," the stranger called back. "Is how you call a bad name. Bastard." There was a brief silence, then the unknown assailant went on, "Maybe I make mistake, mister. I don't shoot no more yet, but you prove to me you are what you say."

"I ain't taking your word you won't drop me if I show myself!" Longarm protested. "Anybody'd who'd drygulch a stranger ain't much in my book for telling the truth!"

"I do not make lies. I will not shoot!" the man insisted.

"Tell you what," Longarm called. "You stand out in the open, where I can see you plain, and put your rifle on the ground. I'll hold up my badge and you can take a look at it. Does that sound fair enough?"

"*Da.* So I vill do."

Peering under the belly of his horse, Longarm got his first look at the stranger. The man stood with his empty hands outstretched, though the green thigh-high wheat sprouting up around him made it impossible to see whether he'd really laid his gun on the ground, or whether he'd only leaned it against his leg where he could grab it quickly. That wasn't important to Custis Long. He knew he could get off two slugs from his own .44 Colt Model T before the bushwhacker could pick up a rifle and shoulder it. Just the same, he studied the other man for a long moment before offering himself as a target again.

Except for his headgear, the stranger might have been any farmer or cowhand. He wore a denim jacket over a butternut shirt, and his jaws were heavily bearded, although his upper lip was shaved clean. His nose descended straight from thick, black brows and flared into a bulbous tip. His eyes were dark, his cheekbones high. Longarm found his headgear strange. Instead of the usual wide-brimmed, high-crowned felt hat that almost every outdoorsman in the West favored in both winter and summer, the stranger was wearing a floppy, round cloth cap with a short, shiny bill.

Satisfied that there was no chance he'd be beaten to the first shot if further gunplay ensued, Longarm stepped from the shelter of the roan's rump and walked slowly toward the fence that ran between the two of them. The other started equally slowly to meet him. Longarm casually pulled aside the flap of his long Prince Albert coat. The stranger spread his outstretched hands wider apart when he saw the Colt that Longarm wore butt-forward, high on his left hip, but Longarm was careful to keep his hands well away from the gun. He moved deliberately, taking the wallet from his inside breast pocket, and let the coat lapels drape forward over the pistol as soon as he had the wallet out.

Flipping open the wallet, he held it up so the man could see the deputy U.S. marshal's badge pinned inside. He said, "Now then. Unless you've got some reason why you'd be bashful about meeting up with the law, that ought to satisfy you."

"You said it is Long, your name?" the stranger frowned.

"That's right."

"How am I knowing this? If it is not yours, the badge—"

Exasperated, Longarm interrupted, "You're the damnedest, most suspicious fellow I've met up with for a while. You act like you're an owlhoot on the prod—which you could be, for all I know. Well, if you are, I'll find out about it, and if you ain't, then you'll just have to take my word that me and the badge belong together."

Unexpectedly the man smiled, showing twin rows of gleaming white teeth. "Now I believe you. If it vas you are not who you say, you vould this minute be trying to proof to me still more. *Dobro.* Me, I am Nicolai Belivev."

"Glad to make your acquaintance." Longarm looked past Belivev for a house of some kind, but saw none. "You live around here close?"

"There." Belivev pointed to what looked like a hump in the ground on the far side of the wheatfield.

"A soddy?"

Nodding, Belivev replied, "Is vhat they are call here. Next year, *pri Bog shini*, I build a real house on top of ground, then ve don't live no more like rabbit in hole."

"You been here long?"

"Four years." The man's voice was proud. "Next year, I come to be citizen of USA."

"Mind telling me where you come from, Mr. Belivev? You throw out a lot of words I never heard before."

"From Russia ve come," Belivev answered. Then, bitterly and with hatred in his tone, he continued, "Mother Russia! A mother like nobody needs!"

"You said 'we.' " Longarm frowned. "You mean there're a lot of settlers around here from Russia?"

"*Da*. Ve are many." Belivev turned and waved his arm. Beyond the hump of the soddy, Longarm saw the mounds of other sod houses, as well as a few dwellings built from wood.

"How'd it happen that all of you picked Kansas?"

"It vas from your railroad line, you see? They send men over to tell us they sell land for a few kopecks that ve pay each year until the land, it belong to us."

"From what you said a minute ago, I got the idea you weren't too sorry to leave Russia," Longarm observed.

"*Da*. Is true. Is not Mother Russia any more, like vhen our grandfathers go there from Germany long ago." Belivev hesitated before adding, "Is not here like vat the men from your railroad tell us it is being, maybe. Mr. Long, you are—" He hesitated, searching for a word. "Law-bringer for U.S. government, is true?"

Longarm nodded. "I'm an officer who upholds the federal laws, if that's what you're asking me."

"*Da,* is vhat. You tell me, then— Is lawful a man puts up a fence to guard his vheat vhile it grows, and other men cut it down so they can run it over with the feet from their cattle and horses?"

"That ain't exactly covered by federal law," Longarm said. He fished a cheroot out of his vest pocket, flicked a matchhead with his thumbnail, and puffed the cigar into life. Then he went on, speaking slowly and thoughtfully. "Fence-cutting's mostly covered by state laws, Mr. Belivev. Of course, here in Kansas they've got a law that makes trespassing on another man's land illegal, but you've sure got a right to put up a fence to keep people from damaging your crops."

"Then vhy the men who raise cattle cut our fences down? And vhy the sheriff don't make them stop vhen ve ask him to?"

"There might be a lot of reasons." Longarm saw no reason to tell Belivev that one of those reasons was probably responsible for his having been sent to Kansas in the first place.

"Tell me them," Belivev asked. Then, before Longarm could reply, he shook his head. "No. A better thing it vould be if you tell them to Mordka Danilov. He can more clear than me explain to the others vhy. Marshal Long, you vill go vith me to see Mordka, *da?*"

"Well—" Longarm looked at the sun, beating down from the unclouded sky as it started its final slide to the west. The heat made a liar of the calendar, which said it was now autumn. He asked Belivev, "Just who is this Mordka fellow?"

"Mordka Danilov is the elder of the *Bratiya,*" the Russian said. He explained, "In your language, *Bratiya,*

242

it means Brethren. This is religion I speak about, our religion that causes us such trouble in Russia that ve move now to your country."

"Uh-huh. Sort of your pastor, you might say?"

"Mordka guides us, he advises us. He does not preach at us."

"Oh. I see," Longarm said, though he wondered at the distinction. He thought for a moment, then nodded. "All right. If you think it'll help, I'll talk to him. Where's his house?"

"If you vill come vith me, I take you there," Belivev offered. "Is not far avay."

Longarm indicated the fence with its stretched wire strands studded by barbs. "How am I going to get my horse on the other side?"

Belivev pointed to the hump that marked the sod house in which he lived. "The path to Mordka's house goes that vay. If you ride around my fence, and I go across through the vheat, then ve get to my house at same time. From it, there is just little vay to Mordka's."

Longarm nodded. Nicolai Belivev turned away, stooped to pick up the rifle he'd laid on the ground, and started trudging through the wheatfield without looking back. Longarm watched the Russian for a moment, then mounted and nudged the roan with his toe. Turning the animal, he rode parallel to the fence until it ended in a corner, then rode along it on a rough path toward the soddy. Before he got to the hump, Belivev came out without the rifle, and was waiting when he rode up. Longarm reined in.

"Which way now?" he asked.

Belivev said, "Ahead. Is not far. I valk by your horse and show you the vay."

With Longarm on horseback and Belivev on foot, conversation between them was impossible as the

Russian led the way along the fenceline to a rambling crazy quilt of a house, a quarter of a mile distant. When his guide stopped and pointed to the house, Longarm dismounted.

"Come," Belivev said. "You can please explain to Mordka about the fences. Is better he tells us in our own language vhat he hears from you. Some of the *Bratiya* don't know so much *yashlkne Ameriska* as like I do."

A tall, raw-boned woman, her head bound up in a scarf, opened the door to Belivev's knock. She kept her pale blue eyes fixed on Longarm while she and Belivev exchanged a few words in their own tongue. Longarm heard the name "Mordka" repeated several times, but that was all he understood. After their parley ended, the woman stood aside and motioned for them to enter. Belivev almost pushed Longarm into the house.

After the bright sunlight, the interior seemed dim, almost to the point of utter darkness. Like so many homesteaders' dwellings, the house had few windows, and all of them were small because of the scarcity and high cost of glass. When Longarm's eyes had adjusted to the lack of light, what he saw was an almost exact duplicate of the homes he'd seen elsewhere in places where settlements were just springing up.

There were a table and three or four straight-backed chairs. A woodburning range stood in one corner of the room. On the walls, shelves held bags, cans, and wooden boxes. Cooking utensils were hung on nails behind the stove. A low bench held a bucket and a washbasin; a towel drooped from a nail over it. At the table, a man sat with a book open in front of him. For a moment the man did not raise his head, and Longarm followed the example of Belivev and the woman, who stood quietly, waiting.

When the man closed his book and looked up, Longarm found himself the object of the scrutiny of a pair of the most piercing blue eyes he'd ever seen. They seemed to shine under bristling, snowy brows that matched the long, square-cut beard rippling down over the seated man's chest. Though the beard was full, Longarm noticed that the man's upper lip was clean-shaven, revealing full, red lips outlined by deep creases that slanted down from a hawklike nose.

"Nicolai," the man said. His voice was deep and resonant.

"*Kum Mordka*," Belivev replied. "*Ero gostya imya Long.*"

"Mr. Long." Mordka Danilov nodded without rising or offering to shake hands. "*Pazhalasta.* I make you welcome to my house." He said to the woman, "*Marya. Sedalische. Sbteen.*"

Quickly she brought chairs for Longarm and Belivev, placing them at the table, with Longarm facing Danilov and Belivev between them. The woman stepped to the stove and busied herself with the steaming kettle and thick, tall glasses. She carried the glasses to the table, set one in front of her husband, then served Longarm and Belivev.

Mordka raised his glass. "To your good arrival, Mr. Long."

Longarm picked up his glass and, following the example of the other men, sipped the hot liquid. He recognized the flavor of honey, diluted by the hot water, and decided that a good tot of Maryland rye would have improved the brew.

Setting his glass back on the table, Nicolai Belivev told their host, "*Sodar Long ero priditi ohpravleny.*"

"*Na zemstud?*" the older man asked.

"*Nyet,*" Belivev replied. "*Centrovley.*"

Mordka Danilov frowned thoughtfully, looking at

Longarm. He asked, "You come, as Nicolai says, from the central government, Mr. Long? From Washington?" His English was much better than Belivev's.

"Not Washington. Denver. That's in Colorado. But I'm a federal officer, so I guess you could say I'm from Washington, in a manner of speaking. I'm a deputy U.S. marshal, Mr. Danilov."

"Ah," Mordka nodded. "You do not belong then to the ranchers, as the sheriff does?"

"I don't *belong* to anybody but myself," Longarm said emphatically. "I've got a job that I do, seeing that the law's upheld. That's all I'm interested in. It doesn't matter who breaks the law, I arrest him, whether it's you or the sheriff or the richest rancher in the county."

"Why have you come here?" Danilov asked. "Who among us is breaking the law? Surely not the *Bratiya?*"

"As far as I know right now, nobody's broken any laws I'm obliged to enforce. My chief sent me down here to make sure there's not any crookedness in the election that's coming along."

Mordka smiled somewhat bitterly. "I see. You do not interest yourself in trespassers who cut fences and destroy crops, then?"

"Not usually," the deputy answered. "That's the sheriff's job."

"If he refuses to do his job, then can we turn to you for help?"

Longarm wasn't sure exactly how he wanted to answer a question of that kind. He took his time in replying, and chose his words carefully. "The law's a pretty broad thing, Mr. Danilov. Federal officers are only supposed to handle cases where there's been a federal law broken. There are times when we've got to step in, like when a local officer breaks a law or doesn't do his job right. But it's not real easy to set up rules in cases like that."

Danilov nodded thoughtfully. "You have not been here long, have you?"

"I just got in last night. Right now, all I'm doing is sort of looking around."

"Nicolai has told you of the troubles we of the *Bratiya* are having?"

"About all he's told me so far is that you're having a bad time." Longarm decided it was time for him to take control of the questioning. "You and Mr. Belivev keep talking about this thing you call the *Bratiya*. Do you mind telling me exactly what it is?"

"We have no secrets, if that's what your question means," Danilov replied. "In your language, Mr. Long, *Bratiya* means Brethren. It is our religion. It is each man's personal freedom to choose his religion in this country, is it not?"

"It sure is," Longarm agreed. "Though I can't say I've picked one out yet for myself."

"You will, someday," Danilov said with a smile. "But if you are not a pious man, I can understand why you would be puzzled by our religion. Tell me, do you know of the Anabaptists? Have you ever heard of the Mennonites? The Amish, I think they are called in America."

"There were some Amish folks up north of where I grew up, I recall. I don't guess I've heard about the others."

"They're much the same, Mr. Long. I'll try not to make my explanation too long and tiresome. The Mennonite beliefs were established three hundred years ago, Mr. Long, by a priest named Menno Simons, who found the rituals of the Roman church too elaborate, too worldly. He began to preach only what is in the Bible itself—simple worship of God and Christ without altars or incense or fancy robes. Menno Simons made many converts, who called themselves Mennonites. They renounced worldly trappings not mentioned in the Bible, and vowed to live in peace with all men. They put aside weapons and all acts of violence."

Longarm broke in, "Wait a minute. That doesn't square up with Mr. Belivev taking a shot at me, telling me he'd shoot me if I put a hand on his fence."

"Be patient, please," Danilov said. "I will try to make that clear later. Menno Simons began his preaching in the sixteenth century, by your calendar. Even before he died, though, in many of the countries where he had made converts, the Roman and Protestant churches as well as the secular governments had begun to persecute those who had adopted Menno's beliefs. His followers refused to serve in armies, or to take oaths in courts of law. The ancestors of our own people, those of us who now live here, were promised freedom to follow their own beliefs by the tsarina of Russia, who came to be known as Catherine the Great. They migrated to Russia, most of them from Germany." Mordka paused to sip his cooling honey mixture.

Longarm took the opportunity to insert a question. "That must have been a long time back. Dates ain't my strong suit, or history, either, but wasn't she the Russian queen a hundred years ago?"

Danilov nodded. "Yes, a hundred years. For eighty of them, our families lived peacefully in Russia. Then a new tsar came to the throne, and he decided that Russia must become one land, one people, with one language and one religion. Our fathers learned Russian, and taught us to speak it, but they would not give up our religion for the official Russian church, and they would not serve in the tsar's army. So the persecution began once more. For a while our families bowed under, but when the tsar sent his Cossacks to imprison and kill those who would not worship as he ordered, or join his church, some of us reluctantly decided that we must fight back. It made us very sorrowful, but we learned to shoot and to do the other deeds a man must to protect his family. Of course we could not do this and still follow all of Menno's teachings, so we kept what we could of our old beliefs and called ourselves the *Bratiya*."

Mordka Danilov paused and looked piercingly at Longarm with his flashing blue eyes. "You understand, Mr. Long, it was not easy for us to do this, and our hearts were heavy. So, when the agents from your railroads came to find people who wanted to come to America and buy the land they were selling so cheaply, we saw that we could be free in America to follow our religion as we wanted to. That is why we emigrated; that is why we are now here in your state of Kansas. But even here we are finding that we must still fight to protect ourselves. Does this help you understand why we ask you where we can find help?"

His face sober, Longarm nodded slowly. "I guess it does, Mr. Danilov. Only from what I've gathered, your troubles here don't come from what you believe in, but from putting your land into wheat, and fencing it off."

"Only partly, I think," Mordka said. "Perhaps if we had chosen to raise cattle, there would be no trouble. But we are farmers. We must work now and raise crops to pay for our land, and even to earn money for our food and clothing."

"Oh, I understand that part," Longarm told him. "The thing is, I don't see much I can do to help you, except to have a talk with the sheriff. Maybe I can get him to keep things peaceful, if he's not doing it now."

"We would be grateful," Mordka said, rising to his feet. Longarm and Belivev stood up also. Mordka went on, "It is close to the hour I spend in meditation.

Nicolai, will you stay and join me? I'm certain Mr. Long can find his way back to town without help."

"Sure," Longarm agreed. He added, "And I'll come back and talk to you some more in a few days, Mr. Danilov. Maybe I'll see some way I can ease things a bit."

"You will be welcome in my house at any time," Danilov said. "And if you are curious about our religion, you will also be welcome at our small church near the town."

"Thanks. And if anything happens that you want to tell me about, I'm staying at the hotel."

Outside once more, Longarm mounted with a thoughtful face and started the roan back toward the settlement. As he rode, he studied the fences that paralleled the crude road. He hadn't been assigned before to a case that took him into an area where Glidden wire was used. The barbed strands of fencewire had appeared on the market fairly recently, and he'd heard the wire discussed—but mostly cussed—by cattlemen who'd encountered it. As he looked closely at the tautly-stretched, saw-toothed wire, he could understand the reason for their displeasure.

At close range, even under the declining afternoon sun, it was hard to see the fence against the growing wheat. At night, or in a storm, unless a horseman happened to notice the posts that supported the fence, it would actually be invisible. A horse moving at any pace faster than a walk could barrel into the sharp teeth of the Glidden wire and scrape cuts on its chest and legs that might cripple the animal. The top strand of wire was just high enough to catch the leg of a mounted man, and against its barbs the soft leather of boot uppers would provide no protection at all.

He could see, too, how cattle being driven across

open prairie could pile up on a fence like that until the pressure of the herd on its leaders snapped the posts. That very pressure would shove the leading steers into the sharp, thin strands and cut them to ribbons as they reared in panic from the pain of the metal points stabbing into their flesh. *It would be easy for a rancher to lose a good handful of steers that way,* Longarm thought as he let his horse set its own pace between the lines of posts.

I guess if I had a ranch around here, I wouldn't cotton to seeing the prairie all cut up this way, Longarm told himself. *I'd be real tempted to carry a pair of nippers in my saddlebag and snip those wires, if it was my animals they were likely to tear up. But it'd be just as tough if I'd put my sweat into raising a crop and had a herd of steers or a bunch of riders cut my fence and trample my land. Damn it,* he thought, *this is one place where a man can have trouble making up his mind who's right and who's wrong, where these Glidden wire fences are concerned.*

His thinking didn't comfort Longarm a great deal. It only aggravated what he'd felt about this assignment from the moment Billy Vail had handed it to him in Denver.

Vail was in a testy mood, and Longarm wasn't happy, either. He'd just seen Julia Burnside off on the morning express; she was moving with her father back to Atlanta, and he hated like hell to see her go. Julia had been good company as well as a good bedmate for Longarm during the several months since they'd first met. Tired after a long night of lovemaking, and two hours late because the eastbound express didn't pull out of Denver until ten in the morning, Longarm snapped back at Vail when he made his usual remark about his deputy's tardiness. Usually the chief marshal's comment was half-joking, but this time it was completely serious.

"Damn it, Billy, I ain't married to this office the way you are," Longarm retorted. "It seems to me you'd allow for all the times I work day and night on a case, when I show up a few minutes late."

"If you call two hours a few minutes, you need a new watch," Vail shot back, glaring out from under his heavy eyebrows. "I've got a new assignment for you, and now you'll have to hump it to catch the noon Santa Fe train to Fort Dodge."

"I'll be glad to hustle, if it gets me out of this office. What's wrong at Dodge?"

"Nothing, except you'll have to stop there to pick up a horse. Where you're going is about fifty miles east of Dodge—some wide place in the road called Junction. If it'll make you feel better, you can ride the Santa Fe spur that goes right to the town, and save fifty miles on horseback."

"Who am I going after at this Junction place?" Longarm asked.

"Nobody. You'll be looking *at*, not *for*. There's a big squall blowing up down there. It seems the locals are ready to fight over who they'll elect to run the county. There're rumors of plans to stuff ballot boxes and keep a lot of people from voting."

"Now hold up, Billy. That's for Kansas to worry about, not us. Hell, why are we sticking our noses into a local election fuss?"

"It's not just local," Vail informed him. "You know this is a presidential election year too, and the big men in Washington are afraid it's going to be a close race. The smart money's betting there won't be ten thousand votes nationwide between the winner and the loser. They say even a few hundred votes are important in this one."

"In a place like that, there can't be much over a hundred votes."

"Maybe not. But when I get a wire from Washington telling me to send a good man to keep an eye on things, I know they're really worrying."

"But, damn it, Billy, it's not a job for a lawman!" Longarm protested. "What you need there is a nursemaid."

The portly chief marshal pounded his desk with a large hand that showed the scars and calluses of a far less sedentary life than the one he was now leading. "Then, by God, you'll be the nursemaid! Now, I don't want to hear any more arguments. You get that noon train, and you see that the voting's honest. If it's not, you can call for a fresh vote. Is that clear?"

"Clear enough," Longarm grumbled. "But I don't like it."

"Nobody asked you if you did," Vail said curtly. He picked up a fresh sheaf of papers from his littered desk, his signal that the time for talking had ended.

Longarm carried the grudge over his new assignment, together with his unhappiness about Julia's departure, on the train that took him down the eastern slope of the Rockies and across the broken Kansas prairie to Fort Dodge. He had to kill a night and most of a day there, waiting for a cattle train that eventually creaked its way across the flatlands on the spur that ended at Junction. His butt sore from the unpadded seat in the caboose, he reached railend a little before midnight, put his horse in the settlement's livery stable, and himself into a room in the town's one hotel. Then, after sleeping late, he set out to scout the territory he'd be working in, and wound up getting shot at when Nicolai Belivev mistook him for a fence-cutter.

As he rode back toward Junction in the red sunset glow, Longarm was more positive than ever that Billy Vail's assignment was going to be a nasty one to carry out.